ALSO BY MARTHA GRIMES

The Old Contemptibles

Send Bygraves

The Old Silent

The Five Bells & Bladebone

I Am the Only Running Footman

Help the Poor Struggler

The Deer Leap

Jerusalem Inn

The Dirty Duck

The Anodyne Necklace

The Old Fox Deceiv'd

The Man with a Load of Mischief

THE END OF THE PIER

The End
of the Pier

Martha Grimes

ALFRED A. KNOPF NEW YORK

TO KENT, BILL AND JAMES W.,

who would tell me, if they knew

Ramon Fernandez, tell me, if you know,
Why, when the singing ended and we turned
Toward the town, tell why the glassy lights,
The lights in the fishing boats at anchor there,
As the night descended, tilting in the air,
Mastered the night and portioned out the sea,
Fixing emblazoned zones and fiery poles,
Arranging, deepening, enchanting night.

Oh! Blessed rage for order, pale Ramon,
The maker's rage to order words of the sea,
Words of the fragrant portals, dimly-starred,
And of ourselves and of our origins,
In ghostlier demarcations, keener sounds.

"The Idea of Order at Key West"
—WALLACE STEVENS

PART ONE

PART ONE

Maud

ONE

The Rainbow Café treated any day before a holiday like big money. Maud wondered as she set the hot beef sandwich and mashed potatoes on the counter just why Shirl expected this surge of extra business. The only people at the counter had been Ubub and Ulub Wood, and they'd eaten what they always ate, the daily special. Ubub and Ulub had other names, but they'd been long forgotten. It was either Dodge Haines or Sonny Stuck who'd decided to call them by the letters on their license plates—UBB and ULB. They drove twin Ford pickups, black and battered. No one could figure out just how they'd managed to get those trucks battered up in the same way, so that the only thing that distinguished one from the other was the tag.

Maud hadn't wanted to go to work this day, and then she had. She had meant to stay home, but it was the Labor Day weekend, so she had settled on going in an hour later than she usually did. Shirl hadn't even noticed, despite her prediction of their getting in a crowd.

She drew a cup of coffee in a white mug and put that in front of Ulub, who didn't say anything; he never did. Maud wondered if he ever had. Since he always wanted the special, Shirl and Charlene always knew what to give him. Ubub did the talking, what there was of it, for both of them.

Shirl was ringing up a take-out order of doughnuts and coffee, sitting on a high stool behind the register and shoving the stuff across the black counter at a teenage kid. She handed him his change and a venomous look as if he'd made her open the register at gunpoint. He left.

When the teenager left and was walking past the window, Shirl started talking about "the little creep" to Maud. Not the one who'd left, but her son. Probably, any kid that age brought her son to mind. His name was Joseph, and she only called him by name when she wasn't in a white rage with him, which was seldom. Everyone else called him Joey. He was "the little creep"; his father, who'd left them flat after Joey was born, was still "the big creep." Charlene kept telling Shirl she should be glad he wasn't getting stoned and flying off rooftops.

"The little creep's too lazy to fly, and of course he ain't doing drugs—it'd cut into his shoplifting time." Joey had hooked some sunglasses from the SuperSaver Discount Store the day before. Shirl had called this down the counter to Charlene as she shoved a plain white bakery box at a customer. Lemon chiffon was always the special pie of the day except at Thanksgiving and Christmas, when Charlene wiped off the blackboard and wrote in "Punkin."

Joey would come in nearly every day for lunch and Maud would get him his favorite—beef stew—and butter four slices of bread for him. He was usually off school, suspended but not expelled, and Shirl acted like a parole officer. The boy had a pale little face and a smile like smoke, hardly there and quickly dispersed, as if there'd been something in the past worth smiling about, a memory that had guttered out.

Shirl would shuffle towards him and start in, calling him "Joseph this" and "Joseph that," ask him all sorts of questions: did he mow the lawn, rake the leaves, shovel the snow? depending on the time of year. She didn't stop until he'd eaten the fourth slice of bread, when she'd stick another cigarette in her mouth and shuffle away. Then Maud would pour him a second cup of coffee. He'd smile that vanishing smile at her, give her his condolences for having to work there, ball up his napkin, and leave. It was a ritual whenever he was suspended from school for breaking into lockers or calling the math teacher a pervert, a sleazeball, a scumbag. Five days a week Maud would watch him come in and go out and remember something about gates of ivory, gates of horn. She'd had three years of college, mostly literature courses, and loved to read. Still, she couldn't recall where those gates were, or just what they meant, except some important passage to somewhere, somewhere final.

As she hung her apron on the peg and took down her coat at seven o'clock that evening, she thought how Joey would be going back to school the day after Labor Day.

Then she stopped thinking about Joey and school, for that only made her think of Chad, and he was gone.

That was why she hadn't wanted to go to work. She had really wanted to come down here, where she was now, to the end of the pier.

Maud sat on the end of the pier watching the party across the water. It had been going on, it seemed, all summer, and she wondered, as people do about the tree in the forest: did it simply stop when she wasn't around to hear it? It had been just before the Fourth of July when she'd noticed the lights and come down here and looked across the wide lake at Japanese lanterns like strings of Christmas lights. The first time she'd simply stood for a while, squinting over the water, hearing the faint strains of music.

The next night she'd come down with her martini glass and sat on the edge of the dock, her bare legs dangling over the edge.

The night after, she'd come with a wood-and-aluminum chair and a cold bottle of Popov vodka, and in the following nights and weeks she slowly furnished the end of the pier.

After the Fourth, she'd brought down a small table and a Colonel Sanders plastic tub filled with ice in which she'd stowed her ready-mixed-martini Popov bottle. Then, when Chad came home from college, she'd got him to haul down an old rocker from the bedroom of the cottage that sat back along the path in the woods.

He told her it wasn't a pier, it was a dock, and he couldn't imagine why she'd want to sit out here for hours at night.

Chad had been sitting in the aluminum chair, drinking beer, looking around the lake frontage, checking out the marshy grass—the pier was in a little cove—and the tree with a heavy root above ground like a bent knee, a tree praying in the matted grass and weeds.

He sighed, world-weary at twenty, and asked her, "Why do you keep working at Shirl's?"

"Because it's dark and quiet, I guess."

He pulled another beer from the carton; there was a little sucking noise as he uncapped it. "I hope that's not what life is, just something dark and quiet."

"If you're lucky," she'd said.

In the darkness his head turned. "Come on, Mom."

It hadn't been the real question, anyway. It wasn't "Why do you work at Shirl's?" but "Why do we live in such a nonhappening place, why didn't you finish college and get your English degree, why didn't you get a great job, become an executive, maybe, or at least marry one, someone we could have lived with instead of *him*, why don't you own your own restaurant, why is that a cube of ice in your glass and not the moon?" Maud said, "Shirl likes you."

He was lighting a cigarette, and the flame from his disposable lighter lit up his profile and went out. "Shouldn't she? I'm polite."

"Polite isn't the point. She doesn't like *anybody*. But she does you. She's always holding you up to Joey, and even *he* likes you." Maud shook the Popov bottle free from ice crystals. "What do you talk to her about? She won't let Charlene or me wait on you." Maud was extremely pleased by this.

"Her feet."

Maud twisted the bottle back into the plastic tub and turned to him. "Her *feet*?"

"She's got corns and bunions. That's why she's always wearing slippers."

"I Concentrate on You"—they liked Cole Porter over there—came floating across the lake.

"It's the first time she ever offered anybody a job since I've been working there, and that's ten years. You liked it up here, then."

"When you're ten you like practically anyplace except jail. Anyway, I don't think I'd've made a fortune in tips at Shirl's. Don't they play any real music over there?"

"You can't dance to the Grateful Dead. They like to dance. I'm not *saying* you should've taken the job—just that she offered it. And Lorraine said Jewel Chapman would've loved to have you work at the feed store."

"There's just not enough money in it. You want me to earn money for school, and there's a lot of house painting in Hebrides—"

"I'm not *saying* . . . Oh, well." Hebrides was twenty miles away; without a car he could only stay here on weekends instead of all summer long.

Today he had left, which was why she hadn't wanted to go to work. But some part of her knew better, that if she didn't go in, she'd just sit around the cottage all day, like a mourner returned from a funeral. They had taken the local taxi to Bakersville to get the small plane to the city to get the large plane to get the space shuttle . . .

Maud stared up at the night sky, looking for an airplane's tiny red light, like a red star trailing across the sky, as if his plane might have doubled back. She thought that pinpoint of red light, throbbing along, must have replaced the sound of a train whistle for pure melancholy.

He'd left early, two days before he had to. "Mom, I was wondering . . . Would you mind . . . ?"

Whenever Chad started with that, she knew she'd mind. "I-was-wondering-would-you-mind" was a group of words that had taken on a life of its own. Yes, she'd mind, though she almost always said no, she wouldn't, because what followed was never truly unreasonable, just painful. It always had something to do with going away, leaving before he actually had to. "Disappearing" was the way Maud thought of it; Chad called it "leaving for college."

The latest addition to the pier's decor was a lamp Maud had found in the crawl space beneath the cottage eaves. It was black iron with clawlike legs and had a stained beige shade of faded roses. She'd got Chad to rig several extension cords together so they would stretch back and plug into the outlet at the rear of the cottage. Maud read a lot. When there was a lull in the party across the lake, when everyone had gone in from the terrace and battened down inside and she couldn't make out the music, she'd switch on the lamp and read whatever she'd brought down with the vodka.

Lately, she'd been bringing to the pier her old college anthology of American poetry. She'd come upon a poem by Wallace Stevens called "The Idea of Order at Key West," the point of which she was trying to grasp. This was not for her a mental exercise or a desire to further educate herself in the world of poetry. It was very important to her (although she couldn't have said why) that she understand this poem. A lot, she felt, would then be revealed to her. She'd read parts of it to Sam, who couldn't understand it either, and seemed more interested anyway in complaining about the lamp.

Sam was always fussing about the lamp, telling her to get rid of it. "It's dangerous," Sam kept saying, though he was pretty vague about the danger. She asked if he was afraid it would electrocute the fish if it fell into the lake, and he said it would probably blow fuses all over the place. What was dangerous about that? she asked him. Just blowing a fuse?

"Well, but don't you think it must look kind of strange if they"—he nodded towards the party—"look over here? And see someone sitting under a lamp? It would look strange, I think."

She told him she needed the lamp for reading.

The only person she knew who understood about books, how they would make you feel rooted to the ground and to the past, somehow, the way TV never could, was Miss Ruth Porte. Miss Ruth came to Shirl's every evening except Thursdays and weekends for her dinner. She always sat in the high-backed rear booth, the side not facing the big television screen that rattled and wept its way through the day. It drove Miss Ruth Porte crazy, she said. Why didn't they bring along a book—Miss Ruth liked Jane Austen—if they wanted entertainment?

Miss Ruth would smooth her hand over her vellum-covered Jane Austen, carefully wrapped in plastic, and say, "It's just like family, her people. It's the kind of thing these new writers don't understand, that readers want to feel this is a family they can almost walk and talk amongst. Writers these days"—it was never clear who they were—"only want to write about breakups and breakdowns, everything unraveling and everybody going to the devil." She would pause then over her menu, open it and close it several times, not satisfied with the expression of whatever notion she had. "It doesn't have to be *good* family—the dear Lord knows most families aren't, and certainly Miss Jane Austen knows it. Let's see, what's the special?"

Maud would stand patiently with her small book of checks and pencil for taking the order. Often she would make comments about whatever book she was reading, not because she wanted to soft-soap Miss Ruth (who was the last of the Porte family and rumored to be rich) but because there was hardly anyone else to talk about books to. Besides Wallace Stevens, Maud was reading F. Scott Fitzgerald, and Miss Ruth was very enthusiastic, saying he was much, much better than Ernest Hemingway, despite what the Book Mark people thought. This was a reading club that met every Thursday night, which was why she didn't come into the Rainbow Café.

Miss Ruth would always inquire about Maud's son, Chad, whom she thought to be "splendid, just splendid," and it was no idle compliment. It was right in line with what everyone else seemed to think, and Maud wished they'd stop talking about him as if he were a visiting divinity. Everyone seemed hanging around waiting to get anointed or something. He knew what to say to people, it was as simple as that. God only knew where he'd got this instinct, for it surely hadn't come from her. She considered herself what they call pathologically shy, which was one reason she liked working at Shirl's. All the customers were used to Shirl's surliness, which had spilled over onto Charlene and Wash, the cook, and even the two part-time girls who came in when there was what Shirl thought of as a rush.

Maud, compared with everyone else, was considered a real find. Shirl's customers were always asking her what she was doing working here, and she would always answer "Just lucky, I guess," with a little wink, and they would laugh. When they all sat in a line at the counter—Dodge and Sonny and Mayor Sims and sometimes even Wade Hayden from the post office, and Ubub and Ulub— and reacted to something in unison, turning their heads right or left, it would put Maud in mind of a decrepit chorus line, and then she would have to laugh, too.

She knew it mystified the customers that she was working as a waitress when she had all of that education. It was hard to make people understand that education or not, there were some people who had no ambition in that way, who didn't want a profession, and who didn't want a lot of money, and she was one of them. So with her three years of college and her timid smile, she imagined they took her for someone with a sad past, like a duchess in exile.

Two speedboats ripped by, crossing in each other's wake. The pier felt the reverberation, the slap of the churning water, before it closed behind the boats, smoothly and seamlessly.

Maud stuck an olive on a cocktail stirrer. The dish of olives sat on the wooden barrel she'd found behind the house. The stirrer had come from a small, flat box of six she'd found in the crawl space. Each had been carefully niched into an inner strip of white cardboard. They were clear glass topped with pink glass flamingoes, the sort of thing people never buy for themselves, but give as gifts. This one had never been used, or never been given.

Another small craft cozied up to the dock over there. By now there were at least a dozen, more than usual because it was the Labor Day party. The guests didn't all come by boat, of course; most of them probably drove down some old road on the other side of the house.

Now from this silvery-white boat emerged the party-goers. She was too far away to see what they actually were wearing, beyond brief blobs of gold or blue or red, but she knew some of them must be wearing long gowns that made it difficult to maneuver out of the boat. The high, trilling voices of the women, the brief whoops of laughter from the men that accompanied their emergence from the silver cocoon of the rocking boat suggested to her that they were rescuing their hems from trailing in the water. Others would come down to the dock, with their drinks and cigarettes—she could see the coal ends throbbing on and off. They helped the new arrivals up and then all trooped back to the party, towards the patio. She wondered where the latecomers had come from. Was there another party farther down the lake that took precedence? That was hard to believe. Probably from their small cocktail parties in their smaller cottages they had met briefly with this as the final destination.

This scene was repeated endlessly, until the dark lake over there was divided by strips of light from the boats, so many that it sometimes resembled a small marina.

Maud had always been quite sure they were not ordinary people and that they were in some way acutely blessed, as one might be who would remain in a state of grace for a season. She never came to the pier during the day to see what the house over there looked like then. And she knew that this was the last party, the Labor Day party, for La Porte was basically a summer place, where the summer people threw open the shutters of the big Victorian houses right after Memorial Day and shut them after Labor Day. Then La Porte became a ghost town. To hear Shirl talk it was always a ghost town; the summer people came in their shorts and Docksiders, hung over and tan as only the rich seem to get, to do little more than buy the Sunday paper and milk.

"Where's the warehouse, that's what I want to know," Shirl would grumble around her smoke. "They all got food at those lake places—where do they get it? One of them's got a helicopter pad—is that how? They fly it in—the caviar, the champagne, the roasted pheasant?"

Maud held her glass by the stem. She hated drinking martinis from a warm glass, and between drinks she shoved the glass into the ice to cool it again. The several patio doors over there were all open now, and she could see them dancing. Sometimes they had a real live combo out on the patio; other times she supposed it must be a stereo. It comforted her, like the book in her lap, that they liked Cole Porter. It was like a party out of the past, something that might have taken place in the 1920s or '30s, something her dead parents might have attended, and danced to "Begin the Beguine."

Several of them—she had to squint to make them out—had come out on the long, long patio and were dancing to it right now. Laughter and glass breaking.

She picked her glass from the bucket, poured herself a drink, and dropped in an olive. If the ghost of F. Scott Fitzgerald walked, it walked there, laughing and breaking glasses on the patio.

But the ghost of Wallace Stevens would not need to get drunk and break glasses. (He had been in insurance, to her great mystification.) Maud even went so far as to believe that the ghost of Wallace Stevens could sit comfortably on the end of the pier in the folding chair reserved for Sam (and Chad, when he was here) and contemplate the party across the water.

She sang beyond the genius of the sea.

(Maud read)

The water never formed to mind or voice,
Like a body wholly body, fluttering
Its empty sleeves—

She replaced the flamingo-topped cocktail stirrer that she used as a marker and closed the book. Sipping her martini, she thought about it, frowning slightly. The sea was formless, apparently. So the singer had to . . . had to . . . She squinted, looking off across the lake . . . What? She shook her head. It would come to her, sometime, what Wallace Stevens meant.

Then there was her favorite line—oh, what a line!

Ramon Fernandez, tell me, if you know . . .

"I wonder who," she had said to Sam back in July, "Ramon Fernandez was."

Sam had been silent for a moment, since Sam rarely shot back answers, and then he said that he was probably some friend of the poet. "When I'm in Hebrides next week I could go to the library and see if there's anything there on that poem."

Maud slapped the book shut and stared. "*No!* All I said was I wondered. Wonder—*wonder!* The answer's something I have to decide for myself." She actually felt a little afraid that Sam might just look the poem up.

He sighed. "Maud. If Ramon was a personal friend—"

"Ramon *Fernandez*. We're not on a first-name basis with him," she snapped.

Sam shook his head. "Well, if Señor Fernandez was a friend of Mr. Stevens, there's nothing *for* you to decide."

"You're so literal. And what do you mean, 'Señor'? How do you know he's Spanish or Mexican, anyway?" Maud was frowning at the Popov bottle to see if there was enough to get her through this conversation. "I'm not surprised you don't understand this poem."

"Cuban," Sam had said equably, as he snapped open another can of Coors.

"*What?*" Maud shot up in her chair, back rigid. "He is *not* Cuban."

Sam shrugged. "Stands to reason. The poet's in Key West, right? Florida. Closest place where somebody might be from named Ramon Fernandez"—he tilted the Coors and drank—"is Cuba."

Maud slapped her hand to her forehead. "Your name is Dutch, isn't it? *Dutch*. Does that mean you commute from Lancaster, Pennsylvania?" She turned a furious face to him. "You're *deliberately* ruining this poem for me." She turned away and stared out over the water. "And it's important." She felt like crying.

"Sorry."

After a suffering silence that had Maud rocking and staring straight across the lake, Sam suggested that if she was so curious about the couple on the other side of the lake he could always cruise around with a disturbing-the-peace complaint. Maud got so anxious that she yelled at him, something she hardly ever did with anyone but Chad, and told him not to dare. She wasn't "curious," and how could they be disturbing the peace when they probably owned a half-mile of lake frontage?

She thought she heard a scrunching on the path, Sam coming along with his six-pack of beer, but when she turned to look, saw that it was the black cat that had turned up a month or so ago and kept disappearing and reappearing. It walked slowly and stealthily onto the pier and simply sat, blinking.

Maud tried not to look at it because it made her stomach tighten, seeing that it was sick and probably a stray. It was the eye that was bad. It must have been a tumor, for the right eye was completely clouded over and bigger than the other. There was no iris to see, just what looked like a hard blue carapace that must have started out small but gotten larger and larger.

This was the fourth night the cat had come, and she had remembered to bring along a plastic dish. A half-pint of milk was sitting on top of the ice, and she poured that into the dish and set it some little distance away since she imagined the cat wasn't all that trustful of people. Maud wondered what the cat did during the day, whether it hung around the pier, catching field mice in the rushy grass. It made no move toward the milk. Could it see the dish, even?

To Maud, the cat's having a tumorous eye was a source of inexplicable dread, worse than seeing it in an old, sick person. What made it worse was that the cat had this affliction but didn't know.

"Why in hell would you want the poor cat to *know*?" Sam had asked. "Wouldn't that just make it worse for it?"

"That's not what I meant; you don't understand."

"Would *you* want to know?"

Maud couldn't really understand it herself, why it was worse that the cat wasn't aware that this shouldn't be happening to it. "Yes. Anyway, that's a stupid question because I'd know whether I wanted to or not."

"Okay, then. The cat *doesn't* know, whether it wants to or not."

"You're just twisting it all around." She had watched the cat that night, sitting as it was now, yawning, not knowing, unaware that something hideous was consuming its left eye. It wasn't that Maud found the malformation repulsive; it was that the cat didn't know that there was an alternative, that its eye might have been perfectly normal.

"Let's just say," Sam had said when the cat first turned up, "that the eye doesn't hurt, which it probably doesn't, the way that cat just sits there and doesn't seem to mind."

"How do you *know* it doesn't—?"

Sam had waved his hand for her to shut up. "For the sake of the *argument* let's just say. Now, for all that cat knows, that's just the way things are supposed to be. One day something starts clouding up in its eye. Does it think, 'Je-*sus*, but I better get me to a doctor,' or 'I'm dying,' or 'I'm going blind'? No. It just takes what comes and doesn't worry about it."

The cat at this point had gone over to the edge of the pier and lain down, as if it were bored by all of this talk about its fate. Then it rolled over.

"You're just reading stuff into that cat's mind. Stuff that cat doesn't have any idea about and doesn't care." Sam had popped another cap on a can of Coors for emphasis.

Maud hadn't answered. The conversation was going around in circles and she couldn't explain. She imagined herself in a room with a window suddenly shuttered against the light, imagined herself starting, sitting up, wondering what had happened. No, she thought impatiently, that wasn't it.

The cat had inspected the dish of milk now, but didn't drink it. Could it see it? That was stupid; it had one good eye. Anyway, it could certainly smell it. Maybe it was too cold. Maybe she shouldn't have put the carton on the ice. Just because she and Sam liked their drinks icy cold didn't mean the cat would.

Why would you want the poor cat to know?

Maud fingered the book in her lap—the book of American poetry—as if it were one of those little stoppered bottles she thought Indians used for magical purposes and it might release the answer. The cat was sitting nearer her chair, looking up at her with its clouded eye. It was worse than pity, what she felt. It was more like remorse and shame. Blood crept up her neck, heated her face as if a torch had been set to it, and she would have poured herself another drink except that a tremor had started in her hand so that she had to set the glass down. It was as if a task had been set for her: she must work out the answer to this problem about why it was worse for the cat that it didn't know.

For the life of her, she couldn't think of one single human situation that might fit the cat's. Again, she thought of a room, imagining herself asleep in the dark. She squinted across the water, where the lanterns were lifting and bobbing. It must be windier there.

The room could not be like a prison cell. It was important that it be a fine room, one with a very high ceiling and pale, prettily tinted walls. And at the end were two very high windows, long and narrow, almost like French windows but not reaching the floor. Curtains made of light stuff like chiffon would rise and fall in the breeze. The curtains were pale yellow. Every morning (except for the last one, when she would rush from the room, terrified, she'd decided)—every morning, she would wake slowly to see these soft, lemon-colored curtains billowing out in a wind blown from . . . where? what? From the water, the sea.

For this room would be somewhere in a warm country—Greece, maybe—where the east-facing windows with their delicate, blown curtains would frame two oblongs of blue sky. Maud rubbed her elbows and searched for the right shade of blue. She thought of her one piece of good jewelry, a ring that had been her grandmother's, an opal. The lemon-yellow curtains (it might be Cyprus, where the lemon trees grew) would blow in a wind off the green sea. The walls would be pink, and the ceiling perhaps garlanded; the bed a sort of filigree ironwork, and no furniture except for a wardrobe that would house her few dresses, all long cotton with straps, no sleeves. She would go with bare shoulders and feet.

Maud started when the music changed across the water, and realized she was a long way from the cat's problem. She was merely dreaming about herself walking in pale cotton dresses, hems to her ankles, walking across the cool stone of the floor.

This was the scene that would meet her eyes every morning. She would see the pale pink stuccoed walls (it might be a villa in Italy) and the frescoed ceiling, the pale curtains and the opal sky.

And then one morning she would wake slowly to partial darkness. It would seem at first like one of those half-dreams, an inner darkness, something the mind knew was only temporary and would soon climb up into full light.

Only in this case it didn't. For one of the windows *would be missing*. The point, Maud thought, frowning, was important. It was not like waking into a slow and awful awareness that you couldn't see out of one eye, and jumping up and calling the doctor. But that the window was *missing*. Where it had been was only the wall, the wall grown over the place where the window had been. On one side of the room everything was dark, the curtains were gone, the pink drained from the walls, the figures holding garlands vanished from the ceiling.

It was all gone; the bed was dark; she could not make out the wardrobe.

And she could not say, "I'm blind in one eye." She could not run out into the street in her terror and yell that her room was disappearing, that the wall had overgrown the window. No one would believe her. They would think she was merely some Greek crazy, gone mad like the one who had murdered her children. She would be completely isolated. She would be alone with no explanation. And this was what made her problem like the cat's.

Now she felt better, slightly. She felt a bit triumphant because she could explain to Sam how much more dreadful it was for the cat not knowing.

She visualized it again, that room, floating over the Aegean. Sea of jade, a sky of opal, the diaphanous curtains of milky yellow like dissolving pearl, a room of pure light, without the burden of furniture, of the past, of the future . . .

With its missing window vanishing from her mind's eye Maud felt her throat constricting.

She was relieved to hear just after that the sound of Sam's car pulling up. Maud squinted back at the headlights, which switched off, and she heard the door slam.

"Evening," he said as he set about emptying the six-pack of

Coors into the tub of ice, shoving five into the space around the Popov bottle and setting one on the upturned barrel. Sam sighed and lowered himself into a chair. Before he said anything, he always had to line up his cigarettes and matches and pop the can of Coors.

Having done that, he settled back in the aluminum and wood-slatted chair, crossed an ankle over his knee, and rubbed the ankle. "It's the big one tonight, I guess," he said of the party, and tipped the can back and drained half of it. Then he offered Maud a cigarette from his pack of Winstons. They sat back and smoked. "Had to break one up over at the Red Barn earlier," he said. "Bunch of kids were on something. Then I had to go over to Spirit Lake and break up a fight at the hotel."

Sam had been La Porte's sheriff for years. He'd started out as deputy and was now in charge of the four-man police department. He was easygoing and well liked.

"That place is crazy." Maud shook her head. Spirit Lake was another summer resort town, two miles away, even smaller than La Porte, and even emptier in the winter. If people thought La Porte was a ghost town, well, it had nothing on the ghostliness of Spirit Lake in dead winter.

"Still, it's Labor Day. Guess you can't blame people for wanting to celebrate," Sam said sympathetically. That was one reason he was well liked; he could make allowances. "Chad get off?"

Maud nodded, looking straight ahead. "I was about to write a letter to him today. I had it all worked out, but—"

"Why were you writing? He only just left. He's off to visit his friend. Isn't that what you said? That he was going to visit his friend in Belle Harbor?"

Maud squinched her eyes shut. Sometimes he drove her crazy. "I *know* where he *is*. Do you have to keep saying it?" Irritated, she tossed her watered-down drink into the lake and stuck her glass into the ice. "I wasn't going to *mail* it yet, just write it, that's all. Anyway, that's not the point."

"Oh," said Sam.

He was waiting patiently for her to tell him the point, but now she couldn't bring to mind exactly the way she'd felt when she'd tried to write the letter. Her fresh drink tasted tepid. "Never mind," she said, though she'd forgotten the point herself.

Her saying that bothered him, so he urged her to go on.

"Well, just don't keep interrupting." There was a silence while she tried to enter into the feelings she had had earlier when she was writing the letter. Trying to. All day at the Rainbow Café she had been fretting over the fight they'd had about where Chad's money was going. So when they'd got to the airport neither one of them was in an especially amiable mood. "This is what I don't understand," she was saying about the letter. "The words were all there, as neatly lined up as boxed chocolates one after the other. They were clearly in my head. Now, why is it they wouldn't simply move down my arm to my fingers and right out along the page? I started writing and it all disappeared. It was like the ink just dried up in my mind."

Sam said nothing, but she knew he was thinking the problem over. Sam wasn't much of a letter writer.

"The words just—frizzled."

"Frizzled?"

"You know—curled up around the edges. Frizzled. Burned. Turned to ashes."

"Hmm."

She knew it took Sam a while to think things like this over. Sometimes he made no comment at all beyond a "well" or an "oh," but that was one reason she liked to talk to him. If Sam couldn't think of a helpful reply, he made none at all, except for the times when he was being deliberately (she thought) obtuse. But usually, when her full thought was out, if he couldn't add to it, he didn't try to take away from it by saying something like others might: "Have a hard time writing myself," or "Try again," or something like that which demeaned her point. And he never tried to cheer her up, even though he often found her in a bad mood, to say the least. Most people would probably have thought his silence strange; after all, wasn't that what friends were for? To cheer you up?

No, friends knew the difference between that downcast, hang-dog, lowdown feeling people called "blues" (music the party across the water never played, for some reason) and what Maud had. And what Maud had was something unnameable and probably unnat-ural, unless you wanted to call it "depression." That was probably the only word anyone could come up with, but it didn't help her much.

After the lull in the dancing the combo started in on "Brazil." She was glad she'd never left anyone behind in Brazil or it would probably have started her crying.

Another boat—or was it the same black Chris-Craft?—ripped by near the far shore. "Isn't that the same one? Where do they go, anyway? There's nothing at the other end of the lake." There wasn't anything at either end as far as she could make out, except for the Red Barn, which wasn't much but what the name said. They sold beer and half-smokes and had a jukebox and one of those big TV screens like the wall of a house caving in on you.

It showed up, the depression, in the way she'd been about to weep over the cat's eye and the loss of the high-ceilinged room. It wasn't natural to cry as much as she did, and god only knew, to cry over *what* she did. Oh, she imagined a lot of people cried over music, songs that put them in mind of their dead sweethearts in Brazil and so forth. But she'd go straight as a board, freeze up right in front of the milk-shake machine at the Rainbow if someone played "Blue Bayou" or Elvis sang "*I'm so lonesome I could cry.*" It was like her hand was electrified, holding the aluminum milk-shake container, unable to release it.

You don't cry just looking at your own cat because she's sleep-ing with her head on her paws; or over a black car because its rear wheels are up on blocks; or at a rock you see by the side of the road; or a band of wrens waving on tall stalks and then suddenly taking off. At least she thought you don't. And it nearly went without saying she'd put away all the pictures of Chad when he was four and seven and ten and even sixteen. It might be that when she had the roll developed that they'd taken before he left, she'd just tuck them in the album without looking at them, as if they might burn her eyes out.

It looked to her like she had two choices: crazy or depressed.

The issue seemed to be settled a few days ago when she'd picked up a copy of *Time* (or was it *Newsweek*?) that featured an article on depression.

It was epidemic, almost. It was growing among young people (which didn't help her own case). But there were different kinds. She read all of the symptoms with interest, not surprised that the tendency to cry was one. Fatigue. That fit. Although you didn't really score yourself, the idea was that if you had perhaps three or four symptoms you were depressed; five or six, seriously; more than six, almost clinically. And it counted, also, which ones you had. Any thoughts of suicide were, of course, rather serious. A *lot* of thinking about suicide was pretty dangerous, and *attempting* it—this seemed to come across to the reporters as a surprise—was the clincher. There were twelve symptoms. Maud checked and saw she had all of them except one.

It wasn't exactly what you wanted to write your mother about. But her mother was dead. It wasn't exactly what you wanted to write your son about, either.

"I don't know," said Sam.

"What? You don't know what?" His voice had brought her out of her reverie.

"Whether it's the same one."

"What same one?"

Sam turned and gave her one of his long looks. "The boat, for god's sake. You asked if it was the same . . ."

Maud had forgotten what she'd said. "You're so literal."

"You forgot, didn't you?" He took a pull at his Coors, smiling in that exasperating way he did when he'd caught her out in some small thing. "You were just sitting here mooning over something and forgot what you were saying."

Her little laugh sounded artificial even to her. "Just because you take everything literally . . ."

"Literal has nothing to do with it. Want some more?"

Sam was tugging the Popov bottle out of the ice, which he wasn't supposed to do, and he knew it, and she put her hand over his and shoved it back down. Maud liked to pour her own drink in a certain way and at certain times.

Holding her glass up to the lamplight, she said, "Well, you're certainly in one of your moods."

"What're you talking about? I don't have moods."

That was true. Even when she knew he was sad, or disturbed, he didn't show it. "You certainly do. Usually, it's when you've been going around at night checking on us."

"Us?"

She turned a patient little smile on him. "Ever since Nancy Alonzo was murdered you've been checking up. I guess it's nice of you to do it. But it makes you moody. 'Obsessed' is a better word."

He just sat there smoking and not answering. When Sam didn't answer, she knew she'd struck a nerve, and pulled back. "It was pretty terrible, what happened. But it happened in Hebrides. You're not sheriff of Elton County, so you shouldn't be worrying about it."

"It might have happened in Hebrides, but she lived in La Porte. That cuts no ice with Sedgewick, though." Sedgewick was the sheriff over there, and there wasn't much love lost between the two men.

As Sam talked about Sedgewick and Elton County, Maud poured herself a cold martini and listened to the music.

From across the water the faint strains of a whole orchestral arrangement scored her thought. It was only the music, but she had long ago learned the words:

The morning found you miles away,
With still a million things to say ...

Maud could feel her scalp prickle and tighten, the skin crawl. It was the exact same feeling that people were always using to describe fear or disgust: "*My skin just crawled.*" It was as if the thoughts had somehow got too large for the skull to contain them, a terrible feeling that traveled down her arms and broke out in gooseflesh.

She would have to practice harder at containing her thoughts. That image of her mother had slipped out from behind one of her mind's bolted doors; at least she thought she'd bolted it, but here it was, opening a crack, and her dead mother slipping out like a child told to stay in its room, and sneaking along the hall to tiptoe downstairs. And then the image became unruly, clotted with other images, unmanageable, for it was as if her mother were slyly opening other doors along the way, doors that Maud had stupidly, momentarily left unsecured. Her mother was letting out the other occupants; there was the blur of her dead father (who had died too long ago to visualize concretely); there was her Aunt Sheba, with her wry, ironic mouth given to caustic comments, who marched resolutely down the hall collecting Chad, Chad at the age of five or six—Aunt Sheba coaxing him out to come along, there was a party, let's not miss it. They were all collecting on the stairs before Maud could control them, herd them back into their locked rooms—*shove* them back behind their doors. There they were, all gathered on the stairs to sit and watch through the banisters the flamboyant party to which they had not been invited. The party that flowed from inside to outside, from the old family drawing room out onto a lawn and then across the lake.

And there was no control: her mind was crowded with old relatives, ones she hadn't thought of for ages, ones that it wasn't necessary absolutely to keep locked up—other aunts, uncles, the cousin who had died of cancer at twenty-eight, and then friends she had lost touch with. They were filling the hall, the wide stair-case, peering over the mahogany banister, searching the lake as if those passing boats might ferry them across it—

> *Return I will*
> *To old*
> *Bra-zil*

There on a lawn somewhere was Chad at five, at ten, at sixteen. *Go back, back inside.* She could never, of course, tell this to another living soul, because how could they understand what she meant? A psychiatrist, maybe, someone like Dr. Elizabeth Hooper, who'd been in the Rainbow that day; but who else? "Possessive," that's what Shirl would say. "*You want to keep that kid locked up, that's all.*" Of course, Shirl would be the least sympathetic of all, since she spent so much of her time yelling at Joey to either stop playing hooky or haul ass out of the house and work. And yet Maud didn't think she was possessive—not in *that* sense. She frowned in her effort of trying to figure out just what it was: that she wanted to be able to go back and see it all over again—not like snapshots (they only caused her pain), but to have all of those stages of growing up out there, like the lines of light thrown by the lanterns across the water.

She clutched at the book of poetry in her lap as she looked across the lake—the music was louder, faster, strident with the sting of some female vocalist—and thought about the woman in the poem walking by the sea, singing. Maud had got far enough in her understanding of this poem to know that somehow the woman singing there had power over the sea. A simple mortal woman had some kind of control over it.

But the singer wasn't simple, Maud admitted to herself, despairingly. Obviously the poet meant the woman was an artist. A singer, a poet, a musician—an artist. She had "genius," and that was the reason she had control, although Maud did not at all know just what the control was, except that it was crucial.

"Tina Turner."

Maud jumped slightly at the sound of Sam's voice. Half her mind had been aware he had stopped talking some moments ago and had been just sitting there, quiet, drinking his beer, listening to the party across the water. "What? What?" She squinted at him.

Sam nodded toward the other side of the lake. "Tina Turner." He yawned, patted his hand politely against his mouth, and looked down at Maud's lap. "You still trying to figure out that poem about Key West?"

It annoyed her—well, *embarrassed* her a little—that he seemed to be able to read her thoughts. Irritably, she asked, "How can you tell that's Tina Turner? You can't possibly. It's too far away."

"Well, I can tell."

He could not; it was just a singer and a fast, jumpy song. Hardly anyone was dancing; there was only a little clutch of tiny figures. She liked the small daubs of the gowns of the women, even though the dark, the distance, and the lantern light muted them, blurring the pinks, turning them lavender. And then she realized she could no more see such mutations than Sam could hear whose voice that was. Someone—a man, she thought— broke away from the group and walked slowly down to the dock and stood there smoking.

"It's not *about* Key West," she said when she saw Sam fold a stick of gum into his mouth. He did this sometimes preparatory to leaving, and she did not want him to go.

"It says it is in the title. 'The Idea of Order—' "

She sighed hugely. "Oh, for god's sake." She started to lecture him and thought she should change her tone if she wanted to keep him there. Patiently, she explained. Re-explained. "It is *about* a kind of order—"

"I figured that out. It says so in the title."

"It is *about* a person's ability to order things. In this case it's a singer making some sense out of the sea . . . No . . ." She held up her palm as if to stave off some objection Sam had clearly not been about to make—yet. "To 'master' it."

"Tina Turner, for example."

She refused to speak to him now.

Diplomatically, he changed the subject.

"That cat's going belly-over off this dock in one more minute."

"*What?*" she shouted.

"Well, for Christ's sake, there's no need to scream. All I said was, that cat—"

She looked at the black cat. It was hunched down nearly half-over the edge, as if it had some serious business under there, something on the underside of the splintered wooden plank. "It's okay." But it wasn't okay with her that now her attention had been drawn again to the cat; at least, though, its bad eye was turned away from her. "Don't you know if that cat belongs to anyone?" She knew the tone was accusatory; the implication was that he was a policeman and he should know the comings and goings of the village's animals.

"No. It's just a stray. It's not wild, though."

Maud fingered out the olive in her glass and sucked on it. "Why isn't there a vet around here? That cat's really sick."

"Well, there's one in Hebrides. You thinking of taking that cat to a vet?"

"The tumor's getting bigger. How can I? I don't have a car."

"There's the Merk."

"It doesn't run, you know that." She knew the black Mercedes fascinated Sam. Where had Maud ever got an old Mercedes?

"Trouble could be in the transmission, the main cylinder."

Main cylinder. What was he talking about? Maud wondered if it was the main cylinder that was burning out or grinding down in her brain. The glass sweated in her hand and she put it down on the barrel top, closed her eyes, and listened to the water slapping out against the pilings.

Sam went on talking about someone on Route 12 who was a transmission specialist, named Paul. A genius at it. "And blind as a bat," Sam said, with a little, wondering shake of his head.

Maud turned her gaze from the dancers over there, who seemed to be drooping against one another like flowers. She knew there were blind musicians but not blind transmission specialists.

"He's got the touch. It's all in the fingers, you think about it." Sam ran his thumb over the tips of his fingers, back and forth, eyes shut, as if he were feeling some delicate mechanism. "You know, if you've got no use for that car, give it to Chad. This is his last year; by summer Paul could have that car—" He stopped.

"*Last year.*" It was an implicit, unspoken agreement between them that Chad's last year in college was not to be talked of as such.

Now Sam was making as much noise as he could crumpling his can of Coors, and talking so fast about cars in general he might have been the auctioneer at the annual police auction of repos, trying to drown out what lingering vibration there might be from that phrase as if it were a plucked violin string. Chad was a favorite, a favored topic of conversation, and so was his time at the university; but it was to be talked about as if it were never-ending, a thread woven in and out of all of the other talk, drawing it together, yet never cut. Bad enough in itself he was away; that this might be more than a mere caprice on his part or Maud's part or Fate's part was not to be looked at. That there might indeed be some final term was not to be spoken of in any concrete sense. Not, for lord's sake, in the sense that a present, a *gift*, would be given to immortalize the occasion of Chad's final departure.

"I saw a nice little Datsun that I think you could get cheap."

"I don't want another car. What would I do with a car?"

Sam took a mouthful of beer, drew in on his cigarette, was thoughtful. "You could get out and around more. Go places."

"Oh, for Pete's sake." She hated it when someone started talking about her as if she were an invalid, someone like Ada Chowder, who lived in the Hebrides Nursing Home and was only released to visit her son and daughter-in-law every third Sunday. It wasn't like Sam to say something so stupid. "You could take it," she said, feeling vengeful.

"What? The Datsun? I've got—"

"No, damn it. The cat. You could take it to Hebrides."

Sam made a tiny, gurgling noise in his throat, the sound of someone who's choking a little on the craziness of a notion. "Don't I have enough to do without carting cats around?" His laugh was deprecating. "Besides, Sims would really like that, wouldn't he? Me using the car to take a cat to Hebrides?"

Mayor Sims spent most of his time in the Half Moon Bar and couldn't care less, but she knew Sam was feeling defensive and in his pause to take several more sips of beer would come up with at least four other reasons why he couldn't take the cat.

"It'd give Donny a laugh, too, that's for sure." Sam caved in his empty beer can, put it in the basket.

"So what. He's only a deputy. You're the loot."

As he was shaking the ice shavings from his next can, Sam looked up, squinting at her. "The what?"

"The loot. That's the word New York cops use for 'lieutenant.' Or at least in books." When she saw Sam's baffled look, she sighed. "I *mean* the boss. The highest-ranking cop in La Porte."

It was the way she looked at the fact of departure; she couldn't help herself. Her scalp prickled; again the skin tightened and she looked stony-faced up at the sky while Sam talked on about cars to fill in the void. Up there was the night sky, as black as macadam, and the hard, unfiltered light of the stars. She felt she was trying to bear its weight to keep it from crashing down around them.

She was supposed to be proud, Shirl kept saying, when pride had nothing to do with it, had no place in any lexicon of what was happening, was a word you could only attach to a Norman Rockwell painting. He must have done one of a boy in a mortarboard between Mom and Pop, all of them beaming away.

The stars looked hammered in place up there, and her glass grew warm in her hand. She had felt something similar when Chad had finished high school. That, she thought, had been bad enough, the end of his living at home. But there were vacations and there was dependence. She'd hear other women saying *"Whew! Time I had a rest from all that"* and wondered to what alien race of mothers she belonged.

Sam's voice came through her thoughts as a low sowing of indistinguishable words; the patio on the other side of the water was a chartreuse blur. As a parent she felt disgraced.

"That boy's done you proud," Shirl had said at lunchtime, taking bites from her jelly doughnut in between drags from a cigarette held in the same hand; with the other she was wiping down the top of the pastry display case—Shirl's two hands always seemed to do the work of four. And she managed at the same time to nod her head toward the far end where Joey sat mopping up brown gravy with a hunk of bread, implying, of course, that she was stuck with "the little creep."

"Not," she added, holding up a sticky hand for emphasis, "that I'm giving *Chad* all the credit. It's *you* you oughta be proud of, raising him the way you did. The way he turned out, that's your doing, don't forget."

That this cause-and-effect mother-and-son relationship must also apply to Shirl and Joey was something she could blithely ignore. It was the *father* who had had the effect there—the adverse effect, of course—and Shirl loved to think Maud shared with her the total failure of their ex-husbands' ability to function as fathers. "That big creep," she told Maud, had taken off one fine day in May and was never heard from again. "One fine day in May," she was always saying, making it sound like an old-fashioned song. "He's up and off, the big creep. Leaving me with the mortgage, the bills, the kid. Not one red cent did he leave me nor did he send me."

"He pays nearly all the bills," Maud said of Chad's father, while Shirl wound out the rag in the sink. "I'd never've been able to send him to that school. It costs a fortune. It costs eleven thousand a year for tuition." The shake she was making done to a thick cream, she poured it into one of the ribbed glasses. It was so thick it stood up around the straw.

"So what's money, girl, I'd like to know?" asked Shirl, apparently forgetting money was her major complaint about the big creep. "It ain't money makes a kid turn out with character and personality. Is that shake for him?" Again she nodded towards Joey. "Christ, is it his birthday or something?"

Maud sighed and walked down the counter with the glass as Shirl called to Joey that he had enough zits already he looked like a potholed road and he could just kiss his chances with Louella Harper goodbye if he drank that shake because he'd sure never kiss Louella.

The six faces at the counter all turned to the object of these words, and as she set down the milk shake Maud could hear Joey mumbling into his drowned potatoes for someone to fuck off. He did not look up to see Maud giving him an encouraging smile, although he did thank her and cleave his hand to the ribbed glass as if this were some way of wreaking vengeance on his mother.

"Living well is the best revenge," said Maud brightly, wanting to cheer him up.

This earned her a squinty-eyed look and a request for a spoon for this "shit-thick" shake.

Maud pulled an iced-tea spoon from a plastic cutlery tray and put it before him. She walked back down to get the coffee pot and refill Ulub's cup. He was extending it, his oil-black thumb holding back the spoon. Shirl could have poured the coffee; all she was doing now was standing smoking, but she no doubt thought that concentrating on bad fathers was more important and picked up where she'd left off.

"Conscience money. That's all it is."

Rinsing off a Coca-Cola glass, Maud said again that Chad's father paid for it, if that's what it was.

Shirl was driving home a point and she wasn't letting Maud deflect her, even though it was Maud's marriage and divorce and Shirl hadn't been there.

"I don't care if he put all the crack dealers in Detroit"—it came out "*Dee*-troit"—"through Yale, it still don't make up for walking out on your wife and baby boy"—she was shoving her close-together eyes up into Maud's face—"for a piece of ass."

Shirl's idea of conversational discretion was lowering her usual bawl to an asplike whisper that whipped down the counter, stinging each customer into looking up before they all returned their eyes to their plates and cups.

"Tight ass at that," Shirl hissed.

Maud's ex-husband had once actually walked into the Rainbow Café with his wife, and that had provided Shirl with a mother lode of conversational possibilities superseded only by God having been around at the Creation. Velda, the new—well, slightly used, given two prior husbands and three years of marriage to Ned—Mrs. Chadwick, was a model and once a Miss Universe contender. She had flyaway cheekbones, a mass of red-gold hair that looked wind-blown but you knew was actually blown by a hairdresser, a pencil-thin figure, and model's shoulders accented by shoulder pads like a football player's. Shirl said she looked like the TV antenna on top of the Rainbow Café, but Maud knew Shirl was just trying to make her feel better. The shoulder pads were stacked under a green silk designer dress. Velda glowed like neon and vibrated on and off, standing there in the Rainbow looking around at its dark booths and long counter with a "how quaint" expression, twisting this way and that—torso, chin, neck—as if Ubub might jump up and take pictures. Probably it was unconscious posing, Maud thought later, charitably, since Velda was probably never far from the cameras and strobe lights.

When they walked in tanned like crisp toast with Chad in tow, it caused a mild sensation—as interesting an event as would ever happen in the Rainbow, Shirl had said, short of an onslaught of hooded Palestinian terrorists. Ulub and Ubub had looked up from their short stacks and eggs; Dodge Haines had nearly slid from his stool; Mayor Sims, who'd come in for a sobering cup of coffee before confronting Mrs. Sims, had stopped in the middle of delivering to Dodge what sounded like an old campaign speech on drugs. There were a few strays (as Shirl called people off the street), who'd swiveled in their booths to have a gander at Velda.

It had been just this time a year ago, a few days before Labor Day, and Ned said they'd come "on the spur" (Maud just *bet*), and Velda angled her way to the counter and cut in with this *super* idea of taking Chad on an "island hop": Nantucket, Puget Sound, the Cape, Martha's Vineyard. And *did* Maud mind *too* very much if they carted this *wonderful* child (Chad kept his face blank, his eyes down, and looked guilty for being there) off just *four* days early and then they'd *whisk* him to school after this *whirlwind* vacation, and it sounded to Maud like they were all caught in a plane propeller; but Velda smiled and smiled, her long, tanned arm half-leaning, half-dropping across the counter as if she were already in the middle of Puget Sound doing a crawl stroke.

And Ned. All he'd done was just bunch his arm around Chad's shoulders, occasionally giving him a fatherly squeeze, playing Daddy Warbucks to a fare-thee-well.

Mind? Of course she minded. Did Mr. Blank-Face want to go? Of course he did, though she knew *he* knew this was completely rotten, Ned and Velda swooping in this way and taking his mom by surprise. And it wasn't as if they were fighting a custody battle; it was only an "island hop." Maud had stood behind the counter in the midst of all of this green glitter and bonhomie and felt like a cow in a field, beige and dull, chewing over her response.

She saw herself reflected in the eyes of the incandescent Velda— Maud with her shoulder-length, straight, sand-colored hair and desert-brown eyes, the ordinarily subdued freckles probably breaking out like a fresh crop of zits. Stood there with a cut-out smile while ribs of white anger shot through her.

But the anger dissolved momentarily, replaced by an empathy for Chad, who had nearly dislocated his shoulder getting away from his father's grip to go over and sit down and start a conversation with Ulub. This in itself was an act of desperation (though you'd never know it from his laid-back smile), since neither of the Woods talked. Ubub did act as main factotum sometimes, placing the orders at the counter. So Chad started up this monologue, offering them cigarettes (which they regarded as if they were strange Indian signs) in order to show Maud he was sloughing off these two tanned people and their offer if that was what his mom wanted.

Maud kept on smiling and said, sure, sure, that was fine, that was very nice, she was sure Chad would enjoy that. Would any sane nineteen-year-old not enjoy going back to college with a tan like the ones Velda and Ned were sporting? Oh, La Porte had its lake, but no sand beaches, and people didn't do much swimming, just boating of sorts. La Porte had seen better days. Once it had been a fashionable little summer resort, but it was pretty down-at-heel now.

Velda and Ned had come to town and left with Chad, who was wearing (Maud noticed) a new pair of Gucci shoes and an Italian jacket that made his eyes look like molten gold. It was so strange, Maud thought, how her own dull coloring had translated itself into that sunlit look.

And Shirl had rooted herself by the coffee machine, drinking in the scene like her cup of coffee, enjoying every revolting minute of it.

It was the first, last, and only time Maud had ever seen Velda.

When Ned had paid for their three glasses of iced tea and called to "Velvet" they'd better be going, Maud heard Shirl make a retching noise over the cash drawer, which had sprung out to slap her in the stomach.

Ned had left a tip.

He had folded up a twenty into a little square and stuck it under the iced-tea glass. That was Ned's version of "discreet."

No one had noticed this but Chad. He had stared at his father's departing back, plucked the bill from the counter, and looked at it as if it were a hand grenade.

It had saved what little could be saved of the encounter when Chad had shoved it back into Ned's pocket without a word.

Maybe Shirl had been thinking of this present Labor Day as some sort of anniversary of last year's and Velveeta's (as Shirl called her) visit, because she couldn't seem to stop talking about the haplessness and hatefulness of husbands, and what she'd have done if the big creep had come back to La Porte dragging the new Mrs. Creep along. Since she was scraping out the hard vanilla from the bottom of the ice-cream container, much of this was echoing up from the nearly empty basin. But her head and hand would emerge, the scoop dipped in warm water, and she'd call down the counter to Maud, who was trying not to pay attention, cutting up the lemon chiffon pie.

Dodge Haines, who was getting the apple pie à la mode, crusty with ice, leered over his coffee, and the others up and down the counter were equally entranced with this playback of the visit of Maud's ex-husband and his new wife; also, it gave a man like Dodge, macho to the core, a chance to exchange his witty keep-'em-barefoot-and-pregnant philosophical views with Shirl.

The only person who had the good taste at least to pretend not to listen was the tall brunette sitting at the counter, the one for whom Maud had just cut up the lemon chiffon. This was Dr. Elizabeth Hooper, a woman Maud could hardly say she knew, for Dr. Hooper didn't live in La Porte, but a woman for whom Maud felt an infinite respect and empathy.

Dr. Elizabeth Hooper fascinated Maud. She came through La Porte exactly once a month, every third weekend, like clockwork. She was tall and elegant, wore simple suits in cold weather, simple dresses in warm. Today she had on a frosty blue linen dress. Maud always studied her dresses and accessories. To the shoulder had been pinned a gold brooch, and she wore a gold bracelet; one long, bare arm rested on the counter, but unlike Velda's, it was pale, untanned. This alone would have sent Dr. Hooper rocketing in Maud's esteem: she was clearly a woman who had other things on her mind besides Nantucket. Maud also liked the way she sat at the counter rather than sitting in one of the dark, high-backed booths, the way the other women who came in on their own did. It bespoke to Maud a certain confidence and carelessness, that Dr. Hooper couldn't be bothered worrying over being a woman alone. For despite the entire feminist movement, Maud had seen absolutely no change in the mouselike withdrawal of any woman from fifteen to fifty, the caginess they felt over being in a *restaurant* alone, as if it were a porn movie house.

Since Maud considered herself terminally shy, it had been nearly two months before she got up the nerve to speak to Dr. Hooper. She could never keep up the friendly chat of Charlene or the constant complaining of Shirl as they moved down the counter and among the booths. Except for Miss Ruth Porte, who seemed so frail and quiet it would have been shameful not to be able to converse with her, Maud hardly exchanged a sentence with the customers; could not be forced to even under the constant agitating of Dodge Haines, who considered himself La Porte's lady-killer and never seemed to look at any woman above breast level. "You'd think my tits was my eyes," Charlene would say, but in such a salacious tone that you knew she enjoyed it. Charlene had a big smile and big breasts and bestowed herself on everyone like a basket of fruit.

All Maud could do to make up for her lack of conversation (except for her book talks with Miss Ruth) was to smile, and her smile wasn't like Charlene's—no wide red lips and flash of bleached teeth. Her smile was little more than a slight upward hook at the ends of her mouth, a shy smile. She tried to smile a lot to make up for her silences—which were at least appreciated greatly by Joey and, she thought, by Dr. Elizabeth Hooper—because otherwise the people of La Porte might think she was putting on airs. It was her college education and her being favored so much by Miss Ruth Porte, also educated and able to talk to Maud about books, that she was afraid might make people think she was uppity. But even though Maud's smile was constrained, she knew it was pleasant. An old boyfriend (a hundred years ago, when there were such things) had told her she had the prettiest smile he'd ever seen. It was the smile of a little kid, of an *infant,* even, the smile of someone who'd just learned and really meant it. It was the most sincere smile, he said, he'd come across. Maud had forgotten his name, this high school boy; but she remembered the grave look on his face, the effort that had gone into describing her smile *just right.*

It was a compliment she had tucked away in her mind like a petal in a book and looked at again and again for thirty years. Only Chad, who'd told her she looked more like thirty than forty-seven; and Sam, who had told her (to her utter astonishment) she was the most comfortable person to be with because she was as serene as a nun (when she wasn't mad)—only they had ever said anything as nice. Ned had never paid her a compliment she could remember.

Maybe it was her "serene" smile that made Dr. Elizabeth Hooper react in kind. It was probably because Maud was the only one in the Rainbow (except for Ulub and Ubub) who hadn't tried in some way to wheedle out of her why she kept coming through La Porte. Charlene had found out Dr. Hooper was a psycho-whatever because a cousin of a friend of an aunt of hers knew someone who'd gone to see her. Or so Charlene said.

But no one could find out what she was doing in *La Porte*, going back and forth, and sometimes staying overnight at Stuck's rooming house near the end of Main. There was much speculation about whether she'd been called in by Miss Ruth to pay personal visits to Miss Ruth's crazy Aunt Simkin. Shirl, who was never hard-pressed to mind her own business, still felt "funny," she said, about asking Dr. Hooper why she came through town.

It was, Maud supposed, because Dr. Hooper was a psychiatrist, and people who'd never read about it or been to one (as Maud had while she was married) thought they could read your mind and probably suck your soul out of your body. The way Shirl talked about them, leaning on the counter, moodily smoking a cigarette and polishing a glass, head doctors were about as safe to be around as mass murderers or that Boy Chalmers fellow who they said had murdered Nancy Alonzo and done the same thing to those two women in Hebrides. She threw down the towel and shuddered. It hardly bore thinking about.

So she went back to thinking about Dr. Hooper. Maud would watch Dr. Hooper's flickering glance at Shirl or Charlene and wonder if perhaps she *could* see what was going on in their minds.

It was Maud who always waited on Dr. Hooper and who always saved back a piece of lemon chiffon pie if they were running short. It was true that Shirl made the best pies of anyone around except for Jen Graham, who ran the hotel over in Spirit Lake, and this particular pie was especially popular: the filling was a pale cloud of whipped-up lemony filling, and the crust was melt-in-your-mouth baked meringue. That Shirl had begged the recipe off Jen Graham and then started claiming the pie was her original creation, just about everybody knew, although Shirl thought it was a deep, dark secret and a real sleight-of-hand performance on her part to wheedle a recipe out of Jen. The Rainbow's big white pie boxes were always carted away by customers after eating a slice of lemon chiffon for dessert. So they often ran out of it. Even Chad loved it, and he hated lemon pie.

Dr. Hooper was in the Rainbow Café the third weekend of every month, Fridays and Sundays, eating her pie and drinking her coffee, and often writing a postcard or two, sometimes a letter. It always amused Maud to watch Mayor Sims maneuver around behind Dr. Hooper, leaning back and staring down his nose in his attempt to make out what she was writing. Dr. Hooper always caused a mild stir, probably because she was their mystery woman. Her appearances in La Porte and the Rainbow were as dependable as the turning of day into night.

It was Dr. Hooper herself who had finally, some months ago, started a conversation. She had asked Maud what school her son attended. It had so surprised Maud that Dr. Hooper knew she *had* a son, Maud had slopped coffee into the saucer when she was refilling the cup.

Dr. Hooper said, "I heard the owner"—and here she looked off towards Shirl—"talking about him. She seems to think very highly of him." Her smile was slow; she seemed to deliberate before every action, and she looked serious even when smiling. "That's unusual," she added, before going back to cutting through her wedge of pie.

Maud held the coffee pot aloft, thinking the statement mysterious, inscrutable, just the sort of non–small talk she'd expect from Dr. Elizabeth Hooper, if she ever spoke at all. Dr. Hooper certainly wouldn't go in for "Well, we're getting weather," as Sonny Stuck had said that day. Still, to introduce the subject of Maud's own son was a pretty heady subject for conversation.

Forgetting specifically what she'd asked, Maud answered, "Well

... thank you." Then, feeling foolish with that response, she'd gone on: "I mean . . . why is it unusual?" Ignoring Dodge Haines and Sonny Stuck holding up their cups for refills, Maud had just set the pot back on the Pyrex burner and got a clean napkin to mop up the spilled coffee in the saucer. Dodge called to her, but she paid no attention. Let Charlene wriggle on down there.

Dr. Hooper said, "It's unusual for older people to be impressed by anyone twenty or so."

"Twenty. He's twenty." Nervously, she began to shine up the milk-shake container.

Dr. Hooper nodded solemnly.

"I have a son myself. He's fifteen. He's in a prep school up north." She fiddled with a menu. "That's why I go through La Porte; it's right on the way. But I usually have to stay overnight, because it's quite a trip. I stay at the rooming house down the street."

As if everybody didn't know. Mildred Stuck, who rented out rooms, thought having a New York *psychiatrist* staying at her place made her Queen of the Rainbow Café, nearly; she'd even had the brass to sit right down in Miss Ruth Porte's booth and start braying about her "clientele." But it was clear she didn't know a thing about Dr. Hooper or she would have told Miss Ruth.

Maud's mouth opened, but no words came out—that's how amazed she was that Dr. Elizabeth Hooper had a son away at school, just as she, Maud, did. She wanted to ask about him, but before she could think of anything sensible, Dr. Hooper went on.

"Adults—I mean *older* adults—" and she smiled slowly again to indicate she didn't mean to suggest Maud's son wasn't "adult"— "usually haven't much respect for younger ones. For young people. And I imagine"—again, she smiled slowly, as her glance strayed toward the end of the counter and Joey, drinking a Coke— "that she'd be hard to impress. She seems rather disappointed in her own son."

Maud blinked, looking from Shirl, who was complaining to

some customer about his handing her a twenty when ("the damned fool must have known") it was Labor Day weekend and all change disappeared on holidays (to hear Shirl tell it)—looking down to Joey, then back to Dr. Hooper, sipping her coffee, and wondered if Shirl was right after all, if there was some sort of mind reading going on. Not soul sucking, of course, just mind reading. How stupid, she thought. Anyone with a grain of intelligence and any powers of observation wouldn't have to hang around the Rainbow for long to know Shirl was "disappointed" with Joey. And this woman was a psychiatrist.

"People . . . parents . . . I seldom hear them paying compliments to young people." Frowning over her coffee cup, seeming to give this point her gravest consideration, Dr. Hooper added, "Indeed, I never do."

As Charlene flounced by behind her and grabbed up the coffee pot (it was *Maud's* turn at the counter, after all), Maud stood her ground and asked with deadly seriousness, "Why do you think that is?"

"Well . . . there doesn't seem to be much respect for young people. Their parents certainly don't have much for them, in the sense they seem to be more problems than people. I expect it might be because everyone feels so guilty—the parents, the children. It goes back and forth, gets passed around the table and back again." She replaced her cup and folded her hands before her, her expression, her position a little like someone kneeling in a pew. "So your son must be quite unusual."

He *was* unusual; but Maud didn't think she should blatantly agree. Out of the corner of her eye she saw Shirl, who was banging open the display case to get at the pies, staring at her. But Shirl would turn to stone before she'd interrupt a conversation with Dr. Hooper, since Shirl herself was dying of curiosity to know about her.

"I guess people seem to like him," Maud said. "I guess he's able to talk to adults more than most kids his age. He seems, well, comfortable with them, I think. I remember when he was, oh, six or seven . . ." This was ridiculous, she thought, busying herself with polishing up the milk-shake container; she couldn't stand here and reminisce. And there was that familiar tightening in her throat; that would be just fine, wouldn't it—in answer to a polite question on this woman's part, suddenly to start crying? Yes, that would be fine.

Dr. Hooper was finished but not leaving, turning slightly back and forth on the wooden counter stool. She slid the conversation effortlessly into something more general. "I don't mean to say that it's just children that have a hard time of it." Her tone was slightly apologetic, as if it were she and not Maud who was making things difficult, conversationally. "So do parents. Parents are so often forced to desperate remedies." She grew silent, her eyes down-turned. "What do you think?"

That Dr. Hooper thought her opinion truly mattered astonished Maud and drew her eyes from her fun-house reflection in the aluminum container up to Dr. Hooper's mild brown gaze. Maud rocked a little on her heels, as if her body were being pushed by the sudden force of all of the unanswered questions she had about herself and Chad, about her depression over the sense of loss, about the . . . betrayal. The word simply clicked into place in her mind and shocked her. "Betrayal." Her face grew stiff with the exertion of trying to keep this disloyal, irrational thought from showing there. But the word dragged a rush of other irrational notions with it—the notion that she'd been tricked, tricked into believing childhood would last forever. Believing it in her crazy, mixed-up way. Face it: what she felt this very minute was that *he* had tricked her, his six-year-old-ness, his child-ness had tricked her; and she felt, even as Dr. Hooper was taking the three one-dollar bills from her purse and still looking at Maud with those luminous eyes—Maud felt the rage beginning. It would spread as it always did, burning in her constricted stomach muscles, raying out through her limbs, upward to her face like a hot, angry blush, and then settling in a tight sore lump that she feared would fester and burst.

All of this went through her mind in a moment, less than a moment, and she saw herself, as if she were standing away from herself, writing up Dr. Hooper's check with a little frown of concentration that was supposed to suggest she was merely considering her answer. Wetting her lips, she wrote down the pie and coffee, a dollar eighty-five, afraid this woman had seen this inexplicable, murderous rage which was subsiding as quickly as it had come. She added the tax slowly, afraid to look into Dr. Hooper's eyes for fear that Dr. Hooper had seen clear through her, through her carefully ironed apron and sprigged cotton dress, her freckles, pale skin, and light eyes, to a woman with all of the characteristics of a psychopath. The question still hung in the air, *What do you think?*, and what Maud wanted to say was, "I think I could kill someone, I could be one of those parents who could kill their own children, and it terrifies me that I could, even for one-tenth of a second, actually stand in that person's shoes, feel that person's arm raising the knife or the gun" . . . but to turn, Maud wondered confusedly, on whom? The knife seemed to twist backward into her own heart, the gun rise to her own temple. And the murderous anger returned while she drew a line on the check to tote up the pie, coffee, tax— returned, receded in waves, and left behind it the stuff of depression like detritus for the birds on the beach.

As she slowly tore Dr. Hooper's check from the pad and repositioned the oblong of carbon paper, she wondered, how in God's name could all of this go through a person's mind while she was writing on a dirty-white check with "Thank You" scrolled at the top in faded blue ink?

She placed the check by Dr. Hooper's cup, fixed the small, tilted-up smile on her face as she slid the book of checks back into her apron pocket and answered the question. "Well, I think most parents don't know how they feel or what to do, and maybe it's because of all the decisions they have to make—not the big ones, the little ones, the ones that seem to come up every minute, and you have to make up your mind in a split second without being able to get anyone's advice, and where the odds are always against any decision being right because what you think is in everybody's best interests isn't at all, since a lot of the time you don't even want everybody's best interests, don't even know what they are, not even your own. . . . Maybe that's why I don't blame Shirl. Or anyone." Maud stopped suddenly, closed her mouth as if slamming a tiny door, feeling that what was behind it, a rush of thoughtless words bursting out, unbidden and unchecked like some horror-film poltergeist, so alarmed her that she just had to clamp her lips together, try to paste on again that little hooked smile to let Dr. Hooper know she wasn't irrevocably crazy.

But Dr. Hooper merely nodded in her thoughtful way. Her long, elegant fingers placed the three one-dollar bills with the check (it was always the same amount) as she said, "I've never heard a parent say that." Her own smile was a little like Maud's, closed-mouthed, tilting up.

Is that good or is that bad? Maud wanted to ask.

But Maud had been surprised that Dr. Hooper had come in just this morning, apparently on her way "up north," for tomorrow was Labor Day.

"Well, he sometimes goes back to school early. Before he has to."

Immediately, Maud felt an even closer bond. She hung on to the silver milk-shake container, her hands jittering up and down, and told Elizabeth Hooper that Chad himself had left early to visit a friend of his. Probably, she couldn't keep the irritation—or was it sadness? they seemed to overlap—out of her voice, and she cut up Dr. Hooper's lemon chiffon pie pretty ruthlessly. Then it occurred to her that if Dr. Hooper's son had gone back to school already, he obviously wasn't riding with his mother.

"He doesn't spend summers with me." Dr. Hooper's dark eyes were on the piece of pie.

Maud could sense that something here was wrong, so she merely said "Oh" and wiped her hands down her apron sides. Yes, there was really something wrong, for Dr. Hooper's hand shook as she raised her coffee cup. Then she said, not to Maud but very quietly to her piece of pie, "He doesn't live with me; he lives with his father. His father has custody."

Maud returned the pie to the display case, looking at, and then away from, Elizabeth Hooper, who was clearly upset. Maud licked her lips and tried to say that she couldn't imagine that someone like her, who went to so much trouble to see her son, could not get custody. God, look at Shirl. Well, that wasn't fair, she guessed; Shirl actually did put up with a lot from Joey and had raised him all by herself. . . .

And Dr. Hooper once again seemed to be reading Maud's mind, for she said, "I could have had custody; I didn't want it." She had affixed a stamp to a postcard and now brought her balled-up fist down on it. Then she looked at Maud with a thin smile. "I'm a child psychiatrist, and that's how smart I was."

Dr. Hooper hitched her bag over her shoulder and collected her check.

He looked down at the drawer of knives he held on his lap and thought of the loneliness and emptiness and the ones who had caused it, and were still causing it, and that it was only right they should have to pay.

It was an ordinary kitchen drawer with a white enamel front. He had pulled it out by its ridged aluminum handle so that he could sit with it and hold it like a baby or a pet. He was sitting on the green slat-backed kitchen chair, his long hands resting either side of the drawer, looking down at the knives, different sizes, different shapes, and the cylindrical, tempered-steel sharpener he used to keep them carefully honed.

Now, he picked up the butcher knife, ran his thumb lightly along its edge, and had to suck the droplet of blood that made a tiny bubble even with so light a stroke. He remembered he had been in a bit of temper when he'd drawn that one swiftly from side to side down the sharpener. He tried the paring knife, the cleaver, the cook's knife, the hook-bill of the knife for dismembering chicken, the two utility knives. The serrated bread knife he didn't bother with. It was no good to him.

His mind was a black well you could drop a body in, and because it was so deep in this blackness, the sound at the bottom would be no more than the splash of a small rock. A well, a vault, cellar, cavern—empty of light.

Not even as much light as he had been able to see when he was very small under his shut bedroom door after his mother had gone. Just a strand of light. He would crawl out of bed and lie facing the door, his eyes seeing nothing under it but that strand of light, could not see his mother, had thought she was gone forever. He would lie there willing her to come back, thinking the sheer force of his will, his concentration, would make her return to his room, that he would hear what had been the indistinct and distant clap of her slippers down the hall growing more distinct, coming back and stopping at his door again. But he figured his mind must not be strong enough, that there was some weakness there, for she didn't come back.

He would lie there on his side, then, looking at the band of light under the door. If he didn't do this, the dark would swallow him, for even if his eyes adjusted to it the things in his room—lumpy chair, bureau, hump between bedposts, posts themselves—would be barely distinguishable, without definition, and melt back into darkness from mere staring to bring them out of it. His best friend back then had been terrified of the Thing in his closet at night, a Thing he'd described as a monster with teeth like panes of glass that he could feel shatter when the monster bit into his throat.

But he, *he* had never been afraid of a Thing in the closet; he had been afraid of the closet itself, of the darkness and the loneliness. For they always came together. The loneliness was not quite as bad in the daylight hours, because he was out of the house doing something. He could feel it, though, always, even then, as a dull ache; for although he was around others, he never felt, being around them, what he needed. What he needed was intimacy.

Everyone needed it, of course; he was no different from anyone else, except that his need was consuming. Loneliness drove him to desperation. He wondered why the doctors left it out of the list: sex, hunger, thirst. Would he kill someone for a glass of water, for a can of beans, for a good fuck? Sex? Why, sex had hardly anything to do with it.

His hands once again returned to the sides of the drawer; he looked through to the larder, looked at the spigot slowly dripping water (he'd have to fix that washer), and thought, reasonably, as he'd never been dying of hunger or thirst, he couldn't say what that would make a man do. And, of course, when it came to sex, he supposed they weren't actually talking about *killing* for it. He frowned. But, then, didn't animals . . . ?

Looking down at the knives that speared back the reflected light of the bright bulb above, he shook his head, trying to clear it. In his childhood room there had been such a light; it would sway slightly above his bed until his mother pulled the metal cord. Sometimes she would lie down with him and he wouldn't even care about her breath, heavy with whisky and cigarettes. No, he wouldn't care.

God knows he had tried other ways to get what he needed. To get rid of the loneliness and find the intimacy. Even the word seemed warm and slightly liquid. If only his speech hadn't been tangled, stupid words hitting, bashing, mangling one another in their rush toward friendship, toward intimacy; and if that hadn't made the women look down, look away, even step back, almost as if (now the face that turned to the drawer had to smile) . . .

As if he was holding a knife on them.

He hated that he had to show them the knife, that they had to know that they were going to die, for although it didn't completely spoil the end, it made it sad, much more difficult. But there was no other way, for they had to see what they'd done and what they were guilty of. How strange was the often held idea that just before the moment of death, in the moments of dying, the expression in a dying person's eyes grew remote, clouded, shuttered. That a shade snapped down, or curtains suddenly pulled to.

To him, it was just the other way around. It was the moment when the shade snapped up, the musty curtains suddenly opened to let in the light. It was the moment of profoundest and deepest intimacy. There was no holding back.

And he had tried, always, and gently, to explain this. Although his holding them had to be rough (how else could he keep them still?), his voice had been gentle (which in itself was a small miracle), and the words had flowed from his mouth like syrup, smoothly. Naturally, they fought it. Some women had incredible strength.

He was sorry that they couldn't, by an act of a merciful God (but, then, there was no God, not really), simply die in his arms peacefully. Yet, if they had, would they have understood? Would their minds have been full of *him* and the fear of the dark? Or would they be thinking about some other person, some lost place, a long, green meadow full of sunlight? They would not be thinking of *him*.

He drove the paring knife into the chair arm so hard the blade broke from the handle; and realizing he'd done this without meaning to, that the loneliness had driven him to this, he started to weep, wiped his sleeve along his eyes, placed the broken knife carefully on the table.

Taking the drawer out, smoothing his thumb along the knife-edges, childish fits of rage—he knew the signs. That the loneliness, the need for intimacy were overwhelming him again and he would have to do something.

But they hadn't screamed.

It had surprised him that they hadn't screamed. Probably because he had been just an old, sad face for the most part, and then, after he had explained and pinioned them and brought out the knife, any scream had been locked in their throats, frozen there, choking them. Yet he had usually had to clamp his hand over their mouths because of the pleas, the whimpers, the "no"s (no no no no no no) that he was loath to hear.

Except Tony. Antoinette. When he brought the knife from under his jacket, she'd looked at him and laughed. Laughed fit to kill. (Now he bowed his head in shame for that lousy pun.) She was something, wasn't she? Had it angered him she'd laughed? Hadn't taken his reasons seriously? Of course not; he wasn't childish. He had laughed with her, out there in the woods. It had been good to laugh; the idea that that last long look of understanding might be one of pleasure was infinitely preferable to the terror later in the eyes of Loreen Butts.

But her laughter had run down like an old car sputtering to a stop when he'd held her against the oak tree. Carefully and slowly he'd explained he wasn't going to rape her; it wasn't sex he was after. It was closeness.

Understand?

Tony had looked at him wildly, her eyes wild over the top of his hand where he felt the hot breath coming.

And then slowly she nodded.

Is that what you want? You want me to fuck you? You want sex?

The look in her eyes changed to something sly and knowing. Again she nodded.

That's what you want, you can have it, of course. Die happy.

To his astonishment, as he stood against her still with his hand over her mouth, she took her own two away where she'd been dragging, clawing at his, and ripped the top of her cheap rayon blouse down with one hand; the other yanked at his fly. He was hard as a rock.

With her head she was trying to nod toward the ground.

You want it on the ground?

Swiftly, she nodded her head, three, four times.

He held the knife to her throat, lowered her to the ground, where she squirmed, panted, and he spread the fingers of his hand and heard her begging for it. He was enthralled; he was fascinated. He brought the knife down from her throat, held the cold steel across her nipples, which excited her even more, and he looked down at his hard cock and shoved it in . . .

Stupid bitch.

Stupid bitch. It might have worked, she might have got hold of that knife if she'd waited until he was pumping away, if she'd waited until he came, if she'd *pretended* to come too, again and again and again . . .

That's the way he thought of it later, after he felt her go for the knife, after he raised it, brought it around, and slit her throat.

Oh, redemption.

Sam

PART TWO

H e was out there somewhere.

He was as much out there as the black slab rocks that marked off Swain's Point, rooted in the dark like the massive pines that surrounded the boarded-up fishing lodge at the end of the Point.

As Sam drove the potholed road that circled the lake, checking the cabins through screens of shrubbery and openings through oaks and pines, he could sense that presence.

Sam was almost positive that it was no vagrant, no passing stranger, who had tied up and knifed Eunice Hayden, which was what everybody had believed and gone on believing for four years since her murder, probably because they didn't want to believe it could be somebody they knew.

The trouble was that Eunice Hayden had not been exactly a model of deportment, there at the end of her short life. No one could understand this: how any child of Molly and Wade Hayden could turn out like Eunice, when all of her childhood Eunice had been straight as a plumb line, and as rigid and strained, like a child in a black bonnet in a Gothic picture. Wade Hayden had been postmaster for twenty years, and his wife, Molly, was always the first person people called on if there was any money to be raised in a good cause, for the church or the library or the school. Molly could be depended on to go out and get it, could look out of her flinty eyes and make you feel completely responsible for the cracked bindings on books or the short supply of pews. And Eunice's father, Wade, people were always saying, was as honest as the day was long. Sam had always wondered why they said it. How would a postmaster display his *dis*honesty? Shortchange you on stamps?

As he drove slowly, catching the occasional shifting blue light of a television, he tried to put these ungenerous thoughts out of his mind. The girl was dead now. And her mother, Molly, was dead too; she'd died, people thought, from the shock of it, six months later. Molly, Sam knew, who looked as tough as a washboard, had always been ailing. Still, the cold-blooded murder of her daughter certainly had hurried death along, he was sure.

So Wade Hayden had had to retrace the same dirt pathway to the same graveyard and the same tree under which his daughter had been buried, maybe even treading in the same footprints, his own, in which the dust had barely had time to resettle itself.

Of course, the family had come in for their share of questions. One always had to look to family. Wade and Molly had been in Hebrides, they said; Molly had gone shopping while Wade did some pinch-hitting for a friend of his at the Hebrides post office, which wasn't much of a post office, he'd often told people, being only a one-man, one-room PO, with hardly enough business even to warrant the one man. Wade would say this with obvious pride in his own position as La Porte's postmaster: even though La Porte was a smaller place, still there was so much summer business it warranted two men. So Wade had an assistant. He was always glad to help out over in Hebrides whenever the postal clerk (as Wade called him) needed a relief person. That's where he'd been, while his wife had been doing some shopping, and they'd been there for the whole of the afternoon, or at least three hours of it, the three hours during which their daughter had been murdered.

So they'd come in for their share; only it was hard for Sam to lean on the bereft parents the way you might on someone not family, the way he'd leaned on Bubby Dubois and Dodge Haines.

It was Dodge who'd found her, and who never let anyone forget it, though he soft-pedaled the fact he'd come in for a fair amount of questioning himself. The Haydens had a small spread a half-mile from the lake, a few acres with a house and a barn and a henhouse. Molly sold free-range eggs, and a number of men you wouldn't expect to be much interested in eggs had been going out there to buy them. Dodge Haines was one. Bub Dubois's kids had been seen coming out of the barn, too. Even the mayor had got to making speeches about factory-laid eggs and started his personal campaign for the Haydens' double-grade-A brown eggs. It was some time before a few people—the mayor's wife, for one—realized it was Eunice who'd been left to see to the selling of the eggs, and that the transactions in the barn might be taking a little longer than was necessary.

Bubby Dubois did not at all appreciate the rumor that his sons, Darryl and Rick, had her front to back.

Dodge Haines found Eunice in the henhouse, trussed like a chicken, blood from her slashed throat and breast in places you would never expect it could fly to—the wooden beams, the manger—as if it meant to cry out for vindication. Eggs were lying crushed all around her, a hen with its neck broken lying beside her, and the stench so bad he didn't even have time to get out of the henhouse before he vomited.

Interference. That was the way he liked to put it. There had been no sexual interference, no rape as such. Might as well have been, according to the doctor who appeared on the scene with the county police, what with the rectal passage a ruin and the vagina cut up that way. It was as if someone had gone at Eunice intending to kill her with sex and, that not succeeding, had used a knife.

It was only Maud Chadwick who'd given voice to his, Sam's, feelings about Eunice Hayden: living with all that uprightness, those pillars of La Porte, what could Eunice do but go a little wild? Even Shirl's Joey had it better. At least, he probably felt a little bit free to tell his mom "Fuck off" once in a while, since Shirl did the same to him, felt no compunction at all about embarrassing him in front of strangers. Molly Hayden had embarrassed her daughter, too, but in such a way no one could really *call* it that; "good works" was what they *called* it: getting Eunice all dressed up when she was twelve or thirteen and going door-to-door to collect for the church bazaar. That a twelve-year-old would probably rather be strapped to a buzzsaw than have her friends think she was doing *good works* apparently never occurred to Molly Hayden, rattling a collection can down on the corner of First and Tremont streets one Christmas, both of them dressed in rags and shawls with holes in them, letting what rich there were in La Porte know that not everyone would have a turkey on the table if they didn't drop their money in the can. Chad had been going just that one semester to La Porte High School (a year during which he'd let Maud know daily that he'd sooner sleep standing up in an iron maiden than go to school); he said Eunice had been and still was the laughingstock of the school.

And the worst thing Molly had contrived to "humble" (for that's how she put it) her daughter was to take her into the Rainbow Café or Wheeler's Restaurant or even the DoNut DeLite and try to get the waitress or manager to exchange a meal for pot holders Eunice had crocheted or dish towels clumsily edged. Eunice had always had to do the talking. Even Shirl, who was proof against any sob story, would go beet red and just tell Eunice to be quiet and for her and her mother to sit down and order what they wanted from the menu. "Damned old cow," Shirl would say after they'd gone. "And the Haydens far from poor. There's a mother for you." And if Joey happened to be down the counter, the comment would be directed at him. Count your blessings.

Suffer little children, Molly was always saying. Well, said Maud, she ought to know. And add to that that Eunice was as plain as a fence post, though broader in the beam, and it wasn't surprising to Maud that she'd do something extravagant. Could Sam imagine, Maud had asked, Eunice giving Wade or Molly Hayden the finger? Wade Hayden even looked a little like Abraham Lincoln—gangly, with dark hair and that long jaw and sad black eyes. Since her mother was so hell-bent on raising money for good causes, perhaps Eunice had decided on a better way to get it, and not have to go door-to-door standing out in the cold. Lie around in some warm, musty hay.

Sam DeGheyn worried a lot about Maud Chadwick. He hadn't liked leaving her alone, especially after her son had just left, since he knew how much store she set by that boy. Sam had never seen a mother so taken with a child and at the same time so convinced she had done it all wrong.

As he neared Bunny Caruso's cottage, Sam pulled off the road to watch what action there might be there, and let the engine idle as he thought about Murray Chadwick. He didn't like his first name, so he was called Chad. Chad was one of the nicest kids Sam had ever met, and he'd met plenty, and under less-than-ideal circumstances. What he couldn't understand was why Maud thought none of her son's good qualities had come from her, not even his looks, and he looked just like her, or like a lit-up version of her.

Sam was recalling the first time he'd run into Maud Chadwick and smiling over the memory. She'd just got to town and had come into the sheriff's office, stood on one foot, then another, until she'd finally managed to get out that she didn't understand about the parking-ticket envelope. Because the meter had run over, someone (and here she'd reddened, because the man in the uniform she was talking to just might be the someone) had put this envelope under the wiper, and she wasn't sure where to take the envelope. She'd put the fifty cents in it . . .

He wanted (not unkindly) to laugh at the desperation in her voice, at the gap between what she was requesting and the effort it took her to ask for it. Sam had just chewed his gum slowly, sitting there with his hands warmed by his armpits, and thought this new lady was extremely pretty—and thought also that she didn't know it. Perhaps it was Maud's shyness, compared to her son's ability to talk (sometimes a little glibly, Sam thought), that made her think they couldn't be much alike.

From Bunny Caruso's cottage there came a crash of what could have been glass breaking or a dozen other things. Sam was used to night-rending sounds coming from Bunny Caruso's.

Where, Sam wondered, did Maud think Chad got all of his qualities? She certainly didn't think there'd been much genetic enhancement from the father's side. Sometimes she'd look up at the star-salted sky as if Chad's good qualities had just sifted right down from the heavens.

As he passed the blued panes of windows behind which TV sets glowed, he'd wondered if it would help if Maud got a television; it might keep her inside at night. That was pretty ridiculous. Imagine this woman, who was trying to figure out why in Key West there was some kind of order lacking in La Porte, watching "Wheel of Fortune"! If the phrase came up "Ramon Fernandez, tell me, if you know," would Vanna White go bananas? He supposed he shouldn't go on at Maud the way he'd just done, because she got so mad; but that was, in a way, why he did it. The anger dragged her out of whatever haunted version of her life she was momentarily entertaining.

Sam's wife, Florence, called her "spooky."

"The Duboises passed by her on that dock several times. You know, they got that expensive speedboat last year"—

That Dubois talked about as if it was a fucking *yacht.*

—"and she just *sits* there in a chair. A *rocking* chair, and with a *lamp.*"

Florence had turned from the microwave—she microwaved everything—and went on: "At night, can you believe it? With a *lamp* dragged down there? How's she get it lit, I wonder?"

Sam was supposed to answer, but he just went on reading the La Porte *Pendant* and said nothing, and again she gave her attention to the microwave, which she had a way of staring at for abnormally long periods of time, the way people look at their wash going round or their TV screens. Through the kitchen door, Sam could see their own television screen and the faces flickering there, mouths forming silent words. The sound was often off.

"And if *that* isn't spooky, tell me—*tell* me. Ha!" Back to him again, she beat a tattoo on her hips with her fingers. Florence was never long on patience. She hated to microwave anything that required her to push the minute buttons. She was into seconds only. She stared at the black glass at the same time she hated the thing. Florence was trying to make him comment; she knew he liked Maud Chadwick. "Weird, that's what the Duboises said. Bubby calls her 'one weird lady.'"

"Bubby should know," Sam said, turning to the personals, seeing who was advertising a reunion and for everybody to come. Some of these people had folks in the hundreds. They couldn't send out invitations; they advertised.

"And what's *that* supposed to mean, Samuel?" The rising inflection hit the syllables like a musical scale.

Florence thought calling him "Samuel" was a massive irritation to him. He had never told her that Samuel wasn't his given name. His parents believed in simplicity. He did not answer her question, but looked over the top of the paper and said, "Is that toast in there? Are you microwaving the toast again?"

"I *repeat*—what's *that* supposed to mean?"

"That you can't microwave toast, that's what." Sam took a mouthful of coffee. It was sludge. She made it in the microwave.

"*Fuck* the fucking toast!" Florence was low on cuss words. "I'm not talking about the toast. I mean that comment about Bubby Dubois. What did you mean about 'he should know'? About weird, I mean."

Florence knew perfectly well or she'd never have remembered Sam's comment all this time. Still, he wished he hadn't brought it up. Avoiding a direct attack on the father, he simply noted the two Dubois sons' behavior. "Darryl and Rick are going to be hauled in one of these days, bet on it. I caught them dealing crack at the grade school; Donny caught them trying to gang-rape the Childess girl—"

The microwave buzzed and she yanked the door open. "A dirty rumor, that's all that was!"

Sam sighed. No sense getting into a fight about the father, Bubby Dubois. Bubby—what kind of man would still go by his baby-name? The thing was, Florence was sleeping with him, and she was eyeing Sam now with those liquid black Greek-olive eyes of hers and fearing he knew. Perhaps *knowing* Sam knew. Everyone in La Porte probably knew it.

He was pretending not to notice that she was standing there with the ceramic plate with his egg, bacon, toast, and that her large, familiar, still-enticing breasts were heaving—he wondered if with anger or with fear.

He could not look at her, because he no longer loved her, no longer cared much if she had a lover or not. And in some strange way this made him feel the guilty party. He almost pitied Florence that she couldn't be doing better than Bubby Dubois, much like a father would worry over a daughter's throwing herself away on some bum, some fucked-up guitarist who did gigs with a second-rate band.

Keeping his head down, he took the plate from her hands. His eyes smarted. They always did when he thought how he wished they'd had kids. Just one, just one.

So he pitied Florence because she was sleeping with Bubby Dubois, who ran a huge used-car business outside of Hebrides, had a cracked and tanned face like pie crust from all of those days with the hoods of cars stabbing the sun right back at him—the cars or the water; hair like meringue, a wispy white cloud of it with little tides of brown tipping the waves. When he wore that peach lounge suit of his, he looked edible.

"Did you have to microwave the damned toast, Florence?"

Staring down at the plate, she said, "*And* the eggs. And bacon."

It was accusing, as if his request for bacon and eggs had presented, together with the toast, a tactical maneuver that not even the Japanese could figure out and the Sanyo was lucky not to have short-circuited. The toast slices were limp as washcloths.

"Just because you've got a thing for Mrs. Spooky Chadwick, you don't have to go turning the tables." There was a glint of triumph in her eyes as she folded into her mouth a limp bacon strip that looked gray as chewing gum. Her face had a morning patina of shine, a slight greasiness that Sam had once thought sexually stimulating—something liquid emanating from the black, shiny hair, from the olive eyes. Florence was a good-looking woman.

When he just sat there blandly drinking his orange juice (the only thing that escaped the Sanyo) and not answering the charge about Mrs. Chadwick, Florence took another shot:

"Or maybe Bunny Caruso? Maybe her?"

He got up and dragged his uniform jacket from the chair, looking at her, shaking his head. What was in her tone and what was in her eyes was fear.

He knew she was scared to death he'd walk out on her one of these days, leave her to her Sanyo and to Dubois, and the very fear of it forced her into these strange tests of how far she could go.

Sam just smiled and said he had to go to work, gave her a kiss on the cheek, and saw the tears spring up in her eyes.

Every woman he knew seemed to have behind her eyes these little stands of water, ready to overflow.

Not just women, either, he thought, remembering his own reaction two minutes ago. Everyone.

Now he lit a cigarette, switched off the engine, and watched the light shifting in Bunny Caruso's cabin, mottling the shabby curtains. If he had walked up the muddy path filled with rain pools that never seemed to dry up to "check on the disturbance"—
"Thought maybe I heard something crash, Bunny"—Bunny Caruso would just stand there, thin even in that long, loose dress she could

slip over her head in one second flat, and tell him (eyes wide with innocence) that Hubert was "up to things" again.

Hubert was neither husband nor lover who occasionally might be beating the living shit out of Bunny. Hubert was, according to Bunny, her "familiar." Hubert was part of the whole rigmarole of Bunny's so-called business: like the crystal ball on its drift of black velvet, and the flickering candle she used during her "sessions" because she had to douse the light bulbs or Hubert wouldn't appear, heaping messages from the dead on the heads of the living. And the mirrors. Sam had never seen so much mirror space. The ceiling was mirrored, and two of the walls. He supposed it was the paraphernalia that made her customers trudge through mud to get a peek at the future (or the past), because it certainly couldn't be Bunny Caruso herself. She had all the sex appeal of the old pump outside of the town courthouse. Thin and knobbly, her legs stuck out of her hot-pink shorts in the summer like spindles. When she wore her strapless halter, she was always pulling it up, because she had little girl's breasts, breasts hardly developed, and the nipples (she made sure they showed through) looking like pencil points.

Sam sat and smoked and wondered who was in there now, having a "session." The mayor, most likely. He was one of the regulars—always consulting Hubert about the next election, or what they should do about the potholes on Tremont Street, or the council session coming up. But it was (according to Bunny) really the *past* that they came for: to be in touch with their loved ones; to hear the grave and gravelly voice of Hubert issue from Bunny's lips and raise the curtain back up in a dead play. "To speak to one's long-lost loved ones, Sammy," she'd told him, her eyes sequined with tears, her little ferret-nose sniffling. "Imagine, Sammy dear!"

Sammy dear could well imagine that the mirrors got a pretty good workout and that the thumpings and bumpings and occasional crashes meant the loved ones were definitely connecting.

According to Bunny, the mirrors in her two-room asbestos-shingle cabin had been installed at the request—no, by *demand*—of Hubert, who in his former life had been a prince of Liechtenstein and had liked to see himself, in full regalia, from all sides.

Leaning against the doorjamb on one of his rare "checkout" visits, Sam had chewed his gum slowly, enjoying almost more than the mirror story itself hearing Bunny trying to wrap her tiny pink tongue around the word "Liechtenstein." He would have invited himself in except he wasn't sure if Bunny's customer could get himself together as quickly as Bunny herself had. Anyway, Sam didn't want to see himself reflected endlessly in the Caruso hall of mirrors.

Not that Bunny never *invited* him in. When she visited the police station, she'd talk about Sam's aura, go through some routine of clutching her knobbly elbows, and shiver "deliciously" (as she put it) at what Sammy couldn't sense. It was because she had second sight and a sixth sense. And Hubert.

Some of these visits were duty visits, although they both kept up the pretense of sociability. Sam kept a rein on Bunny: he'd suggested she bring in a medical report every two months or so. It was, naturally, understood that he was just a little worried about her and acting not as an officer of the law but in simple friendship. He was worried about her nerves, that her bouts with Hubert were probably exhausting, and from what he'd seen in the movies, mediums could have a pretty rough time of it. They could *collapse* from their exertions. If she'd rather not go to their local doctor, any doctor would do—maybe one in Hebrides.

Sam even elaborated upon this unnerving business of Bunny's by telling her about a famous writer (Maud had gone on about) named Georges Simenon, who always had a total, complete physical examination, a complete check-up, before he trotted off to hole himself up in some hotel or other to write his next book.

Bunny was fascinated. Wide-eyed fascinated. "How many books did this George write?"

Sam tried to remember what Maud had told him. He leaned

back, nodded gravely, and said, "Somewhere around two hundred."

"Jee-*sus.*" Bunny had clasped her hands over her tiny tits—but not as a come-on, just because she was probably used to grabbing at them—and said, "Sammy, do you think I *could?*"

Sam frowned, pushed his dark glasses back on the bridge of his nose. He always put them on, even inside, when he saw Bunny coming along the sidewalk; otherwise she'd see the laughter in there. "You don't have to have a *total* physical. Just a little blood test, maybe."

She waved her hands like a woman drying her nails. "No, no. Write a *book.* You think I could write a book like this George?"

He quickly folded a stick of gum into his mouth so it would have something to work on other than the laugh that threatened. Bunny was never even sure how to spell her name: sometimes she did it with a *y*, sometimes with an *ie*. She was only a couple of years younger than Sam, and he remembered how, when they'd been in La Porte High School together, people had tittered over Bunny not even being able to spell her own name—the old joke come true.

"Well, Bunny," he'd said as he opened and shut a couple of drawers, "why don't you try? The thing is, we need to watch your nerves. Okay?"

Between them they'd never mentioned that blood tests generally weren't a requirement for dealing with imminent nervous collapse. There'd never been a case of AIDS in the county, and Sam wasn't particularly worried about the men in La Porte carrying it around, but God only knew who Hubert might be dragging in from worlds as yet untested, and Sam sure as hell was taking no chances.

The spelling of her name might once have been problematic for Bunny, but she wasn't so dense she didn't know that Sam knew her body wasn't being used as an empty vessel through which Hubert, Prince of Liechtenstein, could speak in the voices of the dead. Thus, she also knew that the invitations to Sam to put him in touch with his dear departed would always be declined. But the ritual visits to the police station were somehow, for Bunny, therapeutic, like confession—as if Sam were the priest, and she the anonymous penitent, screened from full view by Hubert and the crystal ball. Both priest and penitent *really* knew who the other was (didn't they usually, in the church?), but the pretense, helped along by both of them, relieved Bunny from strict allegations—not from Sam so much as from herself.

The fantasy was nurtured by both of them. The clean bill of health she slipped across his desk in the little brown envelope might have been like the fifty cents for a parking fine.

And the allegations of others, Sam ignored. Mabel Sims and her bridge cronies most likely had a high old time around the table talking about the goings-on in that cabin on Swain's Point. If Mabel (and Helen Haines) knew who Bunny was going on *with*, they might have sung a different tune. As it was, the penny-colored eyes of Mayor Sims's and Dodge Haines's wives tracked Bunny's every step from Tremont to First Street before they went into Cooper's Drugs to strangle their soda straws and talk to each other in the big mirror behind the counter. The Sims contingent referred to Bunny as a "loose woman."

That actually made Sam smile, sitting out here in the dark, butting out his third cigarette in an ashtray that wouldn't close; it made him smile to think that some of the La Porte townspeople were stuck back in the fifties somewhere, watching reruns of "Father Knows Best" and surprised to hear Liberace had been dead for all these years.

As far as Sam was concerned, Bunny Caruso was doing La Porte a hell of a lot less harm than the Red Barn, where his deputy, Donny, had told Sam he wasn't at all sure what was really in one of the glass sugar holders and should he get a search warrant? They'd had Darryl Dubois in twice for possession of crack and angel dust, and he'd managed to unload the stuff someplace between the bar and the door of the Red Barn.

Running his fingers through that meringue-cloud of hair, Bubby Dubois had expressed the opinion that Sam DeGheyn was out to get him, and the expression in his eyes had added, "And we know why, don't we?"

Bunny, with her clean bill of health, was dealing in fantasy, not cocaine or crack.

And god only knew, everyone, Sam was thinking, needed some kind of fantasy to get through this life.

"Loose woman."

Helen Haines had used the same words about Eunice Hayden.

It was this, and not curiosity about whether Dodge Haines or Winfield Sims or any other loose men were in there, that had Sam sitting here for fifteen minutes in the dark watching Bunny's cabin.

About ten months before the murder of Nancy Alonzo, there was a woman by the name of Loreen Butts found in the woods behind the Oasis Bar and Grille outside of Hebrides. She was found with her panties down, her clothes ripped off her, and her throat and stomach slit. And nine months before that, Antoinette Perry was killed the same way and in very nearly the same place. The thing that was different about Tony Perry's murder, though, was that her body was found in a section of the wood that made it hard to tell just whose jurisdiction it fell into. The Oasis Bar and Grille was near the county line. Sedgewick had claimed the Perry murder—had done so rather heatedly, Sam thought. But he'd been forced to share it, and Sam never did think he'd really gotten to see all of the evidence Sedgewick had turned up.

Boy Chalmers had been the chief suspect in the Butts murder. He was a handsome young fellow who'd been in the Oasis with Loreen several hours before she was killed. He'd been with her and fighting with her, fighting inside and out in the parking lot, according to some of the customers. He hadn't had an alibi for those few hours when he claimed he'd just gone on home. Well, there was, supposedly, motive, the fight having been pretty rowdy; there was, supposedly, opportunity, too, given his inability to prove he'd left the Oasis grounds. But Sam thought he'd been convicted on flimsily put-together circumstantial evidence, nonetheless.

And, of course, when Boy Chalmers had been taken in for the Loreen Butts murder, there'd been a lot of talk about Antoinette Perry. Boy had hotly denied even *knowing* Tony Perry, which might have been a tactical error on his part, since just about every man in Hebrides knew her. Still, there was absolutely no evidence to show he *did* know the Perry woman; no one had ever seen him with her in any circumstances, much less intimate ones. But since the method was identical in both killings, lack of evidence connecting Boy and Tony Perry wasn't going to stop his being charged with that murder too.

There wasn't much question about Tony Perry's being tight or loose. Tony Perry had "companioned" (as some had heard her put it) a number of men within the twenty-mile radius that took in both Hebrides and La Porte. She was very good-looking—very; indeed, she'd reminded Sam, when he saw her lying in Francis Silber's mortuary, a little bit of his own wife, Florence. Even dead, Tony Perry exuded heat and smoke, as if her body was not so much breaking up, but was instead sending out a sexual effluvium that not even death could dampen down.

Tony Perry had left behind her two small children, who in the end had been transported upstate to a home. Probably, life would go on for them much the same as always, for it was well-known they'd gotten little care from their mother. There was no father— that is, no man who would own up to it.

Loreen Butts had lived in a mobile home with her little boy, Raymond, and her husband, a truck driver who was away a lot. There was some talk about Loreen, also, speculation that she too had been bestowing her favors on more than one man in and around Hebrides. It wasn't Sam's county and it wasn't his case. They'd let him talk to Boy Chalmers, though, and Sam just had a feeling about the kid—he was twenty-two or -three—that he was telling the truth. One of the reasons for this feeling was that—for all Chalmers's height, girth, muscle, and golden-boy looks (hence the nickname: the kid's mother had adored William Holden in *Golden Boy*)—he sensed that the kid was gay. And fighting it every step of the way; he couldn't admit it even to himself. All the time Sam had been sitting there at the table in the incident room, he'd talked about his mother. Mom. Mom was wonderful. Mom was Alexis Beauchamp Chalmers. Mom was from the South, from Charleston, and he ought to meet her sometime, she was beautiful.

If there was anyone Boy Chalmers wanted to kill it was Mom, Sam had decided.

Boy and Loreen: well, they'd had this fight in the Oasis and he'd walked out. Yeah, he knew there were plenty of witnesses to the fight. He'd walked out around ten o'clock and Loreen, fuming, followed him outside.

"Shit, man, she was mad. No one—Loreen thinks—walks out on Loreen. Shit, she starts fooling around with this wank at the bar, and what am supposed to do? Take it? You don't know Loreen."

According to the sheriff, Loreen had hung around until nearly closing time, which, that night, had been near one a.m. Sam wondered why the Chalmers kid would stand around for three hours outside waiting for her to leave, when the fight (according to the witnesses) was pretty routine for the Oasis clientele, even if it was also pretty loud. It consisted mostly of shouting on both sides and Chalmers's banging out the door red-faced, with Loreen Butts going after him, into the parking lot. So what puzzled Sam was, why would Boy then come back to stick around for three hours? If he was going to kill the woman, why not then and there, in the heat of battle? And some "wank at the bar" putting moves on your woman hardly seemed a great motive for murder. Unless she'd done it to you again and again and you were her long-suffering husband. Maybe then you might brood, walking around in the woods, brood and stew and come back with a knife. But Boy? A casual date and some drinks in a tavern? No, it just didn't figure.

Sam wondered a lot more about the husband's having an alibi than Boy's not having one. Carl Butts had been nearly a hundred miles away with his rig, sleeping at a truck stop just this side of Meridian. No one, Sam had suggested, had stayed awake all night to make sure that Butts was actually sleeping like a baby while his wife, Loreen, was being raped and carved up outside of Hebrides. You think we're idiots? asked the Elton County sheriff. You think we don't know it's usually close to home? You think we didn't check the mileage? You think we—?

Husbands, Sam had agreed, generally don't bother raping their wives before they kill them, though he imagined it happened sometimes. Hadn't everything? He didn't go on to say: Christ, any truck driver could set back an odometer; any truck driver had so fucking many good ol' buddies along the route he could probably produce enough witnesses to fill the back of his rig.

Sam didn't say it because he didn't really believe it. It felt too much like a story he himself was constructing because he thought the Chalmers kid had been railroaded into the county jail. Sam didn't mind telling them—Sims and the state's attorney, Billie Anderson—he thought it was a disgrace. He thought no one had been overly zealous in a search for the murder weapon (never found, but the pathologist thought the blade was that of a common kitchen knife). He thought the FBI should be called in. County lines were being crossed, and none of them had the forensics experience of the FBI people.

Just the mention of taking this matter out of her hands was enough to drive Billie Anderson crazy. And Billie, cold sane, wasn't really anyone Sam wanted to deal with. She was worse than Sims because she was smart, she was shrewd.

But the Eunice Hayden killing—no, they couldn't hang that one on Boy, because Boy had an alibi: he'd been in his bike shop with four kids whose bikes he was repairing. Boy had four witnesses to

his whereabouts for the entire afternoon and part of the evening of
Eunice Hayden's death.

Sedgewick and State Attorney Anderson had tinkered in every
way they could with that alibi; the four kids had been talked to
again and again, and their testimony questioned because they were,
after all, only ten or thirteen. But they all remembered, because
one of the kids was going into the hospital the next day, and Boy
had fixed their bikes, no charge. Boy Chalmers was popular with
kids; that in itself told Sam something.

If one-tenth of the effort spent in trying to break down Boy's
alibi had been spent in trying to find the truth of Carl Butts's,
Sam thought they might have gotten somewhere. Cuckolded
husbands were pretty likely suspects. The police in Meridian had
checked out the truck stop, but without much assiduity; after all,
the Highway in the Skyway truck stop was their own favorite
eating joint, and they weren't about to yank around their friends
there.

Sedgewick was not at all pleased that Sam was messing in the
Butts case: it wasn't Sam's case, and he was sorry if Boy Chalmers
had charmed the pants off Sam DeGheyn (Sam just chewed his
gum at that one), but get the hell out of the Elton County jurisdiction. Tony Perry might have been half his, but Loreen Butts was
all Elton County. Sedgewick said it as if the two of them were
bickering over prom dates.

So Sam had waited for over three months before approaching
the Elton County sheriff again, hoping that Sedgewick would have
forgotten his massive irritation by then.

Sam had stopped in the sheriff's office in Hebrides to invite
Sedgewick for lunch at the Stoplight Diner, a popular little place at
a crossroads just the other side of Hebrides and one Sam knew
Sedgewick liked. He had a case on a waitress they called Tater,
some holdover nickname from the "One potato, two potato"
childhood game that Tater had been particularly adept at.

Sam had deliberately left his uniform behind and worn jeans

and a quilted hunting jacket over a checkered woodsman's shirt, and a cap with a brim. He hated hunting; Sedgewick loved it. Sedgewick was a hell of a lot better at stalking deer than men, had more patience with it, had more respect for the intelligence of what he hunted. Men, he'd often say to Sam, couldn't teach him no new tricks. He was a great hunter and a sloppy cop. Fortunately, he had no ax to grind, had no career ambitions, or he'd have been more suspicious of Sam's casual request to be allowed to talk to Carl Butts.

The request was made over the third mock-frosted mug of Coors, and Sedgewick was very busy watching the swaying rump of his henna-haired waitress, Tater. Sam only wanted to satisfy himself as to the character of Loreen Butts, that was all. Just curiosity, nothing official. Sedgewick told him it damned well wasn't, and maybe he could have a word with Carl Butts, but not if he was going to harass that poor man. Boy Chalmers was in the county jail, with his next stop the state prison. Appeal turned down; case closed and neatly tied up. The discussion of the two murders was casual, what with the sheriff dividing his time between his beer and Tater; he'd reach for her thigh, growl, and look lecherous as she passed by, giggling. Sedgewick was a lecher; indeed, Sam wondered if the talk about Sedgewick and Tony Perry had anything to do with the sheriff's vehemence in wanting so much to claim that first murder.

Right now, the sheriff was happy enough to go one step further and be helpful by telling Sam that Butts was probably home because he'd seen him in town that morning. He drove his rig four days and got off three.

"And don't you go harassing that man—he's bought his share of trouble and grief."

The only thing Carl Butts had bought that Sam could see was three cases of Bud tallboys and a half-gallon of Jack Daniel's.

Sam knocked on the trailer's storm door, still with the summer screen insert in it. That autumn, Sam remembered, had been especially chill, the air musky with the smell of leaves someone was burning illegally on the other side of the dank river that narrowed between its high banks as it slid through the trailer park grounds as if trying to shoulder off the debris: rusty tin cans and bread wrappers and empty plastic detergent bottles. The sheriff's office had served the trailer park's owner, Nicholas L'Amour, with several warrants, demanding he improve the conditions. But the L'Amour Trailer Haven (its dirty buff sign decorated with hearts filled in with information about lot size, price, and amenities—kiddies' playground, for example, that no kiddies went near; sauna in a lean-to where you could see through the boards) never saw any improvements; money was changing hands, but not between the owner and the grounds keeper.

Carl Butts, though he didn't leave his chair, was a man of probably only medium height, but squarely built: square jaw set on thick neck, square shoulders and torso—the type of man that put you in mind of a trash compactor, pressed down hard and heavy inside, a lot more than meets the eye.

Sam guessed it was a lot less, the way he stayed glued in the TV chair, the tube of flesh beginning to overshadow the belt, and the rather whiny voice that called to someone in the dark environs to get the door. He was sitting almost within arm's reach of it himself, but the person who came to it was a woman. It must have been from her that Butts got his sweetheart looks and general ebullience. She had narrow eyes and a mouth like a mail slot—thin, squared off, and with a way of clamping down on words. Sam wondered idly, as he answered the question as to what his business was here, if Grant Wood had made his first pit stop here at the L'Amour Trailer Haven; Mother Butts was right out of *American Gothic*. Finally, she let him in, and then quickly reclaimed her seat before the TV, as if Sam might steal it.

Butts looked up briefly from the soap they were watching,

grunted out something about his day off, and returned his eyes to the screen. Neither of them asked Sam to have a chair; both of them wore equally puzzled looks, prompted by a witless dialogue between two interns and the open-mouthed, wide-eyed expressions of two nurses (meant, probably, to register shock, but managing only to look stupid). The Buttses were as intent on figuring this out as if it were the Idea of Order at General Hospital, an intellectual puzzle capable of being patched together only by a roomful of Harvard professors.

Sam folded his arms and watched for a minute. He'd seen bits and pieces of this one; it was Florence's favorite. He started burrowing his way into their attention by addressing the woman as "Mrs. Butts" and discovering he'd been wrong.

"Grizzell. That's 'Griz-*zell*,' mister, accent on the second syl-*la*-ble—not like them papers kept calling it, 'Grizzel.' Made it sound like "gristle.' " She had a whiplash voice and the same punishing eyes as the grammar school teacher who'd walked between the third-grade desks with a narrow birch rod.

At least he'd got her attention for a moment. "Mrs. Grizzell. Sorry. I guess I just supposed you were Mr. Butts's—relative." He didn't want to say "mother" in case she turned out to be not more than ten years older than Carl Butts. "Newspapers aren't known for being accurate. But you'd think they could get a name spelled right, wouldn't you?" Sam smiled his damnedest, realizing this was the mother-in-law, Loreen Grizzell Butts's mother.

She eased a bit in her rocking chair and nodded. "Think so. Now, what's police coming back for? They got that Boy Chalmers that murdered my Loreen." Her attention went back to the soap, where a discussion between a toffee-haired girl and a tearful woman had replaced the one between the doctors.

Same talk, different people, thought Sam. "I'm real sorry about your daughter, Mrs. Grizzell. I'm sorry to intrude upon your grief, ma'am."

At that, she had to look up and look grieved, and pull the wad of handkerchief from her sleeve. But her eyes were still gorging on the soap.

"Carl, offer the man a chair. What did you say your name was?" she asked, as Butts rose to drag over a folding chair with an orange vinyl back and seat. The color clashed with the pink petunia pattern on the slipcovered easy chair in which Butts sat. He grunted when Sam thanked him.

"DeGheyn," said Sam in answer to her question. "Sam."

Her eye strayed from him to the ceiling, the cobwebs there, and she repeated the name, mouthing it carefully. "De-Gin."

"Well, more 'Da-*Geen*.' Long *e*. Rhymes with 'beguine,' if you remember that old song." Sam smiled.

As if she didn't quite trust his pronunciation, she asked, "Just how do you spell that name?"

"D-E-G-H-E-Y-N."

That floored her; she stopped her rocking, then picked it up at a rather reckless speed, all the while shaking her head. "That ain't no American name. What kind of name *is* that, anyways?" Her eyes narrowed.

"Dutch." Sam smiled, offered his cigarettes around. She shook her head, but her son-in-law took one, his eyes still clamped to the swimming greeny-blue of the TV. They'd both forgotten he was a policeman, apparently. "It's a funny spelling, all right. And even funnier, it's *really* supposed to be pronounced without any *g* sound, and with a long *i*—'Da-*Hine*.' You'll appreciate why I use the *G*."

She just shook and shook her head in wonder at the vagaries of oddly spelled names. "Hine? *Hine*? Well, I never did hear any name so peculiar that don't sound like it's spelt!" She shook her head in wonder. "Yes, I most certainly *do* appreciate you use the G. You American?" Her eyes narrowed.

"Born-and-bred U.S. of A. So was my mother and father. It was my great-great-great-grandfather that was Dutch." Sam had no idea if this was true; the origins of his name were lost in the swirling mists of the Atlantic crossing. What he had discovered was that it was the name of a famous Dutch painter, but looking at the picture on the Butts wall of a twelve-point buck, gold antlers painted on black velvet, he thought he'd leave that detail out. Yet Mrs. Grizzell seemed satisfied by this, for she nodded and smacked her lips. Sam went on: "And I'll tell you, it's annoying—I mean, when I hear someone pronounce it who's *read* it, or just looks at the name on my desk. I have to keep correcting them."

Soul mate, her eyes said. Oh, she knew all about *that* problem. "Carl, shut that damn thing off. I never could make out what those fools was doing, anyways."

Butts made no move, beyond mumbling something about "the damned fools." He referred to her as "Ma Gris" as if his mother-in-law were a French perfume.

Sam had seen five minutes now and then of this soap because it was Florence's favorite. Walking through the living room, coming or going out, he'd picked up bits and pieces. Now he said, pointing his cigarette at the screen, "I think *she's* supposed to be in love with that doctor there. Only he's married. That's what she's tearing her hair out about."

"Floozy," said Ma Gris, rocking, arms crossed, hands holding her elbows.

"It ain't *her* causing the trouble," said Butts, topping another tallboy. "It's *him*—it's that intern or whatever. Want a Bud?" He held up a can and Sam thanked him kindly. Butts tossed it to him. "Bunch of assholes, anyway."

"So shut it *off.* I wish to talk to Mr.—" Carefully, she said "DeGheyn," as if the word were a delicate china cup that might crack under the weight of the two syllables.

Sam did not want the set shut off; it might provide him with an opening. Inclining his head toward the women who were rabbiting away near the nurses' station, he said, "Now, that one looks like that woman on 'Dynasty.'"

Ma Gris's head swiveled round to the screen; her eyes narrowed to slits, as if even this were a suspicious statement. "What woman's that?"

Sam thought for a second. "Angela—something?"

"That ain't 'Dynasty,' " she said, spitting it out.

" 'Falcon Crest,' " said Butts, scratching at his belly. "That's Jane Wyman you're talking about. This one don't look like her, does she, Ma Gris?"

Hell, thought Sam. Well, given in his whole life he'd clocked up maybe one full hour of the soaps, he thought he was doing pretty damned well. Nothing lost; let them chew over Jane.

"I got no use for that woman, none," Ma Gris said in deadly level tones. "Do you know she *divorced* our *President.*" A sort of hissing whisper emphasized the devilish nature of Jane Wyman's treacherous deed. "And let me tell you something." She leaned forward and tapped Sam on the knee with a ridged fingernail. "The Betty Kelleys of this world, they ought to be drawn and quartered, drawn and *quartered,* think they can sling dirt against our President's wife." Ma Gris rocked furiously, arms locked forthrightly across her skinny chest, nodding to Sam as if in approbation of his, not her, judgment.

"What the hell you going on about, Ma Gris? Who's Betty—?"

"Do *not* swear at me, Carl Butts. It's that blond-headed floozie of which I speak."

Sam quickly got out his pack of gum and shoved a stick into his mouth, clearing his throat and also biting the tender flesh of the inside of his upper lip. A week's pay, *step right up to the bat and give a week's pay,* he thought, to have Maud listening to this. When he could trust himself to speak, he said, "I most certainly agree. Gossips like her deserve to be horse-whipped." His mind was clicking, clicking over any way to introduce the topic of murder. The attempt on Reagan's life might do, but any venturing near the Reagan household, with Ma Gris in the party, could have him here until the snows came to cover him up. And no closer would he be to Loreen Grizzell Butts.

The charge of "floozie" came this time from Carl Butts, who hadn't forgotten they'd been talking about the soap-opera life of the hapless Jane Wyman. "You got the wrong gal, mister. You're thinking of Krystle." He took a long swallow of beer and looked at Sam with an air of superiority.

Who was Crystal? he thought. Ma Gris leaned forward. "With a *K*," she said.

Sam thought for one insane moment she could read minds. And then he realized it was just her passion for justice in name-spelling. "Dynasty," that must be it. He smiled broadly and said, "Listen, I got to tell you this story about 'Dynasty.' *You'll* appreciate it," he added, as if no one else had the intelligence to do so. "I was watching"—meaning Florence was—"one afternoon and saw"— oh, shit, what was the apparent hero's name?—"saw Mr. Hand- some Gray-Hair go backwards straight down that long flight of stairs. Shot to death—"

"Blake," she said, rocking frantically, and all ears.

"That's right. Blake. Well, he was just lying there, and there was Miss Platinum"—it had to be Krystle—"Krystle with a smoking gun."

Both Butts and his mother-in-law clearly wanted to leap into the account, but Sam held up his hand and smilingly shook his head. "But let me just finish. That *night* I was watching"—in other words, Florence had been—"and there's Blake walking around as healthy as could be. Hale and hearty, no damage done. But that afternoon he was dead as a doornail. Looked it, I mean. And there was Krystle just loving him up as if that afternoon had never happened."

Neither Butts nor Ma Gris laughed. It was far too serious a subject for ribaldry. Sam chewed his gum ferociously, remember- ing telling Maud about all this, how it was the quintessence of the soaps: get shot in the afternoon and resurrected at night. The whole of soap opera. The two of them had laughed so hard she'd nearly knocked the lamp off the end of the pier.

He didn't expect the Butts contingent to laugh, and they didn't. Carl explained to Sam he was seeing a rerun in the afternoon. "That's a real popular show—been going for, oh—how long, Ma Gris? Seven, eight years, maybe?"

She didn't answer her son-in-law, but instead addressed Sam. "It should be disallowed." When Sam's puzzlement showed, she went on, rocking the harder as if to firm up her argument. "See, the reruns spoils things—like it did for you, to see Blake killed and then a few hours later, walking around bold as brass." Unmindful of the inanity of her comment, she smacked her dry lips in satisfaction.

Sam felt nearly sucked into the vortex of this total illogic; he almost felt he should convince her that any "Dynasty" freak would already have seen Krystle trying to stiff Blake.

It was Butts who answered her. "Well, now, Ma Gris, why get mad at Blake? It was Krystle's doing. Right?" His head turned toward Sam.

Sam was afraid they'd all start getting involved in the "Dynasty" family squabble and opened his mouth to divert this. It was unnecessary, for she counterattacked.

"You men *always* side!"

She didn't need to add "against the women."

Sam couldn't have written a better script himself to open up the Loreen Butts case. He laughed slightly. "Now, though, Mrs. Grizzell—in this case, she *did* shoot him."

Ma Gris slapped her hands on the arms of the chair in the act of rocking forward and answered ferociously: "Drove her to it! That man *drove* that poor woman—"

"Hey! Now, just you hold on, Ma." Butts nervously fingered a cigarette from a pack tight in the pocket of his fatigue-green T-shirt. "Just you hold on now." He lit the cigarette and tossed the matches in the full ashtray angrily. "I'd say just hold on." He puffed in quick little jabs and kept his eyes trained on the blue-green images on the silenced soap opera.

After a moment Sam said, "Well, Krystle *was* under a lot of pressure."

Smack went the knobbled hands down on the chair arms. It must have smarted, but Sam had given her her opportunity. "God *knows* the poor woman was—"

Butts was still feigning interest in the faces floating like ragged water, but now his face reddened as he said, "It ain't Krystle you're talking about, is it? It's *Loreen*. You think I *drove* Loreen to seek companionship elsewhere."

His prim way of putting this rather astonished Sam.

Mrs. Grizzell said, "Why, no—that—"

"Don't tell me no. You been near to sayin' it straight out ever since it happened." He stubbed out his cigarette furiously.

Equally surprising to Sam was the mother-in-law's equable answer. "Now, your job did take you away a lot, Carl. And Loreen left alone here to see after the boy."

"That's *my* fault?" He punched his thumb into his chest. "And she never did much seeing to Raymond, anyway."

"Raymond's my grandson. Looks the spit of the Grizzells, if I do say it." Smoothing her skirt, she went on: "Never said it was your fault. Man has a job, he's got to do it. But look what the papers made of it, of my Loreen being . . . you know. Now, Loreen was *never* one to go about with other men—not like that Perry woman. Everyone knew she was a common whore. Went off and left them kids of hers with no one to take care of—"

Butts cracked his knuckles; his biceps rippled beneath the thin cotton. "Took up with Boy Chalmers, though, didn't she?"

"Never 'took up' a*tall;* you know her and Boy was friends from grade school. That's what Boy Chalmers was, just a friend."

"All he could be," murmured Butts to the silent hospital corridors, where the nurses soundlessly belabored their patients.

Sam had moved not a muscle, had hardly blinked for fear of disturbing the current between the two. Now he brought down the front legs of the chair he'd been tilted back in. The tiny, sly smile on

Carl Butts's face vanished at Sam's movement; he looked at Sam furtively, and his jaw clenched like a vise. Sam said nothing.

Loreen's mother went on, unmindful of the implication of her son-in-law's comment. "To tell the truth—and I don't mean to pain you, son—but I always thought Loreen and Boy would . . . you know." Her eyes widened, the cold blue of them covered with a glaze of rime. She brought out her handkerchief again, kneading it in her lap.

Butts said nothing, but Sam saw his mouth crimp. He looked at his shoes.

To Sam, Ma Gris said, "Let me tell you about Loreen. That girl was shy. Shy and quiet." She swiveled to glare at her son-in-law. "And don't you go trying to paint a picture like the papers did—that my Loreen was a tart!" It was the even, deadly tone she'd used before, the last words brought down neat as a cleaver.

Carl Butts flinched. "I never said that. You know, I never."

"But smart," she went on. "Loreen was smart as a whip. Clever. She could've been an actress." Here she looked at the TV, the doubled image of the toffee-haired girl. "Better than *her*. Could have acted rings around her. Could've been better than Jane Wyman and Krystle put together."

"Well, she could rile a man, Ma; you know that." He sounded almost apologetic. "Tart as green apple pie, Loreen could be."

The woman nearly screeched: "Don't you go calling Loreen a tart! Yes, she could rile a person, but only if pushed, Carl Butts. It is a *bald*-faced *lie* to make out anything else."

"Ma Gris, I only meant—"

But what he only meant cut no ice with her. To Sam, she said, "They got it *all* wrong—the papers, the police." And she suddenly sat back as hard as if Butts had shoved a fist in her chest. Ma Gris must have remembered it was police she was sitting here jawing at. "Just what do you want to come bothering us for, Mr. Du-*Geen*?" Spite stung the syllables.

"Sorry, Mrs. Grizzell. You see, I kind of agree with you, that we got it all wrong. See, I talked with Boy Chalmers, and he didn't seem the type to do this."

"Goddamn right he wasn't!" Butts all but shouted. His jealousy, his questioned manliness finally overcame his better judgment. "That man's a fag!"

Ma Gris paled. "Carl Butts!"

With as mean a look as Sam had seen, he leaned toward her. "Queer as they come. Mr. Handsome-Boy. Has everyone fooled."

"Including Loreen, do you think?" asked Sam.

The mother-in-law kept opening and closing her mouth like the wide-eyed nurse on the TV screen. She was speechless.

Butts waved a deprecating hand at Sam. "Oh, hell, man. Women can hardly ever tell. A real man can, that's all." And he looked Sam up and down as if calling his manliness into question, since apparently Sam hadn't figured out Boy Chalmers.

But the look changed when Sam said, "So neither one of you thought he was guilty."

In the silence, only the creak of the rocking chair was audible; and even it stopped, finally. Neither one of them would meet Sam's eyes.

They knew what he was thinking: that the two of them had kept silent because the other main suspect was Carl Butts.

Butts began defending himself against Sam's silence. "Well, the jury thought so. And maybe they're smarter."

Ma Gris leaned towards the TV set, switched it off, sat back. She said nothing, nor would she look at Sam.

Sam stood up. "I guess I'll be going. Thanks for the beer. Mr. Butts . . . Mrs. Grizzell." He nodded toward each of them, though the eyes of each were now fastened to the dark screen.

Sam let the door swing quietly behind him and walked down the rubbishy pavement. In the gathering dusk he saw the faint gleam of a firefly, ready for the dark.

Nearly a year ago, that screen door had shut.

He'd gone through half a pack of cigarillos sitting out here in the dark watching Bunny Caruso's house.

He hadn't expected that any talk with Carl Butts would have turned up new evidence, and it hadn't. Even if Butts and Loreen's mother had agreed to testify to the characters of both the victim and the alleged murderer, it wouldn't have been enough to turn the case around. A mother is obviously going to say her little girl wasn't "that type"; and though the husband was as sure as Sam himself that Boy Chalmers was a homosexual, it was a supposition on their parts. The kid wasn't a *practicing* homosexual; Sam had spent plenty of time with his friends and family, obliquely asking that question. A few of the men who knew him were inclined to wonder about Boy's sexual leanings, but, again, he was so well liked no one wanted to come right out and voice their suspicions.

Anyway, wondered Sam, starting in on a fresh cigarillo, what the hell would it have proved? Even if the kid were a rampaging fag and everyone knew it, who's to say a gay might not in a moment of gross and perverse behavior try to rape a woman? Sam didn't believe it, not about Boy Chalmers, but it wasn't something anyone could *prove.*

So Boy Chalmers had by now lived out a year of a life sentence.

When Tony Perry and then Loreen Butts had been murdered, Sam had remembered the Hayden crime—not that he'd ever really forgotten it—and walked into the mayor's office and told him he thought the Eunice Hayden case should be reopened, that he, Sam, should be given access to the files on it, and that Sheriff Sedgewick should cooperate in every way possible.

This was before the murder of Nancy Alonzo, and Mayor Sims was in the fourth year of the throes of his re-election campaign. He could never stop campaigning, because he must have realized how tenuous was his hold on the job and seen an opponent behind every tree. Unfortunately, there weren't that many who wanted the position—a young attorney here, a chairman of the board of education there, but no one seemed to be taking it seriously. You get into the habit, Sam supposed, of seeing the same man turn up in the Rainbow on the same stool talking about the same town business. For Sam to walk in with something so politically inflammatory as wanting to drag out an old murder and tie it to a fresh one made the mayor wave away his curtain of cigar smoke (he honestly thought that his cigars and seersucker suits would put people in mind of Spencer Tracy) and look at Sam as if he'd gone crazy.

"You trying to tell me that that murder-rape over in Elton County a couple years ago and that Eunice Hayden case—you trying to tell me that because of this you think there's some Jack the Ripper type out there?"

"No."

"Then you trying to tell me you think the same sombitch did all these women?"

"Yes."

"Just because there's been three murders in four years—four years, mind you—"

Sam interrupted. "All of them done the same way. And I'd say that sort of thing in two tiny places like La Porte and Hebrides might suggest our women better bolt their doors."

Sims leaned back and smiled meanly. "Well, I guess I know what your problem is. You never did find who killed Eunice Hayden, so you want to make it look like neither did Sheriff Sedgewick find who really killed the others. That it?"

"No, that's not it."

Sims's mode of argument was to ignore answers and repeat himself. "So since you never did discover the Hayden girl's killer, you want to throw up a little dust to make it look like maybe Sheriff Sedgewick over there didn't do a good job?"

"I think maybe he didn't. I think the wrong man's in prison. I also think the criminal justice system showed signs of working pretty quick, for once."

"And just what's that supposed to mean? You inferring there's something fishy?"

"I'm just saying Boy Chalmers went inside as quick as the jurors went out."

This was too much of a conundrum for Sims. He stared at Sam through squinty eyes and tossed down his pen. "My god, but you got crust. There's nothing to show Boy Chalmers ever even *knew* Eunice Hayden, so the Hayden case, that's got nothing to do with these two others. Why, not even our state attorney could get past Chalmers's alibi, and she's tough as they come."

Sims loved Billie Anderson, who was just as political as he was. What Sims was too stupid to see was that his own argument was circular. Follow it around again and it would show that if Boy Chalmers hadn't killed Eunice Hayden, it was a good bet he hadn't killed the other two women. But all Sam said was, "There's nothing to prove Chalmers knew Antoinette Perry, either. It was just assumed, wasn't it?"

Apparently, the mayor was so certain he was right that his anger drained away and his small, wet mouth twisted into a pearly little smile as he leaned back, hands locked behind his neck. "Well, you do take the biscuit, Sammy, you really do. First off, that Perry and Butts woman, they were *raped*. Eunice wasn't ever *raped*."

"Oh. What would you call it, then, that knife stuck up in her? 'Interfered with'?"

"Watch your mouth, DeGheyn. The doc said she wasn't raped. Now, I'm not a big-time policeman like you, but even I've heard of what is called an MO. Then why wasn't the Hayden girl done the same things to as the others? You tell me." Mayor Sims drew some papers toward him and started signing—his indication the interview was over. "Now get outta here and check the parking meters." He looked up. "You just might be needing a vacation, Sammy."

Meaning: lay off or you'll be taking one. Sam hadn't expected cooperation, so he wasn't especially disappointed; as far as the threat was concerned, he couldn't care less.

But Sam didn't lay off; he kept on asking questions about Boy Chalmers. What he found was that Boy had never had a serious love interest, though he was extremely popular—one girl thought he looked like Robert Redford, and talked as if Boy's incarceration couldn't be really happening, that it was more like a movie, and maybe Paul Newman would come along and somehow get Boy out.

And two months ago, back at the end of June, Boy *had* gotten out. It hadn't been with the help of Paul Newman, though; it had been Alexis Beauchamp Chalmers.

A little over two months ago, at the end of June, Boy's mother had gone to visit him in prison. It was Boy's birthday, and Alexis had been permitted to take him a cake. Oh, there'd been no files, knives, or guns in it; it was pretty much hacked up and kind of pasted back together by the time Alexis and Boy sat down to blow out the unlit candles.

But because it was his birthday and because Boy had been a model prisoner, they were allowed to sit in one of the detention rooms with a guard at the door, to celebrate.

The guard told the authorities later that Mrs. Chalmers had even offered him a piece of cake—a real nice woman, Mrs. Chalmers—but of course he'd just put the slice of cake aside. "You don't think I been stupid enough to eat it? Coulda been drugged."

But Mrs. Chalmers had become violently ill, and he had gone quickly for help. And the chain of events, the several flukes from then on, from that unguarded door all the way down the hall to freedom, was a warden's nightmare. Another guard had been in the john; still another had left his post at the bidding of two other guards who were having trouble containing a prison fight. And the last guard, the one who stood between him and the outside world, Boy had managed to overpower. It was a small prison and not a maximum-security one.

People figured Alexis Beauchamp Chalmers was the best little actress they'd ever seen. But they could never be sure, because she really *had* got sick, and the pretty little pink-icing rosebuds had turned up traces of salmonella poisoning. What had passed between Boy and Alexis, sitting there eating that cake, no one knew. Since he hadn't got sick, people figured Alexis must have planned the whole thing.

It was only twenty-four hours before they caught Boy in Dubois's used-car lot, trying to hot-wire an old Ford. He'd been stupid enough to run back to Hebrides and right into Sheriff Sedgewick's arms instead of running hell-for-leather in the opposite direction.

For Boy, it was the wrong twenty-four hours. This, at least, was Sam's thinking; for, in spite of the awful coincidence of Boy's escape and the murder of Nancy Alonzo in that same wood, near the spot where Loreen Butts was murdered, Sam still didn't think Boy was guilty.

The mayor, on the other hand, seemed hardly to be able to contain his jubilance at proving Sam DeGheyn one hundred percent wrong.

Right after Boy's recapture, he'd gloated. "I guess that pretty much shuts you up about Boy Chalmers, don't it, Sammy?"

All Sam could think of, looking at Sims's mouthful of teeth, which he'd happily punch out, was that the mayor could stand a visit to the dentist. The rise of anger he felt was at Sims's ability to laugh in the face of this horrible tragedy. Sam hadn't known Loreen Butts or Tony Perry personally, but he had known Nancy Alonzo.

While Sam just stood there, his hands under his armpits, his arms hugging his chest in an attempt to smother his rage, Sims had gone on signing whatever documents were on his desk, signing them with a flourish. And talking.

"Yeah, I reckon Billie Anderson'll throw the book at him this time. No more birthday parties for Boy. Now maybe you can use your energies on something more useful, huh? Maybe you can start earning your salary."

Sam didn't answer. He just stood there, and although there was a trickle of sweat down his back and dampness under his arms, he felt stone cold as a statue.

"Cat got your tongue?" Mayor Sims smiled broadly, showing those teeth again that seemed to be shrinking away from the gums, as if the teeth weren't too happy about being so close to Sims, either.

Sam just stood there.

The smile disappeared suddenly. The goading wasn't working, and Sims didn't like that. "Now, I heard you don't agree with some of the evidence. I heard you think that crime-scene officer was wrong." When Sam didn't answer, Sims leaned forward. "Well? What did you think that man who's got more experience and smarts than you ever had was wrong *about*?" When Sam still didn't answer, Sims went on, but with increasing uncertainty. "Hell, she writes his *name* in her own blood on the ground there and you *still* say maybe Boy Chalmers is innocent. My godamighty, man! What kinda proof you need, anyways? Man's a jailbreaker and out one day and *another* woman gets her throat slit? I mean, what *kinda* proof—?" Pure exasperation stopped him. Sims just shook his head at Sam's foolishness.

But when Sam still didn't answer him or move a muscle, Sims got up, leaned over his desk with his hands fisted, and nearly bellowed. "Let me just tell you something, fella! This Alonzo case is *closed*. I don't give a tinker's damn if she *was* a La Porte girl, or if she *did* do cleaning at the court house here, or if she *was* a friend of yours. The case is *closed*. Now, why don't you get out there"— and here he waggled his arm in some general "out there" direction—"and maybe do something useful. Drag your Deputy Donny Dawg out there to the Red Barn and clean up the sugar bowls." His face was mottled purple.

Sam nodded and turned away.

"You hear me?"

"I hear you, Mr. Mayor." Sam's voice was without expression.

Sam had been the sheriff around here for too many years to give a thought to Mayor Sims's temper or Mayor Sims's threats; he was as much a fixture as the courthouse pump, a town relic, a piece of history the people could no more do without than their Labor Day parade.

He was the loot. Sam smiled.

He heard voices, a man's and Bunny's, her piping voice which sounded eternally surprised, and looked through the screen of pines. Bunny and her customer were standing on the tiny, slanting wood porch, and she was waving away moths that had fluttered in when the porch light flicked on. Fireflies thronged the patchy grass, and mosquitoes hung like a veil of gauze over the water holes. The man was slapping the back of his neck, uttering some obscenity. Then he laughed.

Sam watched Bunny Caruso, standing there in her long, loose dress—her "medium's gown."

He wasn't thinking of loose women; he was thinking of misfits.

Tony Perry had lived alone with her two children, never been married, hadn't had much to do with people, except the men she slept around with. Sam frowned.

Eunice Hayden wasn't Sam's idea of "loose"; whatever Eunice had been up to those last months before her death, Sam could still remember her as the washed-out young girl he'd seen standing on the corner of Tremont and First like a shipwreck victim, marooned.

"She didn't make friends easy," her mother had said, probably meaning that Loreen, as a youngster, didn't have any at all. Maybe the girl had been smart; maybe not. Smart can kill you socially at that age.

Bunny Caruso, who was giggling on her front porch, had been counted the school idiot, more or less—laughed at, kept forever on the fringes of the crowd. Got fired from one job and then another; treated with contempt by some of the La Porte people long before she'd found her True Calling. A misfit, to say the least.

Willow Pauley, who lived her agoraphobic life, had reported someone watching her house: a man in the trees. "Swingin' from them, Willow?" Another woman alone; another misfit.

And Sam's favorite misfit: Maud Chadwick.

Watched her through the trees.

The memory of watching her through the trees rose in him like thick black smoke. If he didn't get at her, he would suffocate.

Sitting here now with the drawer of knives, he found himself gulping air.

He had run his thumb over each one, meaning to choose the one that drew blood with the lightest touch. He barely caressed the blade of the hunting knife—his favorite; drew it easily and smoothly along until the thread of blood came to the skin's surface.

He breathed easier.

Letters, he had been thinking, were bad news. One had been propped on the cold potbellied stove, and it wasn't even to him, but to that sorry old drunk with his sharp whiskers and callused hands he'd had to call "Dad." He'd had to call him that or his mother wouldn't lie with him anymore. And the letter had been for that old drunk.

Letters. Women. They came and they went. The women around here saw him and didn't know they'd seen him. They didn't know he was imprinted on their eyes.

He thought of Sam DeGheyn watching through the woods. Now, that was really funny. He giggled, thinking of it. The sound rose in his throat like froth. It was so funny, he cut himself deeper, running the knife blade absently across the palm of his hand.

Licked it. He didn't care; he didn't often feel pain. In his crotch he felt pain, the pressure from that thick coil of smoke rising upwards through his limbs, engorging.

Watching from the woods, he knew just where she went, and when.

And what was funny was that Sam thought he was out there all alone, watching them.

Yet there he'd been while Sam was watching.

The sheriff's shadow.

Now, that—that was funny.

Both of them—with a gun, with a knife—watching through the trees.

Oh, that was a scream. He was out there somewhere. That was a scream. He felt a pressure in his throat rising and he tossed his head back.

Beyond the window the sparrows took off.

THREE

Bunny Caruso's coy giggle was matched with the man's hawking laugh that sounded more like a man having a seizure than a man having a good time. They stood on the tiny porch.

Because his back was partially turned, Sam couldn't make out who it was. At first he thought it might be Dodge Haines's brother Rob, but then he heard that laugh. Sam thought he recognized it; and when the screen door creaked shut and Bunny's friend's lounge suit moved like quicksilver toward his car, Sam gaped.

Bubby Dubois.

His first reaction was a short gasp of astonished laughter; his second was a molten anger that seemed to twist his stomach muscles as if he had a cramp. He felt, he supposed, the way a father must who finds his daughter's young man screwing another girl. Why he thought Dubois, unfaithful to his own wife, would be faithful to Sam's, he didn't know. Why he should feel what would be Florence's own humiliation, he didn't know, either. He felt betrayed.

The engine of Bubby Dubois's Cadillac ticked over with the precision of a time bomb, and Sam pulled his dark glasses from the glove compartment, put on his cap, drew on his black gloves, and got out of his car. To avoid slamming the door, he left it open and started across the hard, rutted road. Smoke plumed from the Cadillac's exhaust. Sam avoided the gravel and came up on the driver's side just as Bubby tossed his arm over the passenger seat and looked over his shoulder and started backing slowly.

"How's your future look, Bubby?" asked Sam, his head lowered to the open window, hands gripping the sill.

Bubby Dubois and the Caddy both lurched, quivered back and forth for a moment, and froze.

"Sam?"

Sam slowly chewed his teaberry gum and gave Bubby a tight, closed-mouth smile before saying, "You bet."

"Well, I'll be damned. Sammy! Long time, no see."

"Small world, Bubby."

Sam could tell, from the way Dubois was running his hands back and forth on the wheel, from the spit-polished look of eyes like dimes, that Bubby was considering, *hoping*, that Sam DeGheyn had come to the cabin on a similar mission. The idea was quickly discarded when the eyes saw themselves reflected in the mirrored glasses.

Sam was leaning against the door on outstretched arms, like someone who meant to roll a car over. "So, how's your future look?"

Dubois slid his sweat-slick palm from the wheel and rocked it. "Aw, you know . . . Little of this, little of that." He smiled; he had a neat white row of teeth, like a kid's.

With a short bark of laughter, Sam said, "Hell, if that's all Hubert can tell you, you wasted your money."

"Hubert?" Bubby stared at the windshield with a puzzled frown.

"Prince of Liechtenstein." Sam removed one hand from the sill to adjust the black-visored cap, bringing it down toward the mirror-glasses. Slowly, he chewed his gum as he watched Dubois trying to conjure up some image that would fit "Hubert." Silently, Bubby mouthed the name.

"Now, Bunny *must* have called on Hubert. How else could you be in touch with your loved ones?" "*Like my wife,*" Sam desperately wanted to add. But his mind could quickly flip through the consequences of that response as if they were printed on Rolodex cards.

"Oh, yeah—Hubert!" said Bubby, with a cunning look. "Well, Hubert wasn't much into things tonight . . ."

Sam watched sweat like spittle snake a tiny track down around Bubby's hairline. Was Dubois really so dumb to imagine Sam didn't know what was going on in Bunny Caruso's mirror-lined room? "Thing is, I heard this kind of crash in there, and I was worrying about Bunny." Sam's face drew a little closer; Bubby's natural reflex was to lean back. "I've been out here for some little time." The glasses hid his eyes; he kept his voice flat.

Bubby's head jerked around. "How long?" The mere idea that Sam had been keeping the cabin under surveillance was the worst thing yet.

"Oh, twenty, maybe thirty minutes. Like I said: I heard this crash . . ." Sam's tone made it clear he was expecting an explanation.

"Yeah . . . yeah." Bubby had pulled a square of white handkerchief from his pants pocket and was pressing it here and there against his face like a powder puff. "It was a lamp."

"Sounded more like a sideboard falling flat. Or maybe a bed breaking up." *Sweat it, man.* "Probably Hubert getting up to something." Bunny Caruso, thought Sam, should really fill her clients in on details. But he supposed only a cop could inspire the colorful account of a prince of Liechtenstein. Why bother to tell her clients? Would they appreciate Hubert? "Seances can be pretty rough, they tell me."

Bubby was making tentative movements towards relaxing a little—putting the handkerchief back in his pocket, lighting a cigarette—but obviously wondering if he should. The hand that held the lighter trembled; the polished corneas glittered. He took a chance and tried to joke around. "Worse'n slam dancing." His artificial laugh was more of a snort, like someone drawing back phlegm. "You ever tried it?"

If the man had winked, Sam would have dragged him from the car and they'd have done a little slam dancing themselves against the concrete abutment of the shack. No. Sam thought for a moment. "I guess I don't want the past back again." Where had he heard that, or something like it? Maud had said it, or read it. It was from one of her books. For the briefest of moments Dubois, Bunny, the shack, the stink of jail cells, of beery trailers, of the debris of broken marriages—all were elided from his mind and replaced by the end of the pier; the party across the lake; the black, unchurned water. In a flash, his mind cut through the anger, the mortification, the desire for vengeance, to the pose, and he withdrew his hands from the window, stood back from the car, and stuck them in his pockets.

The pose was Town Loot, Mr. Danger, Black Leather. At what was he angry? With whom? Did he really think he was out in the dirt road in front of some honky-tonk saloon, the sheriff with his gun hand just above the holster, about to protect some lady's honor? If he didn't love his wife, and his wife was screwing another guy, and that guy was doing the same with someone else, what the hell was that but ironic and trivial? What infuriated him was a marriage acted out before a microwave instead of a bed; that his wife was a foolish, fearful woman; that he wasn't really trapped but that he felt like it. And that he'd like to slough everything off.

He really didn't want the past back. He didn't much want the present, either.

"Sam?"

Dubois's voice brought him out of this haze of thought. The name was spoken plaintively, as if Bubby were some kid requesting the teacher to let him leave the schoolroom to take a piss.

Sam slapped the hood of the car. "See you, Bubby. I've got places to check out yet." He made it sound as if Bunny's was merely a stop on a long list.

Bubby's body went slack with relief. Immediately, he twisted the key, gunned the accelerator. "Swell seein' you, Sammy. Be sure to give my love to—" The name stuck in his throat. Bubby looked alarmed.

"Florence," said Sam, looking over the hood of the Caddy.

"Sure." The car shot back, turned at the road, spat up gravel as it shot off.

Sam didn't look around but kept his eyes on Bunny's cabin. The windows had darkened, lights gone off as soon as she'd left the porch.

He'd been fooling around here, playing cop, when he should have been over at Wade's house.

As he crossed the road to the patrol car, he told himself he'd cut his ritual visit to Wade's short; he wanted to get back to the pier. Maud would be sitting there alone.

Sam slammed the door, started the car, stared for a moment through the windshield.

He was out there somewhere.

It was hard for Sam to imagine any sort of violent act taking place on Hayden property. It was almost as peaceful as that old pier, and far less illusory. Or was it? Sam frowned as he drove down the road with the big white house up on his left and into the tarmac area near the barn where Wade's white station wagon was parked beside a Jeep pickup.

Ever since he had started spending hours talking with Maud and looking out over the lake, Sam had begun to wonder if he could put his hand through stuff that looked solid but might turn out to be mist and fog.

Sounds were muted; objects seemed to have dropped where they stood. Off to one side of the tarmac was an ancient Chevy, up on blocks. It had taken on the air of sculpture or statue, something immutable, unchangeable, marking a spot whose significance everyone had forgotten.

No one had forgotten the Hayden place, though. Not Dodge Haines, certainly, whose cigar it must be sparking up there on the porch, and whose truck was parked on the tarmac.

Occasionally, Dodge came for a visit, probably to still any lingering doubts in Wade's and the township's mind that Dodge had had anything to do with the death of Eunice Hayden.

As he walked across the close-cropped grass, his shoes wetted with ground mist, Sam was aware of lingering doubts about Dodge Haines, a man he had never much liked, even before the Hayden crime, a man who was mostly bluster and bad jokes, and another client of Bunny Caruso's. Dodge (who'd got his nickname years ago because of his loyalty to Chrysler) considered himself a hellion with the ladies. The Rake of the Rainbow Café was stuck back there somewhere in the forties; he thought that mock kisses, pinched thighs, ogled necklines got the women all worked up.

There was no love lost. If Sam disliked Dodge Haines, Dodge hated Sam DeGheyn. After the murder of Loreen Butts, Sam had knocked on Dodge's door so often that Mayor Sims had finally told him it looked like harassment.

"There was just as much circumstantial evidence to indict Dodge Haines for Eunice's murder as there was to convict Boy Chalmers for the Butts woman's," Sam had said.

"Jesus, but you're full of shit, DeGheyn," Sims had replied, dragging his height and girth around his desk like a man in manacles. "Haines found her, didn't he?"

"So he says."

"Hell's *that* mean?"

Sam shrugged. "I'm just wondering when he got there."

"The Moffits said they saw his truck parked by the barn."

"Sure. But they don't know when it pulled up."

"In the man's sworn statement he says he went out to see Hayden, walked into that barn, and there was Eunice 'trussed up like a chicken.' That's what he said. And the rest." Sims looked at Sam blackly.

"I know what he said, Mr. Mayor."

"Get off my back, Mr. DeGheyn."

"Coffee, Sam?" asked Wade, holding up the dented aluminum percolator that seemed as much a part of the Hayden place as the house and the cows and hens. He brought it out to the porch on these Sunday nights and set it on a hot plate so he wouldn't have to keep going back and forth to the kitchen. The porch was his favorite venue, the ladder-back rocker his favorite chair.

Dodge was sitting in the swing, whose chains creaked when he moved. He nodded curtly, looked off into darkness.

"I don't mind, Wade. Thanks," Sam said as Wade handed him the white mug. "How's business, Dodge?" Dodge had a construction company that Sam thought might be getting too much county business. Dodge and Mayor Sims were great pals.

Dodge shrugged. "So-so." He rocked his hand just as Bubby Dubois had.

Everyone must be going broke around La Porte. Dodge wasn't drinking coffee; he had a pint bottle in a brown paper bag. It was part of a persona Sam had never quite placed. Tough guy? No frills? Down-to-business? Sam didn't know, and neither, he figured, did Dodge. The Seagram's in a paper bag was meant to underscore the cowboy boots, the wide belt with the heavy buckle, the string tie. He had a hound's face—heavy jaw, jowls, drooping and bruised-looking tissue under the eyes.

"Want a snort?" Dodge held up the bottle. He still called them "snorts" and often drank Seven and Sevens. Dodge had to be civil to Sam, even, at times, convivial, to make sure no one would get the idea he harbored a grudge, which might also make them wonder why.

Sam smiled slightly. "I don't mind," he said again, holding out the mug of coffee, into which Dodge dribbled whisky. Sam thanked him and leaned back against the railing of the big wraparound porch, freshly painted every three years. The whole Hayden spread looked painted in place, it was that neat.

Talk was sparse with the three of them there. In addition to Sam's lingering doubts about Dodge, and Dodge knowing the doubts lingered, there was Wade himself, a still sort of man. One-on-one, he didn't mind talking. When it got up to three, Wade seemed to consider it a party, and he wasn't much good at parties.

Sam remembered him hovering with his paper punch cup when Mayor Sims had cut the ribbon for the opening of the new post office on Main. It was neatly laid pink brick, more efficient, bigger, air-conditioned, square, and charmless.

Sam made some comment about Wade's tomato crop; and Dodge said about Wade's horse, Fleetwood, "Oughta race that horse over to Brewerstown races someday."

"Well." Wade rocked and sipped, sipped and rocked.

"No, you ought," said Dodge, as if it were an argument. "That's one damn fine horse." He unscrewed the bottle cap, took a mouthful, and put the cap back on. He wasn't cheap, but he seemed to like to husband his whisky, as if he were drinking on a dare. He'd have loved Prohibition, Sam thought, if he'd been old enough to drink back then. Dodge was somewhere in his mid-fifties.

Comment about the old sow, about the half-dozen cows that Maud called "a tragedy of cows," with their thin white faces all looking hopeless and alike, like actors in a Greek play wearing masks.

Dodge apparently thought he'd earned the right to leave, had appeased the gods of doubt, and rose from the swing. Sam told him not to go, that he himself had just stopped by for coffee and couldn't stay long.

But Dodge just stretched and yawned and said he'd had a long day and went clattering down the porch steps. With his pint under his arm and his hands gouging his pants pockets he went whistling phonily off to his pickup.

"How you feeling, Wade?" Sam asked. It was no casual inquiry. Often, in the last years, Sam had got to worrying about Wade. He was a somber man, but very mild and pleasant, and much liked by the people of La Porte. In his tall, lanky way, he was almost handsome, too. The double deaths of daughter and wife had brought the women out in droves with their freshly baked pies and chicken casseroles. It was the first time Sam had seen Ella Ponteen in a fancy dress and carrying a covered dish. Women, Sam had thought, from the time their kids were born, always thought of food as salvation. Eat your spinach, drink your juice. Maybe they were right.

Sam's question was taken, too, as serious, calling for a serious reply. Wade put down his coffee mug for a moment, stretched his arms so the large hands clamped onto his knees, and looked past Sam and the porch rail. "I been better, Sam. I been better, as you know."

Sitting thus, his posture for serious speech, Wade started to talk. The shyness and hesitation in speech disappeared as he progressed, and his progression was along familiar lines. Sam had taken Dodge's place on the swing, was pushing himself back and forth with one foot, arm across the swing's back, head on fisted hand. It was pretty much always the same speech, and Sam wondered if that was what therapy was all about: the same speech over and over, the same events culled from memory, chipped away at in slightly different words, as if the experience were a piece of sculpture turning a many-faceted precious stone, but the heart of it never changing. It was always the same stone.

Was this what Dr. Hooper listened to—over and over again, the same details? Sam looked off, hearing Wade's voice as a kind of muted background music, and thought he'd ask her on one of her passages through La Porte. Maybe even tomorrow, Labor Day. She was staying over at the Stucks' rooming house. He'd seen her earlier, coming out of the Rainbow, and had to stop and stare. Sam hadn't told Maud that he considered Elizabeth Hooper a mysterious and beautiful woman who appeared almost out of nowhere at an appointed time and place and who carried within her the remnants of other people's lives, torn memories, rags of feeling.

". . . All of four years now, and I *still* just can't work it out in my mind, you know, how someone coulda done such a thing . . ."

Despite his reverie, part of Sam's mind still following Wade's drift—although it was always much the same study in loneliness, guilt, reprisal—Sam never knew but what the man's words might not offer up a clue, some new way of saying it. So he listened, staring off into darkness towards the barn.

Sitting with his hands locked on his chair arms as if he meant to shove himself out of the chair, Wade was saying what he'd said many times before, that the loss of a child was the most bitter loss to be borne. That it was difficult for Sam to understand, perhaps, he being without.

"Being without." It sounded as if the barrenness of Sam's marriage were a judgment, and that such aridity prevented compassion.

"What's terrible is, he got away with it. It's not to be borne that someone could do that and get off scot-free. There's times I wondered was it that Chalmers fellow."

Sam stopped the swing. How many times had he heard Wade say it? Wade just couldn't take in that Boy had an ironclad alibi for the time of Eunice's death. But he supposed it must ease the pain a bit for Wade to think there was someone he could look to. He turned his gaze from the far fields, indistinguishable one from the other in the dark. "I'm sorry we didn't find him, Wade."

"Hell, I ain't blaming you, Sam, you know that." Wade's voice was tight, and his jaw was working on a piece of tobacco. The hard way he chewed, it might have been gristle. Then he sat back and picked up his mug, two fingers through the handle, thumb on the rim. "Dodge said you was rooting around—that's his words, 'rooting around'—and that you had been ever since Eunice . . . well . . ."

Sam studied Wade's profile, the way the flesh beneath the cheekbone, the socket of the eye had hollowed out more over the last year. "When'd Dodge tell you that, Wade?"

The tall man shrugged. "Couple months ago. Round the time that Alonzo woman was killed. Dodge said it'd started you asking questions about the others. That Butts woman, and Eunice." Slowly, he turned to look at Sam, and his tone was slightly accusing: "You never told me nothing like that, you know."

No, he hadn't. Sam had said nothing to Wade about his suspicions regarding Boy Chalmers, though it had meant possibly short-circuiting some of Sam's own unofficial investigation. He would himself have liked to get Wade talking more concretely about that day, replaying it over and over again.

"Well, Wade, I wouldn't say I was 'rooting around.' It's been a long time, after all—although I have been thinking about it, that's true."

"I'm glad to hear that. I thought the police just closed the case and forgot all about Eunice." He took another swallow of coffee.

"Hard to forget, Wade . . . a thing like that." Sam shook his head when Wade raised the pot again from the warmer. "No, thanks." He drained his cup, rose, and set it on the table. "It's nearly twelve; got to be going."

"I don't guess Dodge and Mayor Sims is too happy about it. About you rooting around." Wade gave a slow smile, almost sly.

"No, I don't guess so, Wade. Well, I've got to be going."

They said good night, and Sam walked off across the hard dirt yard lit only by a cold half-moon.

FOUR

"I wonder where they go when the summer's over," said Maud, trying to stretch two fingers farther into the narrow olive bottle, scissoring them around an olive that kept falling back. Besides the cut-glass olive dish there was a little plate of lemon twists and cocktail onions. And a garlic clove. It was always there, and Sam knew she was waiting for him to ask about it. He didn't.

"Far as I know, Raoul and Ev—"

Her head turned quickly to Sam. "I didn't say I wanted to *know*, did I?" Irritated that he might tell her, still she was glad Sam was back. It was nearly midnight; the party across the lake usually crested around now, and she was getting depressed. Getting? Wasn't she always? No, this was different; it was superficial, even facile depression, a relief from the real thing.

"You said," said Sam, the fresh beer balanced on the arm of the folding chair, " 'I wonder where they go.' "

"That's *wondering*. *Wondering* is totally different from wanting to *know*. Like wondering about their names. You told me their names. When I said 'I *wonder* what their names are,' I didn't actually mean I wanted to *know*." She would much rather run a few possible names through her mind, pick one, discard it, start the process over again. Knowing the *last* name (which she didn't, but she suspected Sam did) would be entirely too real; last names pinned you right down to a phone book, a street, town, city, country. And, of course, if the name was ordinary, that could be near fatal to her fantasies about the people who owned the house across the lake. "Raoul." That wasn't the real name, she was sure— pretty sure. Sam had let the first names pop out, and when she'd reacted with a mild kind of violence (knocking the lamp over), he'd smiled rather slyly and retracted. Or half-retracted: he'd asked her if she really believed "Raoul" and "Evita" could possibly be the real names of the couple over there. Sam was very quick, though; very quick. He could have pretended he'd just made the names up in order to hide the fact he'd revealed them.

The thing was, she rather liked the names, and she imagined they very well *could* be real, given the Hollywood glamour going on over there. She was afraid of their real histories—God only knew she didn't want to find out they lived in Yonkers or even Manhattan. And what if they came from some palsied mid-sized city like Omaha? What if they had a regular house on a regular street in Des Moines? No one named "Raoul" or "Evita" could possibly be a full-blooded American, though, and therefore they would probably drive off a cliff before they'd live in Des Moines. She didn't want to know the real histories of the owners, or even the guests, because she was afraid of their possible mediocrity. Her imagination could really go to town working up ports of call for Raoul and Evita.

A few times there had been complaints, she'd heard, about noisy parties "over there," but Sam, with his customary delicacy, had refrained from identifying the culprit house. Anyway, it was no more than drunken cavorting in the driveway—which Maud couldn't see and which, consequently, didn't exist for her. God knows she had nothing against drinking, as long as the glasses were perfect, the gestures of raising them elegant.

Sam had said, with that eerie perception he sometimes displayed, that he hadn't intended to give away their names. "You don't even know but what I made them up, do you?" and he'd looked out over the moonstruck lake with that tiny smile . . .

"Sorry," said Sam, who actually did know where they lived, and did know their names, although he had very little contact with the summer people, the ones who owned the quarter-million spreads

on the other side of the lake. He drove around back there sometimes in the dusk and marveled at these houses, at the way they
had tucked themselves, architect-designed and long and low, into
the landscape, burrowed there like moles. Big as they were, they
had surprised his eye, separating from their camouflage of trees,
plants, and shrubs only if he looked closely.

Maud didn't have to worry about reality barging in from over
there, jumping off the dock swimming towards her, waving, yelling, singing, drowning. If she ever drove along the old roads on the
other side she would find them just as dreamy.

He had thought up "Raoul" one night after he and Florence
had been to La Porte's single movie house to see *Kiss of the
Spider Woman*. The name "Raul Julia," Sam thought, had got to
be about the best in the book if a person wanted to conjure up
exotic, mysterious people and settings. What a name! It was definitely a Mother Grizzell name. Ma Gris would absolutely make
a meal of that name. He wondered if the two of them were still
in that trailer, sitting as they'd sat a year ago. Perhaps she'd died.
For all of her wiry aggressiveness, she hadn't looked all that
strong to him.

The "Evita" he'd stumbled on when he'd been flipping through
the chrome jukebox menu of numbers in the Rainbow Café and
found "Don't Cry for Me, Argentina." Evita Perón. He'd thought
"Evita" went extremely well with "Raoul." It was a marriage made
in heaven.

God knows it was better than their real names, ordinary as La
Porte names. Maud would have fits.

"It's all right," Maud said, giving her attention to the olive jar and
finally loosening up the one that was wedged in, so that all the
olives rolled out into the olive dish. From across the lake came the
jumpy sounds of "Anything Goes." There was a little stirring of
the guests. Some had come out to the patio, and she loved the daubs
of color the gowns of the women made, even though the distance

and the lantern light muted them, blueing the greens, or the greens yellowing the blues. *In other words,* she admitted to herself, *you can't really tell.* It was too dark to see such mutations; the patio was like a little chartreuse island.

They sat in silence, Sam humming a few bars of the music, smoke drifting up from his cigarette.

She was glad he'd come back before going home. Often, she wondered about his wife, Florence, who occasionally came into the Rainbow to buy pastry or order a cake for a special occasion. Maud had never talked to her; Shirl always waited on her up there by the cash register. Florence was quite good-looking, she thought, in a smoldering, Italian way. Sam had smiled and said she was second-generation Greek.

She also wondered where he went on these nightly excursions ("just to check on things") around La Porte. Did he circle the lake and drive past the backs of those houses over there? Probably not. But he could be gone for two, three hours, and although he'd said he was going to Wade Hayden's, she couldn't really imagine sitting around with Wade Hayden for over two hours.

This was not because she disliked Wade. She didn't even know him except to see him behind the counter in the post office, where he would always say, " 'Lo, Maud" and " 'Bye, Maud," with nothing much happening in between. His smile would be reserved as he'd stamp a package "Priority Mail" that she'd be sending to Chad. He was very remote. Reserved and remote. Maud wanted to laugh. Beside her, Wade Hayden was probably Times Square. They should have got on like a house afire, standing there together on opposite sides of the counter.

She'd forgotten about that poor girl of his, Eunice, and the sudden memory brought the rocking chair down with a small thud.

Sam turned and looked at her. "Something wrong?"

"I just remembered Eunice Hayden. I swear, but I just can't put that together. It doesn't make sense."

"Does murder ever?" Sam picked up the binoculars and fiddled with them.

"Well, of *course.* Take Detroit or Chicago or New York City. There it makes sense. The very senselessness of it makes sense."

"You've lost me." Sam turned the binoculars over. "Zeiss. These are good. Where'd you get these?"

"In the attic. But listen: that's what those places—I mean Detroit and New York, for instance—are *like.* Killings are part of the puzzle. But not here. It's like someone took a piece from the wrong puzzle, a piece of blue sky, maybe, and forced it into a black pavement. Thumped it right in, I mean. And spoiled the whole design."

"Maud, for lord's sake, what's the difference? You can't force a piece of sky into a New York street, either." He adjusted the focus.

Her fist curled and her eyes squeezed shut. He recognized the signs of a snit coming on.

"The sky's always falling in the gutters of New York. And don't be so damn *literal.*" The eyes opened and the fingers mauled around in the jar of olives. "I hate it when the pimento gets out." She tossed the bruised olive into her glass and pulled the bottle from the ice. "Now *this*"—and Maud made a sweeping motion with the Popov bottle—"makes sense. There's the lake, the moon over it, and the little boats; there's us on the end of the pier; and there's the party across the water. The arrangement is perfect." She made a circle with her thumb and index finger.

Binoculars raised to his eyes, Sam said, "Um . . . Well, there's some people wouldn't agree it's perfection."

Maud gave him a soppy smile. "That comment is beneath you. What are you doing with my binoculars? Put them down!"

Sam dropped them, and they dangled on the narrow black strap. "For Christ's sake, that's what they're for. Distance. What do you do with them, count your toes?"

Maud started rolling her hair up the side as if the lake were her mirror. She knew the gesture irritated Sam. "The rule is, we're not supposed to see the party up close."

Sam sighed. "The rule. You just made that up."

With feigned sweetness, Maud said, "I never needed it before. The rule is, you do not try and see the people over there any closer than you can see with your naked eye. I don't know why, so don't ask me. It's the rule. I think it's because—" Maud stopped to sip her drink and stir the glass flamingo—"it would spoil the design. It would break it all up." She gazed up at the night sky. "The moon would crack, the lake would shatter like glass, the patio would tilt, and the pier would collapse."

For a moment Sam looked at her. "That is certified shit."

As if there were crumbs in the lap of her skirt, she brushed it smoothly, slowly. "That is because you are blind. You can't see anything if it isn't in perfect focus."

Sam swung the binoculars from around his neck and set them on the pier. He pulled a Coors from the bucket, snapped the cap. At least she'd got off the subject of Eunice Hayden. So he was, really, pleased to sit there and listen to her ramble on about some fucking room or other she'd seen in a vision.

"I didn't say 'vision.' I'm not clairvoyant—which is one of my favorite words. It's musical. . . . Anyway, I was talking about a room in my imagination. I keep seeing it. It must be in Spain; there are Spanish tiles on the floor. Or in Mediterranea. The weather—"

Sam's head snapped up. " 'Mediterranea?' There is no such place."

She sighed and dropped her head in her hand. "I mean, as any fool could tell, any country or place around the Mediterranean Sea. God, can I just tell about this room?"

"Shoot."

"The weather is fine. I mean, it's not just sunny; it's silky or gauzy. There's a bed with an iron frame, and a big wardrobe, and a wooden chair pulled up at a sort of dressing table. Peachy-shaded powder is spilled a little over the table. One of those old Pond's powder boxes is sitting on the glass . . . though probably in Mediterranea you can't buy it. The curtains are as translucent as chiffon and billow around the window that looks over the sea. There's a small wrought-iron balcony that I can walk out on—I wear a loose dress and I'm barefoot—that I can walk out on and look out over the sea. The sea is the color of jade until the sun starts setting and tosses this dazzling scarf of light over it at six o'clock and turns it to topaz. At night it's grape-colored. And it's always moving. I can't see the waves breaking on the shore because my room is very high up; but I can see the waves barely forming out there in tiny wrinkles. At night if the moon is very bright, which it usually is, I can see narrow bands of white foam, just a ruffle of white." Maud stopped to take a cigarette from his pack and tamp it down. She had her own, but she enjoyed filching his.

"Is the ice bucket on the balcony?"

She squinted past the blue flame. "What?" Then she looked around at the tub and frowned as if it were some newfangled thing tilting precariously on the end of the pier. "No," she snapped. "If there was an ice bucket I'd have said."

Dangerous waters, but Sam stroked through them. "Well. It was only because the place sounded a little like here . . ."

Her eyes were as wide and wild as a gazelle's as she swept them over the scene around her. "Here? *Here?* Well, fortunately not. The polizia don't go around arresting the wrong people in Mediterranea." The rocking chair thumped back, and she smoked in quick little jabs.

Sam was wary. "What're you talking about?"

"As if he didn't know. Those women raped and murdered. Nancy Alonzo and Loreen Butts and the other one." She looked at Sam. "That Chalmers fellow you arrested—"

"Boy Chalmers. And *I* didn't arrest him—the police in Hebrides did that. And the mayors in both towns were extremely pleased. Not to mention the state's attorney." Maud was rocking the chair gently to the rhythm. " 'Moonlight Becomes You.' Can you imagine? Remember Dorothy Lamour? Someone told me she lived in Baltimore, Maryland . . ."

"You certainly know the right thing to wear . . ." Maud sang. She had a light, sweet voice that put Sam in mind of a tall, pastel summer cooler—the sort of thing you held sitting on white wicker on a wide green lawn . . . Christ, he was getting as bad as her.

"She wore hibiscus in her hair. Dorothy would be better off in my room than in Baltimore. I wonder if she sells real estate. I think someone told me she did." Maud shook her head. "That doesn't fit, either."

Although she appeared to have forgotten about Boy Chalmers and the rape-murders, Sam knew she hadn't. Maud rarely forgot any of the threads of her conversation, any more than Odysseus' wife—what was her name?—would have given up weaving that endless tapestry. "Tell me some more about the room. It's interesting."

"Why should I?" She sang a few more words:

What a night to go dreaming,
Mind if I tag al-looooong . . .

"Well . . . I'll tag along to your room." He thought of Florence. Had she been out going dreaming with Bubby Dubois? How could anyone go dreaming with him?

Maud's voice came through the image of that blubbery body humping his wife. Her sly voice. "Why don't you ask me if there was anyone else in the room?"

Better sly than hurt, so Sam said, "Okay. I'm asking."

Maud stilled the rocking chair and leaned over the arm, closing in. "Nooo." Now it was sly sweetness. "Nooo. There're no chairs on my balcony, so I'm not sitting out there looking over the water with some knuckle-brained, ham-fisted member of the polizia." In a grand gesture, she made a curve with the hand that held her martini glass and the liquid went flying out, sparkling the air, as if she were baptizing the pier. "Shit," she said, looking into its emptiness.

"Sounds like your room's in Venice." It appeared to be a neutral comment, but he just couldn't keep the fecklessness out of it. He knew well enough that she didn't want to qualify her room or place it anywhere in particular beyond its Mediterraneal bearings. He knew she was looking up at him from under the veil of her hair. "Because of the water," he said. He was really more interested in why she was so sure Boy Chalmers was the wrong man. Probably just to be pig-headed.

"It most certainly is *not.*" She grabbed the vodka bottle and wrung another drink out of it. "There's no jade sea around Venice—at least not in the postcard I saw of it. And, anyway, Venice is on the *Adriatic.*"

Anyone who didn't know *that* was surely too witless to be the repository for her great dream. "Oh. Well, I guess I'm not swell enough for Mediterranea. Or even Adriatica." Sam stretched out his legs and dropped the mirror-sunglasses down from their resting place on top of his hair. "So tell me why you think Boy Chalmers is innocent."

"Who?"

He had interrupted her fantasy-telling, and now she was going to be difficult. "The wrong man. The wrong man I arrested."

She had herself picked up the binoculars now and was training them across the lake. He knew she would refuse to talk about Chalmers unless he noticed what she was doing. And commented. Sam sighed. "Well, you're breaking your own rule, aren't you? Didn't you just say we're not supposed to be looking through the binoculars?"

"I'm not."

If he didn't know Maud so well, he'd've thought she was drunk silly. But she was never drunk, just silly. Sam stared up at the black sky. He was tempted not to comment, but he supposed he'd have to. "You're not. But you're looking right through those binoculars."

"My eyes are closed."

Oh, for Christ's sake, her eyes are—Sam couldn't stand it; he reached out and wrenched them from her grip. Which was, of course, just what she wanted—to drive him to distraction. She was smoothing out her skirt and humming "Moonlight Becomes You."

As he wound the strap around the binoculars and then set them on the dock, he said, "I'd appreciate it if you'd tell me why you think the Chalmers kid didn't do it."

Dignified silence reigned.

"Maud?"

Making a long sausage curl of her hair, she rolled it slowly up above her ear. She knew it annoyed him, which is why she did it.

"I'd really like to hear what you think. Since we seem to be the only ones who think it. Sims thinks I'm nuts."

He must have hit just the right mendicant-on-the-street-corner note. "*He's* the nut. An alcoholic old nut who shouldn't ever be mayor." She stopped in the act of pulling the little beaded cord of the lamp off and on, off and on, as if she'd just discovered the wonders of electricity. "He hates you because if you ever ran for mayor, you'd win. Still, I hate to say it, but it would be just too much of a coincidence that on the very day Boy escapes from prison there's another murder." She looked at Sam, worried.

He popped another can of Coors. "Oh, I'm not saying it's coincidence. I guess I'm saying whoever's doing these killings took advantage of Boy's being loose."

Maud frowned and went back to pulling the cord. It illuminated and then plunged into darkness the edge of the dock where the black cat was snoozing. "That's certainly possible, I guess. Do you know Chad said that?" When Sam looked at her, eyebrows raised, she nodded. "He did."

"Chad?"

"Um-hm. He was talking about him a few weeks ago, down here. He was setting up the lamp for me and all the extensions . . ." She looked behind her.

Impatiently, Sam prompted her to go on. "Why didn't Chad think it was Boy like everybody else?"

"Chad is *not* like everybody else." She sighed and dug around in the ice for a cocktail onion, which she plunked in her glass before pouring a fresh martini. "I guess he's like us." And she sighed again, as if she, Sam, and Chad belonged to some alien race of folk who because of their greater perception and subtlety had to live beyond the fringes of ordinary society. "Did you know he met Boy Chalmers once?"

"Hell, *no*, I never knew it. You never told me."

"That's because *I* never knew it, until that weekend. Chad was riding that ancient bike out on the road to Hebrides—oh, way over a year ago, I think he said. One of the tires gave out, and Boy was coming along on his motorcycle. He stopped and fixed the tire. To do it, he had to go back to his bicycle shop and get a pump and patch, or whatever, but Chad said he was really *helpful*. He went to a lot of trouble."

"Why didn't he ever tell you this after Boy was up for Loreen Butts's murder?"

She was pulling the little metal cord of the lamp. Off. On. Off. On. "He says he did. He says I forgot. But I didn't forget. He just forgot to tell me. You know how he is." She kept twitching the cord.

"No, I don't know how—will you stop fucking around with that lamp? A person would think you'd been living by gaslight all these years. You shouldn't have a lamp down here, for Christ's sake, Maud!"

She looked at him evenly, said coolly: "Then tell me, how else can I read my book?" She lifted the book of poetry.

"Read *inside*. I'm surprised Chad would help you set this up." Sam turned and looked behind him. "You must have a dozen extensions trailing back there to the house. Have I ever seen anything so stupid!"

"I don't know. Have you?" Maud was reading her poem, mouthing the words silently and elaborately.

Sam gritted his teeth. "You could have an accident. You could topple over into the lake and that lamp right on top of you."

Maud did not look up from her book as she replied, "I've often thought of going swimming with the lamp, yes." Quickly, she reached up and tugged the cord. Off, on.

He should sic her on Mayor Sims. No, Maud was only like this around him. And Chad, too. He drank his beer and looked over at her as she sat there pretending to read that poem, dramatically mouthing the lines and now fluttering her hands a little, just in case he wasn't noticing that she was ignoring him. She turned a page. It rustled elaborately.

Sam knew the reason he'd got on her case about the lamp, and knew the reason he was so irritable, was because it made him terribly nervous, Maud sitting out here alone for half the night, unprotected except when he could be here with her. "Go on about Boy Chalmers. What else?"

"Chad didn't say anything else." She closed her book, a stage prop not immediately useful to her. "He just said he didn't see how Boy could possibly have done these murders. Boy was just too fucking *nice*. Those were his exact words." She looked meaningfully at Sam. "I don't approve of people always saying 'fuck this' and 'fuck that.' It's a word that should be used sparingly, if indeed at all. Some people must always resort—"

Oh, shut up, Sam thought, listening to her ramble on about the impoverishment of the language. "Did Chad say anything at all else?"

"No. But Boy must really have made an impression on him for him to believe he's innocent when he'd rather not."

"How do you mean?"

"Chad would rather think he's guilty." Maud turned to him. "That would mean whoever's guilty had been caught. For *that* would mean I'm out of danger." She folded her hands in her lap and looked out over the lake with the most self-satisfied expression Sam could imagine. Chad worrying about her pleased Maud immensely.

But she was right. Chad would certainly rather think the killer caught.

"Thanks," he said. "Thanks for telling me."

"Yooo-rrr welcome," she said, rolling her hair up the side of her head again.

Smiling slightly, he leaned his head back and studied the night sky. "Wish we could all live in Mediterranea." He felt her grow still, probably pleased he had remembered about her dream room.

"The *carabinieri* probably don't need a new loot." She plucked the Popov bottle out again and held it up to check the vodka line. "I guess if you could have anything you wanted, anything at all, you'd take that room."

Looking disgusted, she forced the bottle back into the Colonel Sanders bucket and set her glass on the barrel.

But he could nearly read her mind: she saw a game in all of this, the what-would-you-ask-for-if-you-could-have-anything game, and he knew she wouldn't be able to resist.

"Well, what would *you* ask for?" Her tone was as stepped-on as the singer over there whining about everything happening to him.

"Depends."

The chair stopped rocking. "What do you mean, 'depends'? If you could have anything you wanted, it doesn't 'depend.'"

"Oh." After a fumy silence in which the vocalist missed planes and got his letters shot back to him, Sam said, "Where would I be living when I asked for—whatever?"

"*What?* . . . *Anywhere,* of course, if you can have anything . . ."

Sam eased down in his chair and rolled the can of Coors across his forehead. "I'm thinking."

"Go ahead, then. Think."

Sam wanted to say "Key West." But she'd read into that reply that he wasn't taking the poem seriously, or her need to understand it. "New York."

Maud stopped rocking and sipping and banged down both chair and drink. "New *York?* Why in the name of god New *York?* You could live anywhere"—she stretched out her arms—"and you choose New *York*? Death Valley, the Mojave Desert I could understand . . ." She settled back again, her face turned to the black sky, and said, "But not New *York.*" Her mouth on the last word was like a little steel vise.

"So now it appears I *can't* live anywhere I want."

"I didn't say that. Did I say that? Just be reasonable, will you?" She paused. "Why New York?"

"Because I have a niece there. Her name's Rosie." Sam did not have a niece named Rosie. He had pulled her out of the air, walking down Fifth, probably because of the tune coming from some old wreck of a piano over there, and a drunken choir of voices: "You are . . . my heart's boo-kaaay." He felt, suddenly, a rush of nostalgia over this imaginary girl who had not even existed a minute before.

Maud folded her arms across her chest, hard. Had she been standing, she would have looked like one of those hardy women in an old pioneer movie. "You never told me about Rosie."

"I don't think about her all that much, I guess."

"Is she on your side or Florence's?"

"I don't think she's chosen up sides." Sam checked his watch. One a.m. Florence would certainly be choosing up any other side but his.

"You know what I mean. You're just trying to irritate me."

Sam smiled. "Maybe. Rosie's my brother's girl." Now he was inventing an entire family. It came from sitting around with Maud, who only touched down on Earth when she was working. He didn't care; anything that would keep her talking was okay by Sam.

Thump went the chair again as she twisted her whole body around to glare at him. "What brother? You've only got a sister. That's what you told me. Don't you ever tell the truth?"

Sam chewed his lip. "He's a half-brother. Mom was married before she married my father. His name's not even the same."

Maud started rocking again. "Half-brother. That makes Rosie hardly any relation at all."

It annoyed him, the way she discounted the niece who had just been born, streaked her way to eighteen or twenty, and was now walking down Fifth, looking in shop windows. He saw her as clearly as he would if he'd been the window dresser, seen her straight through the sun-sparkled glass. She had a filmy blondness that looked as if it were etched in sunlight. Wide blue lake-water eyes . . .

"So, you haven't yet said what you'd want most. Living in New York, that is. If you could have *anything*. A stretch limo, for instance."

Having turned Rosie into the merest wraith of a relative, Maud seemed a little content, tapping her fingers to the music. The guests were out on the patio again. If he squinted his eyes, he could make out a tiny figure dressed in blue with pale yellow hair. "Valet parking."

The cigarette she was raising to her lips dropped. "You're supposed to choose the thing you want *most*. You're not playing."

Sam yawned and slowly rose. "I am. Valet parking. This is New York, remember."

Maud tossed the cigarette into the lake. "Good God, you could have the Trump Tower if you wanted it."

"Then I'd *really* need valet parking. Listen: I want you to go in now. I don't like you sitting out here all on your own in the dark. You never know what sort of weirdos are hanging around. I have to get home." He was not going home; he meant to continue his rounds. Sam leaned over her, resting his hands one on each arm of her wooden rocker. "And unplug that goddamned lamp." He walked away.

"It's *Labor Day*; it's the last party. I'm sitting here and watching. And I don't see why you have to leave. You've got late shift tomorrow, haven't you?" Sam turned on the dock, looking at the back of her head, at the rigid way she held herself. Then she said, "She did write his name in her own blood."

Sam stood there for another moment and then went back to put his hand on her shoulder. "Are you talking about Nancy?"

"That's what they said she wrote: 'Boy.' "

"I don't think she meant Boy Chalmers."

Maud looked up at him, squinting. "Who did she mean, then?"

"Her son. Her little boy."

"*What?* You don't mean you think he—?"

"No, of course not. He's only seven years old. No, I think she was trying to leave him a message. You knew Nancy, didn't you? Didn't she once work in the Rainbow for a while?"

Maud nodded, staring up at him. "Washed dishes."

"Well, you remember she worked for us too, cleaning at night. We used to talk."

"In the Rainbow she'd never talk to anybody. I guess that's not surprising—you'd end up talking to Shirl. She was so shy. Nancy, I mean. I tried to get her to talk. But she'd just keep her eyes on the dishes. It was terrible the way her husband must've beat her up. It was terrible they took the little boy away from her, as if it were all her fault."

"You know what she called him, Maud? 'Dear boy.' "

"Oh." It came out a breathy, drawn-out "ooohh." "Dear boy." It seemed such a sadly old-fashioned way of speaking. Maud suddenly remembered her mother using it, often, when talking about her younger brother, Maud's uncle. And he was dead now, too. He was dead of an aneurism; he'd fallen off a bar stool when he was barely forty-five. Everyone else thought this was funny; Maud hadn't. *Dear boy.*

"I believed her, the story she told about her son falling down the cellar steps. I was out at their house. Those steps were deadly. There was this big hook—lord knows what it was for—sticking out of the wall. The kid could easily have fallen and broken his arm on those steps. After all the other accidents that happened to the kid when that drunk of a husband was around—Rick Alonzo, what a deadbeat—I guess the social worker thought the boy'd be better off in a foster home. It was hard on her, really hard."

Hard? Maud could well imagine. It made her hold her breath even to think of it.

Sam went on. "She'd be mopping the floor, wringing the mop out and talking about him. 'Dear boy,' she'd say."

Maud listened to the birdcall of the clarinet across the lake.

"Billie Anderson nearly laughed me out of her office when I pointed out that I didn't think Nancy had written anyone's name. There was a smudge, another word in front. And that *b* wasn't a capital *B*."

Maud felt a near-unbearable weight on her heart. "Oh, Sam. You think she wrote—"

" 'Dear boy.' "

They were silent for a long moment, Maud rocking, Sam standing there. Then he said, "I'll see you later," and walked off the dock.

He heard her voice again, at his back, and turned and shook his head. What else, how else would Scheherazade keep him hanging around here?

"I guess that means I can't continue my story; I can't tell you about the drowning." She reached up and pulled the bead cord on the lamp. Its shaded glow threw a cone of dull amber over her hair.

"What drowning?" His arms were crossed over his chest. He knew her.

"Mine," she said simply, reaching a languid hand toward her glass. "It happens quite beautifully in the molten sea beyond the room I was telling you about. Well, good night."

The molten sea, for Christ's sake. "How do you drown in this vision?"

In a stagy manner, she turned her profile to him. "I thought you had to go."

Sam stared at the moon and shook his head. "I can come back in about a half hour. Just to make sure you haven't drowned in the molten lake. So give me a quick synopsis."

Maud cleared her throat as elaborately as a diva and said, still facing forward, "I don't know how, but suddenly I find myself above the sea. It's like a net of gold. The sun's setting. I'm in this long, long dress of filmy gold, and I simply drop—no, I don't drop—I *sail* gently down and I lie floating on the sea. I blend with it . . . my dress, my skin, because of the reflected sunlight, and it's as if the sea closes over me, but you can't tell the difference. I fit it. The sea, I mean."

She fell silent and he waited. Then she turned around and said, "I'm the perfect puzzle-piece."

For a few moments he stood there several feet behind her, frowning, feeling a chill. "Turn off that goddamned lamp and I'll be back in a while."

FIVE

He stood right off the path through the woods where she'd had to walk on her way home and breathed in the moist night air.

What had delivered her into his waiting arms but the wish of his dear dead angel mother, to make up for the pain she'd caused him? She'd left her last letter to that bristle-bearded old man who'd done nothing but sit at the kitchen table and drink their money away.

The queer had escaped from jail! It still made him snigger. The queer got out and gave him a perfect reason for doing it on that particular night, when he'd been hanging back because he thought it was too soon—too soon after the Butts woman.

It wasn't because he thought he was in danger. No, it was because he liked watching her.

He liked watching her walk down Main, skittering along with her head down, her feet hardly touching the pavement. She was like a leaf, a pale brown leaf, thin and ribbed and blown about by any wind.

He sighed, tonight, remembering.

And remembering, he found the cold handle of the knife jutting up from his hip. He could almost hear the rustles in the woods that he'd heard that night in June when she moved along the path. Coming towards him.

He leaned back against the tree, leaned his head back until his face was pointing upwards through the branches, his neck taut, as taut as hers had been. He ran his fingers smoothly up and down, up and down, and felt the answering tautness below, could feel his jeans begin to strain.

"Nancy."

He whispered it even now and could imagine her all over again.

She'd started, out there in the unshadowed darkness, a dark so complete that only the stark whiteness of the ash trees in the cold moonlight could pierce it.

And his eyes. But his eyes had burned out patches of these woods, turned the hard dry leaves beneath their struggling bodies to cinders.

"Hullo, Nancy."

He heard her intaken breath, could see her fighting with the dark, trying to make out where the voice had come from. He giggled.

She'd tried to yell, but it came out a gurgle that he simply reached out and cut off, one hand around her neck, dragging her body towards him. Before he drew out the knife, he would make her understand that he was master and she nothing more than a pitiful wood creature, a squirrel or a rabbit.

He'd clamped his hand around her chin, squeezing her mouth up to his, felt his tongue like an asp darting, darting at her teeth as if he'd sting her to death.

And then she was on the ground, both of her hands held as if roped by his one hand, and, dreamlike, the knife appearing in the other, cutting into her clothes, her flesh like butter, trailing straight down from her chin, and all the clothes fluttering and unresisting beneath the tip.

As he plunged into her he shrieked. He felt the pure righteousness of it. Her eyes were hollow, white, turned back in her head as if she dared not look at his blinding eyes.

He brandished the knife in the air and waited for her to recognize this world he had ushered her into.

Her eyes stared up at him.

He smiled and slit her throat.

Tonight, he had to shake himself out of this remembrance.

How could she still have had a breath of life in her? How could she have had strength to leave a sign, a word in her own blood on the ground?

And *why?*

Why had she written that faggot's name, who'd never have the balls to do what he had done—why write that name in her own blood?

Ever since that night at the end of June, he'd puzzled over this. It nearly drove him crazy, wondering. All he could think was that it was the hand of god or his dear angel mother, who wanted to make sure the evil were punished. And the righteous went free. Nothing else could explain it.

It must mean he was on the right track. That it wasn't too soon. And god only knew this one deserved to die, too.

He would have liked to stay here in the woods a little longer, one hand on the knife, the other on his neck, remembering.

But he must move off now down the path and get to a place where he could watch to see if she'd be out tonight as she usually was, and which way she'd go.

If anyone deserved to die. If anyone deserved to die.

What he thought she was doing was drinking. Someone in La Porte might have said that Willow Pauley's being a secret drinker was hard to believe, but Sam had no difficulty believing it. He only wished people in La Porte would pull their shades down or draw their drapes and, occasionally, lock their doors.

Sam had walked back to the police car and was watching Willow Pauley in her brightly lit, white kitchen, where she stood near the sink, moving a glass to her lips and then lowering it, and then bringing it up again, rhythmically. He saw all of this as if a dark cutout against a white background had moved.

Willow's house was not isolated like Bunny Caruso's. It was a sturdy frame-and-brick that sat in its large lot facing Main Street. But it did have a privacy that others on the street lacked, as it was spiked around with trees, mostly ash and pine. Before he died her father had run the nursery just outside of town. He loved trees so much he'd even named his two daughters and one son after them: Willow, Ashley, and Oak. Mr. Pauley had planted enough ash, pine, and oak around the house that by now the property was heavily wooded in back.

And it was the back that Sam always checked out. The old dirt road that ran all the way around the lake trickled off like rivulets from a stream and wound around and narrowed down into little more than ruts. One of them ended up here. The place could be approached from the rear, and Sam had got out and made a brief tour in and out of the heavy cover of trees.

Now he was sitting as he had outside of Bunny's, wishing that Willow would lead her life behind a down-drawn blind.

It was spot checking, that was all. It was all he could do, but he didn't do it on company time. Even if his idea about the killings was totally wrong, there was nothing to lose. He yawned and looked at the luminous dial of his watch and back at the window. One-fourteen a.m. and Willow was apparently cooking. Cooking and drinking. She raised the glass again, and the angle of light showed it to be a wineglass, a large, globelike glass.

Sam studied the spokes of the steering wheel and thought about Nancy Alonzo. She might have been thirty, thirty-five even, but she hardly looked twenty. Working as hard as she had all of her life, and only her hands had aged. He remembered how she had stood there, wringing her red, rough hands, asking Sam if he could help her get the boy back. *I never hurt him, Sheriff. I would never, ever hurt that dear boy.* Sam told her he knew she hadn't and wouldn't. He'd tried like hell to get the agency to reconsider, but with all the other "accidents" the child had suffered through, well, now it was broken limbs, and this was just too much. Poor Nancy.

Poor Nancy. Even now, two months later, Sam could hardly believe that Nancy Alonzo's reward for all of her hard work and suffering was a horrible death.

Sam raised his head from his crossed hands and watched Willow's window. Sims had no trouble, Sam thought, believing it. Sims treated the killing of Nancy Alonzo and the escape of Boy Chalmers from prison almost as if they were calling cards from heaven, something he could whip out and hand to the sheriff.

Sam squinted through the windshield at Willow's back door, the little wooden porch, and the steps going up. The door probably wasn't locked.

The trouble was, there were artificial limitations he had set. He had made big assumptions; he was aware of that. But if he began with the gut knowledge that Boy Chalmers hadn't done that murder near the Oasis tavern, and the sure knowledge that the Hebrides and state police hadn't done much looking around, then he could at least start from there. Someone else had done it, and in order to move at all, he assumed that it was someone from these parts. Sedgewick kept talking about Hebrides and La Porte, that they were two different places. But the murder of Tony Perry had taken place in that no-man's-land of woods; and the Oasis Bar and Grille, that was as near to La Porte, almost, as it was to Hebrides.

At any rate, if he was to do anything at all by himself and on his own time, he had to leave out trying to do any more spot-checks in Hebrides. He didn't know the women there; he didn't know their habits; and it was bigger than La Porte. It was also out of his jurisdiction, though he didn't give a fuck about that.

If he was wasting his time, it was *his* time.

He sighed, turned his eyes to the rear window of the brightly lit kitchen, and saw Willow actually lighting a candle, as if she might be expecting a suitor. That old-fashioned word simply came unbidden to his mind. Willow Pauley wasn't a woman to have a suitor.

SEVEN

He had watched her for nearly a year.

He watched her now coming down the steps of the house, holding on to the wooden railing and carefully placing her feet in the way of someone old or infirm. The crown of her head was down; she was looking at her feet, and light from the street lamp capped it with silver. She reached the pavement, turned up her coat collar, and walked north to where the pavement ended suddenly. It was as if the La Porte boundaries were sharply defined.

From where he now stood, fitting the blade of the serrated knife into a leather holder he'd made especially for it, he could see both ways. He couldn't have found a better place to stand and observe whoever passed up and down Main Street. No one could see him; no one knew he was there.

Clever, that's what he'd always been. Lowering his head, he giggled. It was funny, it really was. Then soberly he zipped up his jacket and moved like any night creature from his place of safety, a fox from its den.

Her coat was white or cream-colored. That made it easier to keep her in sight in the darkness relieved only by the sickly yellowish glow of the vapor lamps. This was the end of town; there was no one about, and no one walked toward the town's edge this time of night, anyway. He had watched too often and too long to make a mistake of that.

In a way, he liked her, would have liked her a good deal, maybe, if she'd been a good woman. She was a person of habit, as he was.

She was dependable. You could count on her to behave in the same way, to do the same things at the same time. You could count on her.

The thought made him hesitate, made him miss a beat in his rhythmic walk, and he felt just the barest tightness in his chest.

The knife in its leather holder rubbed against his thigh. He pulled it out and ran his thumb delicately along the blade.

Even if he fell back and put more distance between them, he could see her easily because of her coat. Her coat was white (*your dress was blue*).

His foot scraped on the pavement as he stopped. He squinted his eyes shut and put his hand to his ear, rubbing the heel of the palm into it, like a swimmer whose ear was engorged with water. Where had that line come from? "*I was dressed in blue.*"

He walked on, heavily. He could see the stand of pines just beyond the end of the pavement and knew she would sleepwalk along the road there. She was a dreamer, a sleepwalker ("*I was all in blue*").

He stumbled a little; the pressure in his head was worse.

"I was all in blue . . ."

Two people. They were singing. The image that flickered on and off in his mind was of a man and a woman sitting somewhere against a painted sunset by the sea, singing. His hand was slick on the handle of the knife. His fingers were biting into his skin. Something was draining out of him, and he felt the tightening in his chest ray out to his limbs. It was not the same pressure that he had felt four years ago, or two, or one. That pain had in it the comfort of the rightness of the thing.

He had gained on her without knowing. Now she stopped. He went cold. If she looked around . . . He stepped into the shadows of the walled drive of the last house.

But she didn't. She knew she had to go down. The others knew it; the fight they put up was for show; it was only a friendly argument.

A friendly argument. His face felt oiled like the knife, only in sweat, and he wiped his arm across his forehead. He felt the sense of purpose leaving him and stubbornly fought to hold on to it. The voices of the singers were intrusive. He tried to shake them off, too, and kept on walking.

Why didn't she look back?

When he saw the woman in the Oasis Bar and Grille, he had not even known what moved him to seek her out, to set his feet in her direction. Her lips had been wet and shiny as red patent, glistening in the smoky light of the Oasis. That silver blouse as transparent as water, that eddied and curled around her breasts and nipples . . . None of that. It was later he had found out about the little boy, *her* little boy . . .

As if a switch had been thrown in his brain, a wire crackled, and his head snapped to the left; his body felt the current. He was crying, losing his will; it was running like sap from a tree.

To steady himself, to draw some sort of boundary around himself, he studied the houses left and right. That was Miss Ruth's front porch, chocolate-brown trim. Willow Pauley's house back off the street, showing edges of light through the trees; was she up? The row of pumps at the Red Bird gas station.

The familiar windows and the square patterns of La Porte made him breathe more easily. Why did she seem always to be coming to the edge of the pavement and yet never entering the dirt road, the woods? Hadn't it been a long time?

"I was all in blue."

The voices of the singers were growing louder, and the scene from an old movie flashed into his mind. She was moving now towards the trees, and he remembered the little girl in the movie, the one that had turned almost overnight into a woman. But her dress was *white*—stark virginal white, with a sash across it as black as sin. His body felt as weightless as the cone of mist thrown down by the last vapor lamp.

She was small in the distance, far ahead of him, the white coat no larger than a moth.

He stepped from the last broken rock of the pavement, walking more quickly, but steadily. Only the movement in his mind was different. In his mind he was tumbling towards her. He was stumbling over the hard earth of the rutted road, his arms outreaching to her as to some point of definition.

He could only lean for support on the knife, which had grown in his mind as big as a tree.

A white moth, fluttering . . . .

The bladelike shrieks of laughter had come from another boat angling across Maud's line of vision. Quickly, she pulled the cord to turn the light off and closed the book.

She had left the lamp on as Sam walked away, hoping he'd stopped to look back and taken note of her refusal to do as he said, to knuckle under to his commands or to shrivel in the face of unknown, unnamed horrors like ivory grins in the night. She had plenty of named and known ones; she didn't need his jungle drums and rustling bushes.

Raised voices, shouts, and laughter issued from a party boat, a square thing on pontoons with a fringed canvas top, which held new guests, she assumed. She squinted to make out the amorphous shape of the boat, which had turned mid-lake and was shoveling across the water toward the party.

Had these people started out together, or had they come from other places, other parties? Had the boat been picking them up all along the shore, heading for Raoul and Evita's?

This cargo of dark figures seemed to fit the near-funereal movement of the boat. Only the coal ends of cigarettes, the tiny, wraithlike flames of globed candles showed the voices were not disembodied.

Maud shaded her eyes, squinting at the far dock. One-thirty in the morning and the party was getting this fresh influx of guests. It could easily go on until dawn and into the morning. The Labor Day weekend marked the end of the season, just as Memorial Day marked the beginning.

Where did they go, Raoul and Evita, when the season ended? It was a question Maud liked to turn over in her mind, for there was such a feast of possible destinations. Brazil was one, for with names like "Raoul" and "Evita" . . .

As she tried to dislodge the two olives cramped together in the bottom of the jar she wondered, with self-disgust, *why* she kept on assuming things about them on the basis of names Sam had probably made up. There hadn't been even a hint of a name until that movie came to town called *Kiss of the Spider Woman* with an actor named Raul Julia. He was very handsome; she had seen it twice. The second time she had sat right in front of Joey, who had then come to sit beside her and share his monster tub of popcorn. He ate it by the handful, pushing the popcorn in with his hand, making comments about the "creepy faggot," the other character, until she had had to tell him *puleeze* to be quiet. So they had sat there in the Empire Theater watching Raul smolder away on screen as if he had a whole grate of burning coals behind his eyes.

It was only after that movie that Sam had come up with that name. She didn't know where he'd got the "Evita," unless it was from that musical. She didn't think anyone in the movie, including the Spider Woman, was named Evita, but it was all very suspicious. Maud sipped her drink.

The party boat, its prow retreating in the mist, could have been a phantom boat, the trailing wisps of fog like a tattered flag, a skeleton crew, the passage of the Damned . . .

Oh, for god's sake, she said to herself. The lake people were anything but damned. They were all probably from New York, Boston, or places in the Poconos marked by stone walls and weathered shingles. Maud saw them all as too wealthy and too savvy to work on an image. The men never bought *Travel and Leisure* in Cooper's Drugs; they just plucked it from the rack and stood there and read it until Bobby Cooper marched up to them and pointed to the hand-lettered sign. They'd just shrug and pay for the *Times* and saunter out.

They had left behind them the days of "summering" in some "quaint" little place they had "discovered" in the Dolomites or spending an entire season in Iceland. They were too smart for that, Maud thought. They had found La Porte by accident, pure and simple, saw it had an enormous lake and a snow machine, and slapped their sides with glee. It was *not* a place you would ever say you "summered in," but only "went to." Rock-hard self-confidence lined with a few diamond mines would probably be the qualification for summer people in La Porte, too far north and too deep inland to even suck up to the fringes of trendiness, much less set a new trend. Maud based her conclusions on rather foggy premises, but she still argued with Shirl, who thought they were a bunch of cheap phonies, that the lakers were simply extremely rich, rich enough they could try and weasel a third refill of coffee without paying the extra thirty cents.

"So they're *rich* phonies, so what?" Shirl would say as she removed a big tray of chocolate fudge cake from the shelf behind her, stared at it, and then returned it to the case. It was a mystery to her why this cake didn't go walking out the door like her lemon chiffon pies and her double-glazed doughnuts. It was another recipe she'd "borrowed" from Jen Graham, who was famous for her chocolate fudge cake; anyone who ate Jen's cake was hooked for life. Anyone who ate Shirl's never ate it again. ("Can't understand it," Shirl had said. "It's even got her secret ingredient." The "secret ingredient" turned out to be a handful of cold coffee grounds that Jen had written into the recipe. Religiously, Shirl tossed in the coffee grounds.) Then she'd slide out one of the trays of her double-glazed doughnuts from the glass case by the cash register and wham it into the glass-fronted shelves behind her. After the lake people in their white togs and designer sunglasses had strewn the Sunday *Times* all over the tabletops and shoveled down their breakfasts and then started buying bags of take-away doughnuts, Shirl's magic moment would come. With the whole tray of unbought doughnuts resting succulently behind her, she could tell them she was "out"; she could lean one elbow on the cash register and the other on her hip and wait for the inevitable nod toward the held-back tray. "Them doughnuts is for charity, for the poor people." "The Poor of La Porte" was always the Sunday banner for Shirl, who, flying investigative-reporter colors, would route the libertine misuses of the township's money and its huge budget deficits right to the door of the summer rich, who, in vaguely biblical language, were those who brought and took away. The Cote du Jours, she called them. And no, they couldn't take home the last green-apple pie, either.

Maud would stand behind the counter dipping glasses in scalding water and listen and shake her head. La Porte had its poor people, yes; but Shirl couldn't have picked one out of a lineup even if he'd been stuffed between Lee Iacocca and Elizabeth Taylor. ("That little squirt? So she's got *eyes*—big deal. I got eyes, you got eyes, even Joey's got eyes.")

Yet they were big tippers, and Shirl hauled in money on Sunday. They thought the place was "quaint," probably because of the scarred wooden booths and the marble-topped soda counter and the rough-hewn, gum-chewing, chain-smoking owner. The men loved the fact that they couldn't bribe her or charm her out of that tray of doughnuts. Shirl seemed to strike them as the Last Gnarled Frontier of Free Enterprise or something, when all she was was plain damned mean.

Maud always asked to work the counter on Sundays (which was fine with Charlene, who got the big tips) because she didn't want to have to see them all up too close. Blurs of white tennis sweaters or caps and (thank heavens) so many designer sunglasses it looked like a spaceship convention were all Maud had to see. She was afraid that she would no longer be able to imagine them in black ties and swishing gowns; and she was especially afraid she might discover Raoul and Evita, might sense who they were, mark the Latin skin, hear the slight accent . . .

Maud shook her head to clear it. Sam had made the names up, she reminded herself. Their names were probably "Kelly" and "Craig" and they lived in the Trump and carried little dogs around. Still . . .

She could hear the party boat disgorge the newcomers, squeals and yaps just like those little dogs.

Her head was lolling a bit, but it came up when the patio door over there suddenly must have opened, perhaps from the thrust of the music itself.

"Brazil."

It was an omen.

So Maud forgot the Trump Tower, but she couldn't put New York out of her mind. There was Rosie.

The party boat had pulled away from the dock and moored amongst the other little boats. And to the music of "Brazil," several of the dots of color had beaded together into what was, yes it was, a line. A conga line. They were snaking all the way to the patio door.

Here Sam had all along had a niece who lived in New York and he'd never told her. Maud looked across the lake now with narrowed eyes.

Unless he'd lied.

Chad

She was a perfect stranger. Why were they lying here in this handsomely draped four-poster bed, among the coats?

Two drunken dances out by the pool, each of them holding a tall drink of bullet-proof rum with an exotic flower spearing it, not dancing really, just leaning against each other.

Bethanne had dropped her French-cut panties the moment they walked into the bedroom, as if she were a guest removing her shoes in deference to Oriental custom. The rest of their clothes were still on their backs.

Voices of more than a hundred guests ebbed and flowed downstairs in the Bonds' double living room on one side and double library—no, it must have been a game room and library. Enough people to make you think half of them were mirror images of the other half. He'd never seen such clothes. They should have had a runway. Teeny-tiny sequined skirts; long, loungy velvet trousers. High-cheekboned faces, enameled lips and eyes.

One of them was here. She could have been twenty, his age; she could have been sixteen—it was impossible to tell about women anymore. He didn't know her last name.

"You don't want to do a line, you don't want to free-base, you don't want to smoke, and you don't want to fuck. Why the hell am I here?" she said.

"You wanted me to pour you into the bathroom next door. You're pretty liquid."

The bathroom's proximity to his room was probably why all of the coats were here. God knows, the Bonds had servants and closets enough to collect them downstairs, but the rich apparently just run up to pee in the marble bathroom and then fling their coats through the nearest available door.

He raised his head slightly to see what covered his stockinged foot. He'd removed his shoes in deference to Ralph Lauren. Silvery fur. Fox fur, maybe. The closest he'd ever got to this stuff was Velda's Russian mink. Was that sable flung over the deep armchair? He didn't want to know what that glimmering white one was. This Labor Day weekend was on the warm side, and these women were still dragging around in their weighty furs.

The girl rolled over, elbow on the pillow, caramel-tanned pointy chin on her palm. She made him think of the crème bruleé on the sideboard of desserts downstairs. Her hair was sun-scorched, long, tendrilly, her dress a metallic sheath of gold that turned russet when the silk moved across her hips.

She fingered his watch; the Rolex impressed her. She walked the fingers of her sinewy, tennis-playing little hands across his shirt front, asking in her breathless voice, "So what *do* you want?"

He'd had three of the rum drinks when he was used to beer and maybe a little grass. She'd taken out her stash of coke, a mirror, and a razor blade as soon as she'd hit the bed, right after she'd discarded the panties. It seemed to be done in one fluid movement, as if the whole thing went together. He told her to put it back, he didn't want to see the stuff. Oddly enough, she obeyed. Then she extracted a miniature solid-silver flask and took a pull on its contents before she offered it to him as she wiped her mouth with the back of her hand.

He smiled at the gesture; it was somehow endearing. Answering her question, he said, "A thousand dollars." Chad stared up at the softly glowing ceiling. How'd the Bonds get that lighting effect? Dragged down a few stars, probably.

"*What?*" Her tickling fingers stopped.

"A thousand. A bank error."

"So call the fucking bank. Now . . ." Tendrils of hair webbed his face.

He blew them away. "They made a mistake. It was a check for a hundred my mom paid into my account. The bank got the decimal in the wrong place."

A sealskin coat slipped from the bed as she suddenly sat up, crossing her legs. "My god, are we going to talk about *money*?" "Money" sounded as if it were a bad taste in her mouth. She rolled away from him, held back her gorgeous hair, and took another drink from the flask.

"Unfortunately, it's spent."

"Like your dick," she said, recapping the flask. Then she snatched something else out of the metal purse, leaned forward over her crossed legs, and started writing.

He wouldn't have thought there was any room in that purse. It must have had a false bottom, a magical gold cube from which she, a magical girl from another world who'd infiltrated the party guests, could call forth all manner of things, balms and anodynes, unicorns and genii.

But here she was, solid and sexy, writing in a checkbook. "If you're so fucking indigent, where'd you get that Rolex you're sporting?"

She pronounced it "in-*di*-gent." Chad smiled over at her where she sat laboriously writing, the tip of her tongue caught between her pearly little teeth. There was something so vulnerable about her that he wanted to pat her shoulder. "Hong Kong." That was a lie; his father had given him the Rolex.

"You people without money are *so bor*-er-ing." She wrenched three syllables from the word.

She had to be kidding. She wasn't. *Zip.* She chucked the check towards him, tossed the checkbook on the floor, rolled over, and started unbuttoning his shirt. He held the check up and squinted at it in that starry light coming from its hidden source around the ceiling moldings. His other hand trailed after hers, rebuttoning the shirt.

"We don't even know each other," he said. "This is for one thousand dollars."

Her hand went to unzip his fly. "Jesus, your pants have little *buttons*."

"I think they're French. Maybe Italian. Borrowed."

Bethanne got her face right down, squinting, fascinated. Then she started trying to fiddle with the little buttons.

He kept staring at the check. Not even her narrow fingers trying to wrench him free made him hard. He was limp, staring at the check. "Why are you writing me a check for a thousand dollars?"

Her hand stopped fiddling, started squeezing. "Because you said you owed it or something. You been doing drugs? My *god*, what's wrong with you? You want me to strip? You want something special?" Now she was trying to wiggle out of what there was of a dress. "You want to unzip?" She turned her back.

He didn't move; he lay there thinking of the thousand he'd have to pay back to the bank before his mom found out.

It had been nearly three months before the bank had recognized its error and one of the assistant managers called Chad. Mr. Frobish had been very understanding when Chad went in to see him. People were generally understanding of Chad. He might have thrown a switch inside, the way he could turn up the charm voltage.

Yes, Mr. Frobish understood that Chad had simply assumed his father had paid the money into Chad's account. Yes, he could allow Chad a certain period of time to see that the bank got it back. Mr. Frobish knew Ned Chadwick was loaded. Yes, two months seemed reasonable enough.

The Bethannes of this world didn't have bank problems. Bethanne's mother was a stockbroker. The way she'd said it made Wall Street sound like a regular meeting place for mothers.

"What's yours do?" she'd asked, out on the terrace, with no particular interest.

He'd been silent, his chin against her forehead. "She's in the restaurant business."

"Hmm. Be nice to own one. It's always so shitty trying to get a decent table."

"She doesn't own it."

She hadn't cared and he hadn't commented.

Her pretense of truculence right now didn't convince him; she was too stoned to bring it off. Unfortunately she was a talker, and she rambled on, ever more sleepily, about how he'd dragged her up here to his room and then—*whish* (the palms of her hands missed each other)—nothin'. "What's wrong with you, Chaddie?"

Chaddie. My god, it was worse than Murray.

Murray was the sort of name he might have expected his father to pick. Murray: not a family name, not a friend's name, not some old blowhard up in New Hampshire (his father's home state) who'd sat around in the general store playing checkers and sucking his teeth. Murray was a name you couldn't do anything with. Murr—what the hell kind of nickname was that? The kids in second and third grade had certainly seen the name's possibilities. With the appropriate swishes and vocal flutings, they'd called him "Mary."

Finally, he'd lied and told them Murray was only a middle name. His real name was Ed. But then friends of his would come around asking for Ed and his mom had to keep telling them they had the wrong house, there was no Ed there. If you're seven or eight you don't feel much like arguing with a mom, because you know they're all probably hiding knives behind their backs, even when they're standing there framed in the doorway looking perfectly friendly, but denying there's any Ed in the house.

"I'm glad something's funny."

Chad had nearly forgotten Bethanne was there. "What?"

"You laughed. Or gargled—I don't know." She was sitting up now, her back braced against the headboard, her knees drawn up, forcing the satiny skirt all the way down her thighs. Her eyes were closed and she was smoking grass, holding a pinched butt between her thumb and forefinger.

Christ, he wondered, what else did she have stowed in that hammered gold cubicle? A water pipe?

"I was just thinking."

"About the money . . . ." Deeply she inhaled, drawing the smoke into cavernous lungs. "Whyn't ya ask Billy? He's got it up to his eyeballs."

"Billy" was what they called him at home. "Zero? At school we call him Zero."

Bethanne managed, with much labor, to wrench her head around to stare at him. "*Zero? Him?* Su'prise he even talks t'ya." The eyes closed again.

"He made it up, not us. It's a pun on his name."

She was too stoned to care what Billy Cooper Bond did with his name. Her arm moved dreamily, an underwater movement, to pass him the roach.

Rather than argue, he took it, hoping that would shut her up. He dragged in on the grass but didn't inhale. He'd inhaled several hundred times too many already. It was grass and coke that had told him that a thousand dollars on his bank statement was perfectly reasonable. When he handed the toke back to her, Bethanne was asleep, suddenly asleep and snoring, sputtering like a tiny outboard motor trying to engage.

It was his mother who'd come up with the solution to his name. After the third or fourth kid had been at the door asking for Ed, she'd finally figured it out. But why was Murray telling people his name was Ed?

He'd been scared but didn't know why. Maybe it was because disowning his name was like disowning her. Like orphaning himself.

Chad sat up, planted his feet on the floor, and looked down at his shoes. Docksiders didn't really go with the designer trousers.

They'd cost forty-nine dollars, and his mother had sent him the money for them. That was just before he'd called her about the hundred he needed. For books.

Textbooks are expensive, he'd told her. So was traveling and so was coke, he hadn't told her.

"Textbooks? It's the middle of the semester. What happened to the ones you bought at the beginning? Did they turn?"

Christ, but he hated when she tried to be funny when he knew his position was arguably weak. "Mo-om." Tone of disgust. "He's assigned another one. So's the French teacher."

"You haven't even used up the French text you bought two months ago. How could you? You don't go to class."

How did she know that? She was guessing. Educated guess, since he'd left his midterm grades lying around the house.

"I go, I go. There was just that time I was sick. Look, I've got to have it by Friday."

"Friday? That's two days from now, Chad."

"Well, can't you messenger it?"

"What was that?"

Oh, shit—now she'd get off on her Hated Words list. His mom loathed words like "enjoy," "make nice," and especially the New Verbs (as she called them), such as "finalize"; and now she'd go on . . .

"I've got a nineteen-year-old with an indigent mother who probably spends most of his time in the girls' dorm and beer-keg parties . . ."

He knew it, she would go on and on, so he put down the phone to go to get a beer. Came back, picked it up from the sprung sofa: ". . . who's flunking French . . ."

Put it down again and sighed. Why was it, for a person who was so shy she was zombified around strangers, that she could rattle on and on and on and on, working up whole tapestries of events from single threads, whole scenarios (one of her Hated Words, "scenario") from casual comments? He picked up the phone—yes, she was still talking. God! the Greyhound would leave Friday with the other guys, and he'd still be here with her talking.

"... nineteen, for lord's sake, why do you expect to have money messengered?"

Couldn't she just say yes or no? He smiled and said, "Okay, okay, just FedEx it."

Silence. He grinned. He could usually shut her up this way. Well, she did it to him all the time. And he knew she was on the other end of the phone trying not to laugh.

"Funny—that's hysterical . . . Look, why did you wait until to-day to let me know about this?"

Because we didn't get the idea until today, he didn't tell her.

Hung up, and felt guilty. He was always feeling guilty about his mother, about the way she worked so hard for so little. And because she made him feel guilty, naturally he got angry. It was much easier to get angry at her than at his father. His father was too distant, a figure in the fog.

So he hung up and felt guilty. And when you feel guilty you just get stoned again.

His father had left them when he was seven, and Chad had always had this murky sort of fear that his mother would do the same thing.

She'd been making one of those sour lemon pies that he hated, running the knife around the edge of the crust as she'd thought it over. "*If you don't want to be one of the family . . .*" That's what she was going to say, he was sure.

"*But there's only two of us!*"

Already, she was leaving and taking the hated pie with her. "*If you don't like my lemon pie . . .*"

But what he feared hadn't happened. She'd just pinched off the dangling cord of crust and asked why he hadn't told her his name bothered him so much. If he didn't like "Murray," well, maybe he could be "Chad." He tried it out a few times, repeated it over and over. It was a *great* name. Especially because it *was* his name, or part of his last name. Why hadn't he thought of it?

Then he wondered why she had. Did she want someone else for her son that she could so easily throw away his name?

He told her he hated that sour pie.

Chad sat up, planted his feet on the floor, and looked down at his shoes. His mother had sent him the money to buy them plus another check to his account when he'd needed more books.

That was the hundred that the bank had magically turned into a thousand. He tried to remember how he had managed, even with the help of a little coke, which is where most of it had gone, how he had managed to convince himself, how his mind had been so fucked up he really could convince himself his mother had sent a thousand bucks. His mom didn't have a thousand bucks. He had reasoned it this way: when he'd told her there was this big emergency (*had* he told her that?), she'd called his dad and somehow got the money from him. Talk about fucked—Jesus Christ, as if she'd ever call his dad for *that* . . .

Bethanne was right; Zero was swimming in money. His father was probably betting a thou downstairs at his private poker game, tossing ten bills into the kitty. But he couldn't bring himself to ask Zero. He wasn't sure why. Self-respect, he supposed.

His only consolation lay in the money he'd managed to make this summer, doing house painting in Hebrides and Meridian. But he'd only managed to earn half of the money that way. If he hadn't had to put out some of his earnings for a room in Meridian, he could have saved more; but there was no way he could commute the distance to La Porte without a car—or even *with,* for that matter. Still, he'd managed to send Mr. Frobish five hundred and twenty-five dollars and beg him for another couple of months' grace. But where he was going to get the rest in a couple of months, he didn't know.

He got off the bed and went over to look down into the dark, the moon in the pool as if it had fallen there. The pool would be covered over soon and littered with leaves after the Bonds went back to Manhattan. Strange how they simply stopped living here in this mansion and started living there in some penthouse, as if their lives were cut in half.

Voices rustled like taffeta coming up the stairs, women on their way to use the john. He wasn't being a decent house guest hanging around up here. He should go back to the party.

The telephone on the nightstand riveted him with its little red snake's-eye of a button that was always on, maybe part of a security system. He stared at the illuminated dial and at the luminous digits.

Chad thought how easy it would be to pick up, call his father, get the money that way. Get twice the money. His father would like nothing better than to get an SOS from Chad, to have the opportunity to pull Chad's chestnuts out of the fire, to act as savior, at the same time giving him some Polonius advice on lending and borrowing and honesty. Or worse, to become, in this little deception of Maud, Chad's confrere, *compadre*—such *compadre*-ism most certainly to include Velda, later on.

He could hear it: "*The kid just seemed to 'forget' that extra zero—isn't that too much, Vel, isn't that rich?*" Chad could picture them over one of their little champagne-and-oyster midnight dinners, bubbling like the wine over the kid's putting one over on his mother.

He picked up the phone and got the operator. He told her he had to reverse the charges; no, he didn't have a phone card.

She let the number ring eight, nine, twelve times before coming back on the line to tell him the party didn't answer, sir.

He hung up.

Hadn't he known the party wouldn't answer? He knew she was down on the end of the pier watching that house across the lake.

At least, he thought, lighting a cigarette, I tried.

Liar.

Without his realizing it, Bethanne had woken, for now she had gotten up from the bed and was stepping into her French-cut silk panties, unsteady on her feet. One thin brown hand gripped the post of the tester bed. Skirt jacked up, one leg in, as if the left and right sides of her body hadn't jigsawed properly. The gold cube dangled from her arm, its chain caught in the bend of her elbow, swinging as she kept trying and missing the panties with the other foot.

For the first time since they'd come into the room, he felt like making a grab for her and pulling her down on the bed. Because for now she'd dropped the act in this woozy concentration on getting the clothes on instead of off. Such an intensity about her.

But he didn't; it would have started the whole thing up again, taken too much time—though time from what, he didn't know.

Bethanne stumbled and swore at some furs ("fucking ermine," "goddamshitty buncha mink") that must have got in the way of her heels—mumbling at them and kicking as if they'd still been on the backs of the slaughtered animals.

Chad still lay on the bed, telling himself to go downstairs again. He did not like this party, he didn't like big parties, and since Zero was the only one he really knew, he felt shy.

He must have dozed off. The next thing he knew was that someone had opened the door of the dark room and thrown another coat on the pile. If he didn't move the coats, the women would be collecting them until dawn.

Half a dozen fur coats. Slippery satin linings, soft mink and sable. And the white one: was it possible for a woman to wear the fur of a snow leopard?

Why are you being so self-righteous? he asked himself as he walked down the hall to the room where he thought he'd seen the maid depositing a carpet of coats. The door was slightly ajar and he went in with his bundle. He stopped dead.

Before the window in a pool of moonlight, the only light in the otherwise dark room, Eva Bond stood bare to the waist.

The Englishman sat on the edge of the bed, fully clothed. Chad heard his indrawn breath, felt his anger at the interruption. Chad did not want to look up from the stack of clothes; he wanted only to manage to leave the room with his head cast down, his eyes on the floor.

He backed out, closing the door on the Brit's expletives.

"Wrong room."

Downstairs there were another hundred or more strangers. The movement and heat of bodies, the clink and ring of glasses and bottles . . . how many cases of champagne had he seen in the kitchen? Where had all of these people come from?

This afternoon, Zero's car hadn't passed another house since the outskirts of Belle Harbor, and that was five miles away. And he doubted any of these people called Belle Harbor beautiful, much less called it home.

He had stopped on the landing. Stairs swept down in an arc on either side to the foyer, which was a huge black-and-white tiled room in itself. There was a teardrop chandelier that turned some of the guests into kaleidoscope bits.

From this height, as if he were standing on a balcony, he thought again of a theater. This was as theatrical as his first view of them on the wide, white steps of the big house early this afternoon, when Zero had parked the Porsche in the drive. His family had not "gathered" on the steps. They looked "arranged" by a slick magazine photographer, or even by some French or Italian director, who wanted to make a point, wanted to let the audience glimpse their inner lives. (Why French or Italian he didn't know, except he thought they were more aware of, or more accepting of, a lack of possibilities.) The Bonds were miles apart just as they were steps apart. The mother stood with her hands locked before her, the glimmer from the noonday sun striking the striped dress she wore and haloing her pale, pale blond hair. Mr. Bond stood on the second step, Mrs. Bond on the other side, and farther up stood Zero's sister. They might have been waiting, frozen there, for the director to call for action.

For a bewildering few seconds, there was no action. And then suddenly Zero's father stepped down with a wide smile and a loud greeting, threw his arm around Zero's shoulders at the same time he was shaking Chad's hand.

Zero had disengaged himself smoothly from the wrap of his father's arm, had made a playful pass at his younger sister, Casey, had acknowledged his mother's presence only by nodding and speaking her name:

"Eva."

Now she was at the bottom of the winding staircase, talking to the Englishman as if they had met, casually, just here, a hostess engaged in small talk with one of her guests. Her gray satin gown slid straight from its thin straps to her ankles; her silvery blond hair had the metallic look of Zero's Porsche lighter, a razor cut that dipped from the nape of her neck to her chin. She stood perfectly still. Even the tulip champagne glass seemed an extension of her hand. She was a beautiful, smooth woman who seemed to husband her energy. When Zero had introduced them earlier, her tapered fingers had slid into his hand in a soundless greeting. No clicks, no clumsiness; simply a cool pose on the wide steps.

He wished that he could retreat, move back up the stairs and come down some other way, but now she had seen him. She looked straight at him, dispassionately. Then the man looked up with a remorseless smile.

Chad kept on walking down the staircase, didn't smile as he passed them, and stopped when he heard the man say, "Come on back, sport—I'd like a word."

"Sport"? The guy was really pushing his luck.

Chad turned and saw that the Brit was still smiling; a master smiler, Chad bet, a real scumbag. Chad didn't return the smile.

Mrs. Bond's "companion" reached out his hand to Chad and said, "I'm Maurice Brett. And you're Chad. Oh, come on. Shake."

Perhaps it was a reflex action to an outstretched hand; Chad shook hands, and when he drew his back, he saw the bills.

Said Maurice Brett, " 'Money.' That's the word." And he held to that infernal lopsided smile.

Three bills. Chad stared. Three hundred dollars.

Eva Bond looked at Maurice Brett. Blood rose from her smooth shoulders to her face, such a strong current it painted a sunset blush across the rim of the silvery gown. Apparently, she didn't agree that "money" was the word, that it wasn't always balm for a seared conscience or a Band-Aid you could slap across a gushing artery.

Like the automatic handshake, Chad's initial thought of deliverance from part of the remaining five-hundred-dollar debt had been automatic. That made him even angrier. He folded the bills into a small square and jammed them into Maurice Brett's vest pocket.

"You don't have to buy my silence. Who would I tell here, anyway? Mr. Bond? The guests? I don't even know them."

Maurice Brett rolled his cigar slightly between his lips. "Billy."

"*Zero?*" He looked from one to the other. Eva Bond had gone back to her glacial pose and was lighting a cigarette without even glancing at Chad. "My God, he's my best friend. You think I'd pulverize my best friend with the information his mother is—?"

Eva Bond's words stopped Chad dead. "I really don't think you need to worry about pulverizing Billy." She was as placid as the lake beyond the terrace.

"I'm a guest in this house, and what you do is none of my business. But are you telling me you don't think Zero would *care*?"

She turned eyes of flint on him.

I really don't think you need to worry . . . It was almost worse than the bedroom scene. "You don't have to worry about me telling him, Mrs. Bond."

He pushed through champagne glasses, caterers, brittle laughter, gowns and tuxedos. A woman whose breasts seemed to be oozing over the top of her cream satin gown grabbed at his arm and wondered why they hadn't been introduced. "I'm Brie Sardinia and you're Billy's friend," she managed to say between sips of champagne as her hand ran down his arm until it was grasping his own hand. The name "Brie" was well chosen, since she looked like a soft, ripe cheese. "My husband spends all night in there"—she looked over her shoulder toward the game room—"playing poker. Care to dance?" They were being crushed against the wall by other gowns and dinner jackets, and Chad used this as an excuse. Too crowded to dance . . . maybe later . . . nice to meet you . . .

"But we could go out by the pool," she called after him.

He pretended not to hear and made his way toward one of the several French doors to go out for some air. He passed the billiard room, where Mr. Bond and four other men were concentrating on their poker game. He recognized a doctor and a man named Brandon whom he'd met and assumed the tall, saturnine one must be the woman's husband, Sardinia. The fifth one looked too cagey and flashy to have hooked up with Brie. His cards were so close to his chest he'd have to dislocate his neck to get a peek at them.

Chad crossed the wide, leaf-blown steps to the section of lawn that was as smooth as a golf course and into which the free-form pool had been set to glisten like an opal in the lights from the house. The surround sound of the Bonds' elaborate stereo system reached out here. Tight little groups had gathered to talk and drink, and the grass was smooth enough to dance on. Zero danced drunk and alone. His arms were outstretched; he snapped his fingers slowly, swaying in time to some old jazz rendition of "After You've Gone."

Then it was Casey, trying to imitate her brother as a sax burned up "Who's Sorry Now?" Slow, easy, hypnotic. Casey was the one member of the family Zero seemed to like having around. She was wearing a figure-hugging black dress much too old for her, with a low neckline and bat-wing sleeves. When Zero saw her in it he said, "Charles Addams would've loved you."

"Mother said I could wear it," she'd whined. Deliberately playing the little-sister role, Chad had thought.

"When did *mother* ever tell you you *couldn't* wear anything?"

Zero had been big-brothering Casey, but he was right: Chad wondered if Eva Bond ever restrained her daughter. The father sure as hell didn't. He obviously adored her. The feeling didn't appear to be returned, Casey preferring instead her unapproachable mother. Perhaps people were like that—the person on the other side of the lake, the one so far off you could only call to, would be the one that you would, finally, make the fatal error of swimming to.

Chad reached the old boat house on the edge of that lake and a dock jutting out from it, whose planks were springy, half-rotten. In the boat house were two rowboats that looked bereft of attention over the past years. They swayed gently with the rise and fall of water. The shelter smelled musty, unused. The paint was peeling from the boats, and one of the oars was broken. He sat on a wooden bench, lit a cigarette, and leaned back against the damp wall.

He wondered about the boat house—why it wasn't used, why the Bonds didn't have some speedboat or catamaran moored here. And hadn't Zero made a perfectly straight-faced reference to a "yacht broker"?

Bilge water lapped at the edge of the planks, and the boats bobbed on the waves churned up by a boat rushing by to nowhere.

Did William Bond know that jerk was screwing his wife?

A poem came back to him: *I dressed my father in his little clothes* . . .

He rested his head in his hands and tried to recall what came after that. *I asked him where the running water goes.*

He couldn't remember the next lines and got up impatiently, thrust his hands in his pockets, and stared down at the little boats. *Down to the sea in ships, set them afloat!* In the poem the father was the son. He was dressing his father instead of the other way around. Yet at the end the fantasy breaks down and the roles are again reversed. Chad wished he could remember the rest.

Water slapped around the boats. Chad looked at it for a while and then climbed down into one of the rowboats, holding on to the planks for support. Even moored safely within the boat house it felt insecure, a thing to be borne away by the smallest wave or the slightest breeze. He lit a cigarette and rested his elbows on his knees, smoking and swaying slightly with the motion of the boat.

Steps came down the gravel. He turned and could tell it was Zero only because of the white silk scarf. Then came the sound of running feet, and the moon slipped out from its cloud cover to shine on Casey's pale face as she ran down the path behind Zero, the long, pleated sleeves sweeping behind her.

"You bored? Right." Zero said it as if boredom were Belle Harbor's specialty. He stepped into the boat, calling for Casey to hurry up. When she too had clambered in, Zero pulled the oars from their locks.

"What in hell are we doing? You're not rowing this hulk out on the lake, are you?" Chad looked around wildly.

"No. I thought I'd take it up on the highway for a spin." He was not an oarsman; he spun the boat so that it hit the dock with a thud.

Casey just sat there, elbows on her knees. "No one can find us," she said with satisfaction.

"There's water at my feet *now*," Chad said.

Relentlessly, Zero kept on pulling at the oars. "You know how to swim."

Chad sat there wishing he'd got hold of his mother. Why? Was she supposed to come running with life jackets?

Why they seemed headed for the middle of the lake he couldn't imagine. Zero hadn't taken off the white scarf, or his dinner jacket, or loosened his tie, as if he were suddenly in a hurry to make a break for it.

Zero released one of the oars and brought out a silver flask and tossed it to Chad.

Chad took a drink and said, "I thought you had a yacht. You said you had a yacht."

"We do. It's around here somewhere," he said without interest.

"You make it sound like you misplaced a pair of cufflinks."

Behind him, Casey was humming; it was that old song about a blackbird. They were about a hundred feet from the dock when Zero finally pulled in the oars from water as black and pleated as Casey's dress.

While Zero was lighting up, Chad said, "So you do this all the time? Do a few dances and then row out to the middle of the lake in a leaky boat? Look, the water's definitely up to our ankles, dude."

"Stop worrying. We're just trying to save you from Bethanne. There's a life jacket right behind you, on the bottom."

Casey stopped the blackbird song and laughed. "She's a nympho, didn't you know?" Back to the song: " 'Where my sweetie waits for me—' "

" 'Sugar's sweet, so is she,' " Zero sang. "Come on, everybody knows that song!"

Chad said, "You sit here in the middle of the lake in a sinking boat singing 'Bye, Bye, Blackbird.' " It wasn't a question, since that was exactly what they were doing.

Suddenly Casey stood up. The boat lurched. " 'No one here can love or understand me—' "

"Sit down!" Chad yelled.

" 'Oh, the hard-luck stories they all hand me.' " Zero was leaning back, legs half-covered with water.

Said Chad, "This boat is sinking."

" '. . . light the light.' "

" 'I'll be home late tonight.' "

The rowboat was sinking in an oddly balanced way, taking the three of them down as if it were one of those fake cardboard cutouts in a musical that moves across the stage on permanent, painted waves. The painted boat would sink behind the painted waves, and the audience would applaud their little number. It was a sedate, an almost patient sinking, almost as if it were waiting for the last line to be belted out:

" 'Black-BIRD . . . Bye-ah-BYE-EYE-EYE!' " The water went up to their shoulders now.

Chad was looking across the dark water with rising hysteria. He was wearing the life jacket, sure. But what about little Casey?

Little Casey was lying on her back, floating.

Zero said, "Well, I guess this calls for some sort of plan. Cigarette?" His legs churning water and one arm out, he brought out his silver case, drew up his legs, and lay there floating and smoking, the boat now probably on the bottom of the lake.

"No, thanks," said Chad. "I'm trying to quit." He spat out water, shook his head to get his hair out of his eyes, held the Rolex to his ear. Were they waterproof? "We've had the warm-up—what do we do now?"

Casey was splashing around, dipping under, coming up, shaking the water from her eyes.

"For god's *sake!*" Chad tried to rip off the life jacket to give to her; after all, he was a decent swimmer.

"She swims like a shark. She swims better than both of us." Wavelets made by his sister's splashing were turning Zero's body clockwise, then back again. "Why are you flailing around? Don't you know about body weight and water? Don't you know why most people drown? It's simple: the pull of gravity."

"Oh, shit," said Casey, who'd been swimming in a sort of circle, and stopped and paddled. "If this is going to be that boring gravity lecture, I'm leaving." And she streaked off towards shore, towards the house, whose undulating length and spaced lights looked like train compartments.

Zero called to Casey, who was by now a third of the way back, her bladelike stroke barely creasing water. "Don't go in the house without us, do you hear?"

A distant reply which might have been "Okay" or "Oh, hell" or "Bye-bye" floated back.

"We just going to flop here all night? That's the big plan?" asked Chad, who was toeing off his fifty-buck Docksiders. Mom will just love that. "You said you lost them? How do you *lose* a pair of shoes? They fell off your feet while you were walking across the campus and you didn't notice . . . ?" That's what his mother would say, getting up steam as she went along.

"You want to go back to that fucking Bethanne? Casey's right— she's a nympho."

His arms were growing tired with the stretching, his legs with the paddling. "Could we continue this conversation sitting in a couple chairs?"

But Zero looked extremely comfortable, floating and drifting about, the end of his cigarette sparking like a star as he drew in, smoke misting the water as he exhaled. He looked indeed just as comfy as he had lying on Chad's bed earlier. Casey, or the water trail of Casey, was well over halfway to land. Chad wasn't really afraid for his life, not in this floating life-raft; but he questioned the sanity of this little outing.

Buoyed up by the water and looking at the stars, he would almost have enjoyed it except that his thoughts kept shifting between that bedroom scene and the drowned Docksiders that must be lying now on the floor of the lake like a sunken treasure ship. He felt the heat of the blush spreading across his neck and face. He'd never given back to her the money he'd saved because the shoes were on sale for half-price.

That and some "loose change" his Dad had sent him had gone for grass, beer. A little coke. A little—he wasn't, thank God, addicted. Sam could have hauled him in that night in the Red Barn.

"But I won't. Just stop using if you're half as smart as I think you are."

"I hardly ever do. I mean, at school a couple times—recreational . . . you know."

" 'Recreational'? Oh, come on. You've got to be fucking kidding."

"I'm not addicted. It's controlled use."

Sam swore softly. "Who the hell do you think you're talking to? Some yobo? Don't insult me."

Sam had gone on. Chad liked Sam, but he couldn't stand being lectured.

"Where're you getting the money?"

Deadly tone.

"Babysitting, maybe?"

He'd started to say something snotty, but he knew better than to fuck with Sam. Not that Chad was afraid Sam would tell his mom. He wouldn't. He liked her too much.

What Chad remembered now was that they—he and Sam—had sat there in the squad car not talking for some time, enjoying, he supposed, a rather companionable silence in spite of the occasion.

He'd been ten the first time he saw Sam. It was near the courthouse; Sam was standing looking at a Rolls parked by a fire hydrant. He had a gun on his hip and shades over his eyes; a leather jacket that barely hid the holster. He was looking at this car, shaking his head. Then he caught sight of Chad, who'd just come out of the matinee, full of Gary Cooper. It was a rerun of *High Noon*. He was thinking how he could tell his mom he'd lost the two dollars so he could go back the next Saturday and see it again. He was thinking of all this and then he'd seen Sam. To come out from seeing a sheriff, especially Gary Cooper, and then to see a real live sheriff standing off there in front of you with his dark glasses and his holster . . . well, that made you think.

Sam had turned those dark shades in Chad's direction and said, "Some people . . ." Then he'd shaken his head again. "Think a Rolls or a Jag isn't bound by the laws that apply to a Ford pickup."

That had surprised Chad—the way the sheriff just talked to him as if he, Chad, were some acquaintance, another adult he was used to sharing his views with, chatting here on the pavement.

Chad had all of a sudden straightened up, made himself a quarter of an inch taller, and made his own assessment of the situation. "Probably one of those lake people."

"Probably you're right. Well . . ."

It was as if they'd been having this sidewalk chat for some time, or ones like it, for years maybe.

"I guess you're giving him a ticket."

"Wish I could think of something that'd make it stick—that people don't go around parking by hydrants. A ticket doesn't mean much to this person. He's got the money to pay it." Sam shrugged.

"If he's got a car like that he's pretty rich."

Sam took out his book, wrote the ticket, zipped it off, and stuck it under the wiper. "Haven't I seen you with Mrs. Chadwick?"

"Yeah. Yes, sir."

"You her son? She has a son, I think."

Chad had been enormously pleased that there was some doubt in Sam DeGheyn's mind, as if Chad might just have been a friend of Maud Chadwick's. "That's right. My name's Chad. My name used to be Murray, but I changed it." He wanted the sheriff to understand Chad had been in charge of his name. "I didn't like 'Murray.'"

"Uh-huh. That happens. I'm Sam DeGheyn. Glad to meet you."

"Me too."

"Well, that's the end of my duty. I'm going to the Rainbow for a coffee. You want to join me, or have you got stuff you have to do?"

For the second time in this brief interchange, Chad had been amazed. No one had ever asked him if he wanted to have a cup of coffee with them. And he liked the way Sam DeGheyn seemed to think Chad might be busy, just the same as anyone else in the town—the lawyer his mother knew, or the doctor, or even someone on the police force. He hated coffee, of course, but that wasn't the point.

So he'd fallen into step with Sam and gone to the Rainbow, where Shirl, then known to him only as a stocky woman with a square face who talked a lot in a loud voice, set up coffee for Sam and a soda for him. His mother hadn't started working at the Rainbow yet.

It was the first time Chad had had any good feelings about La Porte since they had come to live there. Before this he had hated it. He still wanted to go back to Sweet Air, but the road out hadn't pointed with such insistence since that Saturday afternoon.

"Look, I'm sinking."

"No, you're not," said Zero. He was floating a distance from Chad, would have melted into the water had it not been for the white scarf and shirt front.

Chad made as many waves as he could, slapping about, bitching, anything to disturb Zero's becalmed mind. Swear to god, he wouldn't be surprised if Zero turned north and just started swimming out to sea.

"Float," said Zero. "Rest up for the small hours. Things can get weird back there."

Weird back *there*? thought Chad, trying to pull up his legs. Well, that was one way of looking at a bunch of people drinking and eating and listening to music while you were floating out here in a dinner jacket in the middle of a black lake. But then as he started to float he felt suddenly pleasurably encapsulated, insulated. Looking at the stars, just buoyed up by the water, he would almost have enjoyed it except that he kept thinking of his mother and the Docksiders. He lay there on his authentic water bed trying to think up a good lie. He didn't think she'd much go for having lost them mid-lake. "You've finally learned how to walk on water, Chad. I always knew you could."

Way off in the dark, a tiny figure waved and called. Casey had got to the shore.

"Might as well go," said Zero, chucking his cigarette and watching it arc in the sky. Then he rolled over and started to swim. "Race you?"

"Oh, shit, shut up. Anyway, my shoes are at the bottom of the lake. They were new."

Zero angled over to him. "So? So you can have a pair of mine. Let's go."

"Not the same." Water was curling from Chad's mouth as he turned his face for air. "Mom paid a hell of a lot. Now what do I tell her?"

Zero was a stroke ahead of him and called back, "The truth. What's wrong with that?"

"Oh, sure." Chad coughed on a mouthful of water, gaining on Zero. "She'd believe this? She's not stupid."

"They'll believe anything, kid. Even walking on water."

They circled a narrow path between the boat house and the front steps. Zero was plucking at the tiny blooms from patches of wildflowers. He snapped off a little trail of leaves from a willow just before they entered the front door. Chad shook his watch. It didn't seem to be working. He took it off and dropped it in a tub of ornamental shrubs and followed Zero.

They came dripping into the large foyer, and the few guests standing by the Sheraton tables or leaning against the staircase turned puzzled, frowning looks on the three and then, bored, picked up their conversations again.

"Come on, Ophelia," said Zero, reaching for Casey, who was heading for the stairs to go up and remove her soaked black dress.

"What's going on?" she asked, the question ending in a whine, for as she said it, Zero swept her up, dumped a handful of crushed flowers and willow leaves on her head, and carried her to one of the arched entryways of the living room, which was nearly the size of a ballroom.

"Close your eyes, damn it," said Zero, "and let me do the talking."

"*I'm* certainly not going to do it!"

"Close your eyes."

The sunken living room was packed, the guests grouping, fanning out, and regrouping. Only a few appeared to notice Zero in the archway holding the waterlogged, flower-bedecked Casey.

Eva Bond, whose profile had been shimmering in the firelight, must have sensed them immediately, even though she hadn't, until now, been facing the doorway.

The three curved and carpeted steps and the archway above framed Zero and Casey in a small proscenium. With an exquisite intonation Chad had never heard from him before, Zero said:

"And from her fair and unpolluted flesh
May violets spring."

Raised voices; a few screams, cut off; and then a collective indrawn breath, before the guests realized it was some sort of joke.

Eva Bond's face was expressionless as she moved with her fluted glass across the room, seemingly unaware of the nervous laughter, the wide-eyed gaping, a fugitive sort of fear. She walked slowly up the three steps and stood looking at her son for a frozen moment. Zero looked past her. Casey shifted and opened one eye.

Then their mother moved past them across the marble foyer towards the billiard room and library.

Furiously, Casey hit Zero on the arm and broke free. "Oh, *why* don't you just give *up*?" She ran for the stairs.

Zero slowly lit up a cigarette; the guests turned away. His smile was a faded imitation of a smile as he said, "No one here likes *Hamlet*?" He walked away, calling back a question: "Bethanne still around?"

Chad didn't care that he would probably catch a fever: in the wet clothes he needed to apologize to Zero's mother. She was moving toward the library, stopping for a moment to respond to whatever comments her husband and his poker-playing friends made as she walked past. Then she went into the library and shut the high doors behind her.

Mr. Bond stopped him: "Chad. Got any plastic on you?"

Chad turned to the gaming table, green baize and walnut. "What?"

"Anything except gold. Just the regulars—AmEx, Visa, Diners,

NatWest. What happened? Did you fall in the swimming pool?"

Chad looked at the ring of laughing faces, five of them, all turned expectantly to him, someone who could solve the problem—except for the doctor, who frowned as he said, "No, no, no. It'd be Diners, AmEx, or *Lloyds* Visa. Who the hell deals with NatWest anyway?"

Chad had never seen square or oblong chips like these before: bronze, white, black stacks; oblong, square, and round.

Brandon, the porky-faced one, who seemed to be holding most of the chips—two tall stacks of bronze, one of white, a few blacks—reached into a big cut-glass bowl where ice cubes were melting into a water pond. Then he plucked up a tiny lemon peel from a matching dish, popped that into his mouth, and pulled over the pitcher, from which he took a swig, and more or less rolled it all in his mouth, mixing. He shoved the pitcher toward Brie Sardinia's husband. Mr. Sardinia held the Waterford pitcher aloft and in Chad's direction. "Martini?"

"What have you got on you? Diners, maybe?" Zero's father asked again.

"Only an Access card."

Mr. Bond shoved back his horn-rims. "A what?"

The doctor cleared his throat. "It's one of those money cards." His voice was low and sad, as if he were back in the hospital, telling Chad's mother the bad news about Chad's condition. Then he tossed down a card. "Yeah, oh, yeah" went the round of smiles towards Chad, the poor pisser who'd be the last to know the headstone and the plot had already been picked.

"Billy!" said Mr. Bond, hitting his fist on the table. Then to Chad he said, "He's got waterfalls of the damned things." Zero's father popped an ice cube into his mouth, followed it with an olive, and then lifted the pitcher and drank. Wiping his chin with a napkin then, he said to Chad, "Ask him, will you? Billy, I mean. I know he's got Diners, Lloyds, so he must have an Express." He slapped down a credit card, its identity downward. The backs were pretty much the same; the signatures had been covered with adhesive. "Do you play?"

The others looked at Chad, if not soberly, at least in invitation. The pitcher was back with Brandon again.

Chad looked around the table. "Never did with plastic. Wouldn't it be easier just to use . . . Never mind."

He knocked at the library door and entered when she called, "Come in."

Eva Bond was sitting behind a large mahogany desk, her arms resting on the top, hands folded. Behind her was a French window, moonlight throwing rhomboids of light across her hair, across the desk where the edges melted into shadows. That eerie placeless light whose source seemed hidden lit parts of the room dimly. This time it seemed to be coming from the bookcases or the wall behind, so that the edges of some of the volumes were bathed in gold.

"Chad," she said, looking him up and down. "You'll catch cold."

"I'm almost dry by now." He tried to smile.

From a dark brown leather armchair with a very high back came the voice of Maurice Brett: "You and Billy make a good pair." His face and hand appeared around the edge of the chair, the smoke pluming across them. "It's a relief you've caught us non–in flagrante delicto." His smile was ruthlessly charming, but still a smile in smoke.

"Sorry I interrupted."

Eva Bond said to Chad's departing back, "Stay, please." It sounded like a command, although he didn't think she meant it that way. "And please shut up, Maurice."

She still sat perfectly straight, hands interlocked, and would have appeared to be some sort of high-powered executive except for the gown. She motioned to the leather sofa. "Won't you sit down?" She smiled. "It's all right."

Chad wasn't sure whether she meant Chad's wetness or Brett's presence.

"Incidentally, sorry about my crass behavior," said Brett, who was nothing of the sort.

"All right." Chad refused to look at him.

"I expect you think I'm a bit of a rat."

Chad said nothing. The leather arm of the sofa was glistening and supple. It reminded him of Bethanne's skin.

"... and make a better offer. A thousand?" Brett was waving his hand slowly, bills wedged between the fingers. "Just what you need, I believe, old sport?"

Chad felt as cold as he had in the lake. "I don't need anything."

"But your mum might. Oh, sit down, for lord's sake. How do I know about the money? I see the question in your eyes. I know it from Bethanne, of course. Funny, she thought it rather charming: someone who couldn't be bought. That's a bit of a giggle, considering. So you still think I'm trying to blackmail you?"

"No," said Zero's mother. "No. You're trying to control him. Why don't you get out, Maurice?"

"Actually, I'm trying to help the poor boy." Brett rose and went swiftly to the table. He wheeled the telephone around. "Go ahead, call your mother."

Chad wasn't sure why he even answered the man. "She won't be there."

Brett checked his watch. "Good God, man, it's after one. Are you afraid to wake her up?"

"I mean, she won't be in the house." Chad looked down to hide a flicker of a smile. "She'll be on the pier."

Brett's eyebrows went up. "Where do you live—Atlantic City? Does she gamble?"

"She'll be on the end of the pier." Chad said it again.

"What the hell does that mean?"

"Nothing to you."

Brett moved back to his chair, repocketed the money, which had never left his hand, lit another cigarette. "What in bloody hell are you kids up to? Take Billy, now . . ."

Eva Bond had risen, her fingers splayed over the top of the desk, her head down. "Leave." Her eyes were riveted on Maurice Brett.

"Of course, darling. It's just this one little thing. Billy—Zero, as you call him—good name—put on more than his usual magnificent performance." He turned to Chad. "What was that all about?"

"Zero's a performer. He's an act, a clown, a nice guy. You wouldn't notice the last. You don't have any children is my guess."

"Thank. God. No." Each word dropped like a stone, and blood rushed to his face.

He's furious, thought Chad. At least there's something beneath that air of condescension.

"Because," Brett went on, "he enjoys humiliating his mother." He paused.

Chad thought that might be more difficult than Brett imagined. "Mr. Brett—"

"Ah! Do I hear a note of respect?"

"No. What I'd like to know is, what're *you* up to? Goodbye."

That, he thought, was one hell of an apology to his hostess. He shivered as he climbed the stairs.

Zero was lying on the bed in another Ralph Lauren room, wearing a silk robe and supple leather slippers, lying there with his hands behind his neck and staring at the ceiling. It looked almost as if he were back there floating on the lake.

The room was dim, the recessed lighting casting watery shadows along the walls and ceiling.

"You look like hell," said Zero, his eyes trained on the wardrobe. "Have some clothes."

"Your dad needs your credit cards."

Zero rolled over. "For fuck's sake, are they still at that stupid game? 'Diners, American Express, Lloyds Visa.' " Zero mimicked his father's voice as his little finger made a motion of knocking ash from an invisible cigar. "I've got an Exxon card; I ditched the others, I get so sick of hearing the names. You know how they pay up at the end of the night? Anything over, say, seven hundred—which is the kind of cash they carry to parties—anything over gets charged. Pops has one of those charge machines. And those chips? Cloak room, hat check—beyond that, don't ask me how it works. You should watch them shoot pool."

Zero swung his legs to the floor. "Might as well go back to the party. Who's Bethanne with?"

"Last time I saw her she was with your best friend. That red-haired dude."

Zero gave him an oddly sad look. "You're my best friend, kid. Was she upright? Prone?"

"They were in the swimming pool."

Zero closed the door of the wardrobe, hiked his legs into some loose-looking pants. Italian, Chad thought. Armani? Ferenzi?

He tucked a shirt into them and pulled on a jacket, loose like the pants. "Open that chest, will you—bottom drawer. I need a scarf."

The bureau was directly behind Chad's wing chair. He leaned around and pulled out the drawer. There must have been two dozen of them. The white silk scarves glittered in the uneven light. Chad pulled one out and tossed it to Zero. Why had he thought Zero had only one, since he always wore it and it always looked fresh?

"Thanks." Zero draped the scarf around his neck, said, "Come over here, will you?" He'd opened the other side of the chest, both doors with beveled mirrors, and was stooped down, looking at the shoes. "Take a look. I've got a couple of pairs of Docksiders in here that I hardly ever wear. I think they're two different sizes, because Eva did the buying and she didn't know what size shoe I wore. Could she pick me out of a lineup, do you think?" For a moment, Zero was silent. "Try 'em on."

"Thanks, but no."

"What in the *fuck* are you talking about? It was *my* fault you lost the shoes."

"You didn't know the boat would go down. You didn't plan to go for a swim."

Zero dropped the shoes on the floor. "For fuck's sake, why the argument? Here are two pairs of the damned shoes, and I know one will fit you, Cinderella, because it's a size too big for me. I never wear them *anyway*."

Why *was* he arguing? He didn't know. "I'll find them."

"They're at the bottom of the fucking lake, dude." Zero was leaning against the wardrobe, arms folded, toeing the Docksiders around. "Now I guess you want the scuba-diving equipment."

Chad sat up. "You have some?"

"You're nuts, kid. You're crazier than I am. No, I don't have any. But I'm sure there's some around. Pop, or his cronies, probably they have some. Send them down to look. They'd love it. Look, what is it about these shoes?"

Chad shrugged. "They're just part of something else."

"The something else must really be worth hearing about." By now Zero had flopped back on the bed again, reached over and opened the door of a walnut bedside table that was really a small refrigerator. He yanked out a beer and tossed it to Chad. "Go on."

"With what?"

"The something else, of course. Whatever it is that's set you on this fucking search for a certain pair of shoes."

Chad avoided an answer by asking, "Where's Casey?"

"Probably in her room, reinventing the guillotine."

There was no delay between the knock on the door and the door's bursting open.

As if she had been called, she had come. Casey stood in the backlit doorway, in silhouette, and in the same black dress, her hair still straggling with water and bits of weed.

"Guess she finished," said Zero. "You don't look too good, either. Where've *you* been?"

"Downstairs, being polite. People are leaving."

"Good. I can get undressed again."

"You could at least go down," she said with no special interest.

Still she lingered, her hand twisting the doorknob. Then she said, "I'm dying."

Zero, who'd been about to hit the intercom, turned swiftly and stared at her. He dropped his head back on the pillow. "Again?"

She didn't move into the room. Chad leaned forward, but he couldn't see the expression on her face. Her voice sounded pretty deadly, though.

"I'm dying. If you think it's so fucking funny—"

"Stop talking like that." Zero threw his arm across his face.

"*You* do it all the time. What kind of role model are you?"

"As good as you'll get around here. What is it this time?"

"You don't care I'm dying."

"The last time was when you wanted to go to the stag party the night before graduation."

"I bet you showed blue movies." Casey picked a weed from her hair.

"Snuff films."

"You're disgusting."

"You seemed to forget you were ten and we were all twenty-one. That time it was . . . yes, rheumatoid arthritis, and you were walking with two canes."

"I was in great pain," she said stiffly.

"Because you fell off that damned horse out there even Kent Desormeaux would be afraid to get up on. Then you were dying from what you called 'subliminal hematoma.' It's 'subdural,' incidentally."

"I had an accident and hit my head and it was months before I knew it. Don't you remember how woozy I was? All right, I'm dying, but you don't care. When you see me floating by the bank just like *she* did, you'll be very, very sorry."

Zero yawned. "Yeah. Well, I'm sorry in advance. So when it happens you'll know I was sorry."

"First I'll have to go insane." The voice was angry but lilting— probably her version of a crazed voice.

"I hope I'm around for that. So what're you dying of this time?"

There was a hesitation. "AIDS."

They were still at it, the bowl and pitcher replenished, the three holes in the credit-card deck apparently filled.

In the few moments it had taken Chad to get downstairs, he had made a decision. He was leaving tomorrow (today, really); he was going back to La Porte, even if he had to hitchhike; he was quitting school, at least for a year. And he was moving in with his mom. Or at least, if that felt too dependent, maybe he could find a room in Hebrides and save up money painting houses for a year.

And during those moments a running stream of guilt simply dried up. But it was replaced, fed by another spring, another stream. Now he felt guilty about Zero, of all people. That he was letting him down.

His hand was in his back pocket, feeling for the hundred dollars he had saved for the trip. His mother had given him a twenty ("in case you have to tip the servants").

The ring of faces looked up at him, smiling. Chad smiled back. They seemed as happy as the dwarfs when Snow White came to call. Then he looked at the big Waterford bowl, the pool of water forming; and then directly across at Mr. Bond, twisting his upraised credit cards in a little wave.

"Deal me in."

Chad had three Waterford-pitcher martinis; bluffed Mr. Sardinia's AmEx flush with only a pair of Dinerses; beat out Brandon's pair of Lloydses with three Visas.

When one of the Bonds' servants touched his shoulder and said Mrs. Bond would like to see him in the library, Chad was sitting with two hundred and fifteen dollars in assorted cloak-room chips from Pierre's, the Four Seasons, and Au Pied de Cochon in Paris.

And he still hadn't figured out the rules.

THREE

Eva Bond was standing at the French window behind the desk, staring at nothing. Nothing, as far as Chad could see, but dark panes of glass.

"I was afraid you might be losing," she said.

"I'm sure they wouldn't have allowed that." He smiled.

She was wearing a lightweight coat in a sour shade of cream that was plain to the point of cheapness. It was a coat that she might have pulled off the rack of the old Hebrides Emporium, a small department store, now shut, where everything looked thin, poor, and out of fashion, even the salespeople, even the very walls. Chad had gone there several years ago to buy his mother a birthday present. There had been only two or three customers, yet the manager and the clerks didn't seem to notice that business had fallen off. The manager wore a boutonniere—a white carnation. The salesladies all wore crisp white collars of linen or lace, and no jewelry. In the cool, dark store, as he went from counter to counter (scarves, gloves, glassware and china), they spoke softly and pleasantly, handling their cheap goods as if they had been silk and Sevres.

He had bought a scarf first. Then a pair of brown cotton gloves that the saleslady had brought out from the display case among other pairs, each contained in its plastic box. Then a long-stemmed glass in the china and glassware section. The woman there had not appeared to think it odd at all that he was purchasing only one glass. Each item had been wrapped slowly and carefully, almost venerably, in tissue while each of the salesladies talked in low tones of the weather, and college, and La Porte.

The store was dark and cool, and exiting to a sun-blanched pavement gave him a shock.

He felt anxious and sad—anxious because he had spent all of the money on things his mother never used. She didn't wear gloves or nylon scarves. And he had realized when the glass had been deposited in its box, closed with a white Emporium seal, that it was not, after all, a martini glass but a champagne glass. Yet to return it, to hand it back to the pleasant woman in the white collar, was unthinkable, just as the sadness he felt when he looked back at the store was unspeakable. It looked doomed.

Six months later the Hebrides Emporium had suddenly closed. Every day he had felt compelled to buy the Hebrides *Banner* to read the store's advertisements and had been relieved in the way a visitor to a sickroom might be to see the patient was still alive. Then the ads disappeared, and he combed the whole paper to see if there was a mention of it. Yes: there was a grim announcement that the Emporium had filed for bankruptcy. And although he knew it was mere fancy on his part, he read into the bleak, brief account of the store's history a self-righteous, sneering tone that implied the town had finally exorcised a dreadful presence on the corner of Walnut and Beech streets.

Chad had taken the local bus to that corner in the business district of Hebrides. The store was padlocked, boarded up, shut-tered, blank, as if it were something too disgraceful to be seen.

He could not tell his mother the story behind the gifts; he did not want to appear unmanly. When she opened one and then the other (gloves and scarf), he said quickly that she needed gloves in the winter, that she should wear them and a scarf, too. She was too careless. He glanced at her and saw behind the eyes and the smile the shadow of disappointment. After all, she had dropped hints to help him out: little things like shoe wax, and where had she ever put her cuticle scissors, and so on. Then she opened the glass and stared at it for some time. And rose and went to the kitchen. When she came back, she was carrying a bottle of champagne. "How did you ever know?" But her voice could only partially reclaim the expectant note from before she'd opened the presents. Smiling, she poured champagne into the fluted glass and said, "Sorry, but you get the water glass."

His own smile was dispirited; he had failed; he had disappointed her, and himself. The disappointment became defensive, and they both retreated into silence. Eventually, after trying on the gloves several times, shaking out the scarf, she said something about presents his father would give her. Last-minute thoughts . . .

But couldn't she see his were totally different?

Yet he wondered why, when all the time he was in the Emporium he had been concentrating on what his mom *would* want, he had bought her what she wouldn't.

All of this went through his mind during the moment that Eva Bond turned from the window and nodded to him.

When he looked at her standing there in that regal designer's gown and the pathetic coat, Chad had his one translucent thought—that this Mrs. Bond was not the same woman who had greeted him on the steps, and possibly never had been.

"Why are you wearing a coat?" He blurted this out to cover a confusion brought about by that single moment of clarity.

She smiled a little, looking down at it. "Oh, just going for a walk. Most of the guests are gone." She moved to the desk. One hand closed around the edge of a large book lying in its center. "I wanted to see you. I wanted to apologize for . . ." She lifted her arm as if she meant to indicate the chair in which Maurice Brett had been sitting, but dropped it again, an unfinished gesture.

"You don't have to." He had been about to add, "It's your life"; but that sounded brutal to him, given she looked now rather thin and very fragile. For it sounded in his own ears as if he wouldn't give a damn if she went ahead and ruined that life.

Again, she went back to the chair behind the desk and sat down. Perhaps it served as a protective barrier. She opened the book, shut it again. Looking at him, she drew out the silence for a painfully long time before she said, "I'd like to suggest something, but you might take it the wrong way. But first I wanted to tell you that I liked the way you shoved the money back in Mr. Brett's face." As she studied some bit of the Byzantine design on the carpet beyond the desk, she smiled slightly. "It was just the sort of thing Billy would have done."

Stunned, Chad stared at her. But she didn't notice and didn't shift her eyes. Whatever she had wanted to suggest that he might take "the wrong way" seemed forgotten.

"Is he popular . . . well liked? In graduate school, I mean?"

"When you have that much money, isn't it hard to tell your friends from your friends?" He smiled. "But, yes, as far as I can tell." And Chad was anxious now. Her question really hadn't to do with the university or whether her son was "popular."

"I wondered. He has friends here, but no one sufficient . . ." She frowned, searching out the right word or words.

"What or who would suffice?" Chad tried to help her out.

She lifted, dropped, her hands on the chair arms. All of her gestures appeared futile. The look she cast him was tentative and quickly withdrawn.

After a momentary silence, she said, "Last March—but you probably know about this—for over two weeks I couldn't find him. I called his apartment and so did my husband. I knew none of his friends. You're the only one he's ever brought for a visit, you see. Finally, I called the dean. It seems Billy hadn't gone to any of his classes for two weeks, hadn't paid his tuition, hadn't appeared at all. The dean was apologetic, but they'd had to take him off the class rosters—until the tuition was paid, at least. It was two months overdue. His father was dumbfounded, given he'd sent Billy so much money." Almost apologetically, she said, "So I called the police. My husband was furious; he said it would hurt rather than help. Imagine the police coming to your door . . ."

Chad remembered it well enough. There had been nearly two weeks in March when Zero had simply stopped like a clock. Stopped going to his seminars (even the Shakespeare seminar), hadn't turned up at a couple of big parties, or Mooney's Bar, or the Qwiklunch—a favorite place, where on two occasions he'd finished up fights with his opponent's head in the crock of garbanzos and stopped the manager from calling the campus cops by stuffing some hundred-dollar bills in his pocket. Chad had checked out all of Zero's haunts, including the Bowlerama. He didn't bowl (didn't do any sports); he'd just grab a dog with mustard and onions and sit and watch the bowlers.

It particularly surprised Chad that he found him after a week sitting silently in the dark, because Zero always seemed to have boundless energy. He walked in any weather with his coat open (cashmere or mackintosh) and that white silk scarf fluttering off behind him. The way he looked, the way he dressed—fitted out by Bill Blass, Perry Ellis, or Armani—had the most glamorous females on campus dogging his footsteps.

Yet the longest relationship Zero had ever had, which only lasted for six months, was with a thin-faced, soft-spoken girl named Paula, nervous and unremarkable in every way except for her brains (the brains of a biochemist) and her kindness. She was the one who'd search through a blizzard for a stray cat. And maybe because she was not beautiful or sexy, word got around that Zero was probably gay, word that could easily have been stopped by one of the three or four good-looking females Zero had dated for very brief periods before he scratched them out as if he were canceling checks. They weren't about to scotch the rumor. When it reached Zero's ears one night in Mooney's, he'd knocked over his beer, and Chad was expecting another Qwiklunch scene. But Zero was laughing so hard he choked. "I can imagine who started that one," he'd said. "That quarterback fern who only scores on the field."

Zero hated beautiful women.

That week in March before Chad pounded on his door, Zero had answered none of his calls. His Porsche had been in place; Chad figured he must be in his apartment.

It was dead dark. Zero had called out, "Enter." Even coming from the relative darkness of a March dusk, Chad had to blink up outlines of sofa, bureau, and Zero sitting at a card table set before the window. He was looking out at nothing except a few dark trees that hadn't yet come into leaf.

"So, Chad." Zero made it sound as if they'd been conversing here for hours and now came the summing-up.

"Where the hell've you been?"

"Sitting here, smoking. And drinking." He lifted a bottle of Jameson Black Bush an inch from the table.

"That all?" Chad made as much of a survey of the room as he could in that light. "No coke? Not even a little pot?"

"I don't do drugs. Never did. You know that."

True. And he didn't sound drunk, either. Never had. In another room the telephone rang. Chad stared at him. "You're not going to pick up?"

"The machine will," Zero said to the window.

The ringing stopped. The faint, metallic sound of a voice ran onto the tape.

"Eva again. She keeps calling. This is, oh, the eighth or ninth one."

Chad was angry. He himself had called a half-dozen times. All right, so it was Zero's business if he wanted to hole up. But it'd been a week now, and this was his own mother. . . . "Why the fuck don't you answer? Your mom is probably climbing the wall."

The silence and darkness deepened as Zero looked across at him. "My 'mom'? Eva?" He smiled slightly. "What about *your* mom?"

"What about her?"

"What's she like?"

"I've told you." Chad felt uncomfortable.

Zero flicked ash from his cigarette with his little finger. "She reads poetry and works her ass off in a diner so you can flunk French and smoke pot."

The look he gave Chad, from smoky eyes under dark brows, was excoriating. Chad felt singed. And more than a little angry. "Who the hell are you to comment on the way I run my life? You don't seem to be doing such a hot job of yours." Immediately he felt sorry when Zero, who had taken no offense at, nor apparently any interest in, this mild attack, turned his face toward the watery windowpanes and the leafless trees, past which the snow fell slowly, illuminated by the globe of a street lamp. And he had, in that instant, an entirely different picture of Zero—Zero of the cashmere coats, the silk scarves, the Italian suits, the Porsche convertible. In that instant Chad knew that Zero had no attachment whatever to the things of this world.

"Dude, listen . . ." Chad began.

"Segue off, will you?" His tone was devoid of animosity, almost pleasant.

But Chad didn't. He sat down there at the table, his presence seemingly unfelt by Zero, and poured himself a shot of Jameson and looked around the room, wondering what to say. But the room revealed nothing, and Chad had, once again (for he had been here many times), the odd feeling that the separately and carefully chosen pieces of furniture did not bear the stamp of their owner.

The room was not filled with the secondhand junk that you could find in most of the rooms around town, purchased quickly and by the roomful from one or another of the dark shops whose cranky owners would never go to the trouble or expense of fixing a broken spring or polishing up a surface and whose living depended on the coming and going, the arrival and departure, of the students. Chad had been in several of these shops with Zero and had felt how he would hate for his livelihood to be wedded to transience and impermanence.

Zero, however, did not buy junk. He had an uncanny talent for ferreting out, amidst broken-springed, legless, stacked-up pieces, a true antique whose value seemed lost on the owners of the stores. In this way, Zero had acquired the Sheraton side-board, inlaid with marquetry, above which hung a handsome mirror of beveled glass; the rosewood writing table; the Elizabethan chair of wood so dark it looked burned black, with a high ribbed back and strange gargoylelike finials at the end of its arms.

Chad let his look rest like a patina of dust on each of a dozen pieces in turn, and he thought how like a small museum Zero's room was, the furniture beautiful or bizarre, but unique. Yet for all of its uniqueness, the room spoke less of its occupant than would a hotel room where a traveler might set out on a bureau a framed picture. Zero seemed like that traveler without a picture, or a visitor who had come and gone and refused to leave his calling card.

Perhaps because of the dark, or perhaps because Chad hadn't wanted to see it, it wasn't until after he'd made his survey of the room that Chad saw the white bandage. The cashmere sweater sleeve had drawn back with the movement of Zero's hand, raised to smoke his cigarette, and the bandage seemed almost luminous, raised there like a little white flag against dark water.

Chad's throat felt raw, as if he'd been swimming against an icy current. It was hard to get the words out. "What's wrong with your wrist?"

"Hmmh?" Zero said dreamily. The glance he gave Chad was more a look turned inward.

"Your wrist. What happened?"

Zero looked down at his arm. "Burned it." His smile was a little slow.

The two of them sat there at the table by the window with the snow clumping now on the sill, skirting the trees, and mounding on the tops of the cars.

The walk glittered in the cone of light streaming down from the street lamp, and Chad said, "Remember Shadowland?"

"Shadowland" was like a code name for that winter when, just before the Christmas break, students and faculty had been stopped from leaving because of a snowfall so dense and deep it barricaded most of the little town behind doors and windows. Chad and Zero had been on the verge of leaving when their flight was canceled, and they couldn't have got to Chicago anyway to catch it because Zero's Porsche was buried under a cloud of snow, a white mound in a string of white mounds by the curb.

Oddly, neither of them was disappointed. They took their white imprisonment as an opportunity and managed to get to the grocery store and the liquor store before everything shut down.

They had been passing the Paper Store when Zero caught sight of some party hats in the window and insisted on setting down the crate of champagne and going in to purchase the hats.

Thus, they had spent five days drinking only Dom Perignon and eating Hebrew National salami sandwiches and caviar, and watching from Zero's shadowy room, the snow plows beetling heavily along the street outside.

They wore their party hats for five days. They made up personae to go with them. There were eight hats, and that gave them four characters each. Zero would sit in the Elizabethan chair wearing the flimsy gold crown and intone lines from *King Lear;* or Chad would put on the frog hat and search for the wizard; or beneath the tall blue cone, Zero would weep, taking on the character of the Princess of Shadowland. She was his favorite character, and her palace his favorite domain. The Princess had woken to find the king and queen and ladies-in-waiting all gone, vanished, until she recognized in the flitting shadows along the cold walls king, queen, ministers, and servants. It was the job of the Princess to turn the shadows human.

There was an elephant hat and a lion hat; there was a hat with a picture of Elvis Presley and his guitar; a black cone with silver stars; and one with a silver Studebaker. (This one really killed Zero; he loved playing the Studebaker.) They had decided that these were leftover hats, extra hats from some job lot of hats for theme parties, and that the bespectacled woman who ran the Paper Store (and didn't look like she'd ever been to a party in her life) had cheaply sold them together in one package. Probably, there'd originally been eight hats for Elvis fans; or a set of animal hats for a kiddies' party; or even hats for a bunch of car buffs.

In the stories that Chad and Zero concocted, each had to participate in the other's tale, wearing the appropriate hat. Zero could continue Chad's plot line, and Chad could add elements to Zero's. There was some sort of loose idea that each would stump the other, but it never worked, because events simply became more fantastical. The lion was fixing flat tires; the frog was making salami sandwiches with caviar for the wizard. The only act to be mastered was a quick changing of hats, for if the frog spoke from under the Elvis hat, you had to pay a dollar. Or if you were at one moment the Studebaker and quickly changed into Elvis, the other person had then to shift his manner of speaking to you (for you wouldn't talk to Elvis as you would to a Studebaker) or pay a dollar.

Zero never had to pay a dollar, for he was able to slip in and out of roles as easily as water sliding through weeds or over pebbles, no sudden hat switch of Chad's too difficult to make his way through or around. But his favorite character was always the Princess of Shadowland.

On the day that Chad and Zero were able to leave for home, all of the characters were to appear together in one tale, or at least as together as Chad and Zero could bring them, hastily taking off and putting on hats, becoming one and becoming another and telling of their travels and travails. Zero said they would all live in Shadowland together, Elvis and the Princess, Lear and the frog, the wizard and the elephant, the Studebaker and the lion.

They were, at the end, each supposed to solve the Princess's dilemma; to come up with a way of turning the shadows back into king and queen and servants. But on that last day, they awoke from their champagne sleep to sunlight so bright and hard they had to turn away from the window. Outside, the Porsche was revealed in all of its geranium red, and people were walking to and fro with brightly wrapped packages along pavements from which nearly all traces of snow had melted.

So, in order to get to Chicago and catch their flight, they had had to scramble, to shower and shave and change and toss their cases in the car.

They never broke the spell; they never solved the puzzle; the palace remained filled with shadows, and the Princess drifted and sighed among them.

That was, at least, the way Chad saw her now, sitting again in Zero's room, watching the snow fall. Saw her walk down colonnades, shadow-sunken. He watched Zero watching the unhurried fall of March snow and assumed he'd never heard the question. "Remember Shadowland?"

And then he assumed Zero wasn't going to answer, for the silence went on and on.

At last, Zero turned from the window and said, "That fucking frog never could drive—he ran over Elvis and totaled the Studebaker."

"What's funny?" Eva Bond asked, with a smile.

The shadowy room in Chad's mind was replaced by this strangely lit one, and he realized he must have been sitting here for some moments without commenting.

Chad shook his head quickly, trying to recall what Eva Bond had said just a moment ago. He remembered. "The police?"

"The one who called me back said there was nothing wrong. Billy looked pale, he said, and tired, but he was dressed, and the apartment was perfectly neat. 'No orgy, Mrs. Bond.' The police-man laughed a little. He was very nice—very. 'Your mother called, wants you to call her,' I told him." Ruefully, she looked at Chad. "That's a wonderful reason for the police to bang on your door. 'Your mother called.' " She sighed. Then she said to him, "I won-der why he wouldn't answer my calls."

Was this it, then? Was he to be the messenger who bears the bad news, who recounts the sad tale of spoil, woe, and death, and gets hanged for his trouble? For reasons obscure to him, he grew angry. "Why don't you ask Zero?"

She stood up, turned to the French window, turned back. "Oh, Billy wouldn't tell me."

"Why not, I wonder?"

There was a silence. "I can hear that self-righteous anger in your voice. It comes, I suppose, from your twenty-year-old vision of what parents should be and do." She smiled. "I find most children to be somewhat pious and preachy."

"Are we?" Chad was annoyed with this unjust assessment, made worse by her controlled little smile. He had to match her. Leveling his voice, he said: "Do you think that's all we are—ingrates?" He couldn't keep his voice down, spotlighted as he felt by her cool stare. "Don't you know you can all make us feel guilty as hell? I wonder: why *didn't* Zero let you know where he was for two weeks? And why did he have to put on that crazy display with Casey tonight?"

Her eyes hadn't left his face. "I thought it was rather good—idiotic, perhaps, a bit like his father's poker game, but quite bril-liant in its way. Billy likes attention."

"Likes *attention*? Can't you see behind it?"

She did not answer this directly but said, "We all had parents once." She started to button up her coat, turning again to the window. "We were all, as the poet said, fucked up in our turn." She paused. "I gave up long ago trying to change the course of things. Things just happen. You can't alter their direction or ward them off, like holding up crosses in the face of the devil." With her hand on the latch of the French window, she smiled. "You really think I don't love him, don't you?"

When she reached the path she turned and gave him a little wave.

He listened to the sound of her heels scraping on the gravel. Then he walked over to the desk and looked down at the large leather book she had been fingering. It was a photograph album of the sort that he had seen years ago and wondered at the patience of the organizer. The corners of each snapshot were secured by small black triangles.

Most were of Zero; many were of Zero and Casey; a couple of dozen of Zero and his mother; fewer of his father; fewer still of the whole family. And they had been taken by many different cameras: Polaroid, thirty-five-millimeter, an old Instamatic.

The album was worn, some of its pages loosened from the metal rings. It had been handled a great deal over the years. As he went to close it, a few loose pictures at the rear fell onto the floor. Chad looked down to see Eva Bond looking almost roguish in her flying gear. She was leaning against the single-engine plane, wearing a leather jacket, helmet, and white scarf. It looked like white silk. For a moment he merely stared, sightlessly, at the figure in the carpet against which they lay. As he reached to pick them up he had the strange sensation he was looking at two lives, lived long, long ago, now fallen into desuetude, irreclaimable. He thought of Zero, sitting in that dark room; he thought of Zero's mother, standing a moment ago at the French window. He felt ill.

At the sound of the car engine, Chad went to look up the little path she had walked towards a garage large enough to house a half-dozen cars. The lights of Maurice Brett's BMW glowed. The car backed up, spat gravel as it accelerated, and nearly leapt towards the long driveway.

What?

He couldn't believe it. Was Maurice Brett by way of being a penance?

Zero was standing at the window that overlooked the path his mother had just taken, looking down at the path with such concentration that Chad had to say his name twice.

He looked around. Chad might have been someone he knew from the past but couldn't quite place. His face was ashen. "Where's she going?"

"What? Who? What're you talking about?"

Zero was across the room in a flash and running out and down the stairs. Chad followed, saw him go into the huge living room, now empty of everything but flat champagne, half-drunk cocktails, sodden food. He heard the yelling. He heard the sound of glass breaking. Then he saw Casey, in the hall, in an old bathrobe and what looked like Zero's leather slippers.

"Go on back to bed," said Chad.

But she stared at him, twisting and twisting the cord of the bathrobe.

When Chad said it again, she turned towards her room. But when he got to the bottom of the stairs, she was still standing there at the top, looking over the banister.

Will Bond was gazing up at his son. He had a drink in his hand until Zero yanked it away and threw it against the wall. Whatever the father was trying to say was lost in the firing of glasses and bottles—against the patio door, against the huge mirror over the fireplace, against the hearth itself—and Zero was shouting, "You knew it, didn't you? You could have stopped her. God damn it, that's my *mother!*"

Zero raced past Chad without even looking at him to the front door. Within fifteen seconds Chad heard the Porsche's engine roar.

Jesus, he was going to drive that car at a hundred per, if Chad knew him. The Porsche might even overtake them, despite the long head start. And could the Bonds' Jaguar keep up with it?

"What the hell's going on?" asked Will Bond, who was swaying where he stood, not from vodka but from the assault on his senses.

"Give me your car keys. Please."

Will Bond made no move, simply looked at Chad from blurred eyes.

"Gimme the keys to the Jag, damn it!"

In a stupor, Zero's father reached in his pocket and tossed him the keys.

The Jaguar careened down the drive. In five minutes he was coming up to the highway and had to decide: north or south? He made a sharp turn to the south and pressed down hard on the accelerator. In a few moments he discovered how powerful this car was.

Chad heard a scuffling in the back, looked in the rearview mirror, and saw Casey climbing over into the front, still in the bathrobe.

The Jag swerved, and they nearly rolled onto the soft shoulder. "Christ! You could get killed!"

The shoulders of the robe moved indifferently. "So what? I'm going to die anyway."

FOUR

How much of a head start had Zero got? Five, maybe ten minutes. But he was driving a Porsche; he could overtake the BMW. The BMW wouldn't be speeding.

The Porsche would overtake it, yes. And then what? Chad could visualize Zero moving up alongside and, like the state police, motioning them to pull over. And if they didn't, the Porsche would keep the BMW in view, even if Zero had to tailgate. But the car *would* pull over. Chad hoped at least that Zero would not be fool enough to try and run them off the road.

Chad tried to imagine the look on Eva Bond's face, the confusion of feelings that would surely overwhelm her upon realizing that she was so important to Billy that he would automatically go after her.

How, he wondered, had this inarticulate, longtime suffering started? And what drove the two of them to go on refueling it?

If he was doing eighty, the Porsche was probably doing a hundred. Fields, farms, fences flew past as blurs, just barely distinguishable one from another. It was too fast; he wasn't used to this car, he didn't know how fast it would go before hurtling them onto the soft shoulder or into the sheet of rock on the left. He dropped to seventy. And even at that speed, two cars hurtled by him, one filled with a bunch of young joy-making, turned-on kids.

Beside him, Casey seemed to have shrunken inside the big quilted bathrobe. She had said nothing for miles; she must have dozed off. And then, coming up on him, he saw the double red and blue lights of a state trooper. *Shit!* He pounded the steering wheel and was about to pull over to the side when the police car barreled past him. Behind it was another, both with sirens blaring, and behind the second car two troopers on bikes. He slowed and began to pull over.

"What's going on?" Casey rose up from her seat.

"Nothing. Go back to sleep."

"Sleep? Who said I was *asleep*? How the fuck could anyone *sleep* with you red-lining it and a bunch of cops after you?"

He pulled the car back onto the highway and ran it up to seventy again. "They're not after me. Just shut up, will you? I didn't want you to come along, did I?" He wondered if she knew, if she had ever had a notion that her mother was screwing another guy.

The pitch of her voice was very low when she said, "We'll never catch him."

Chad wondered if Casey meant it literally or figuratively—or both. She sounded very sad.

Then he heard the *wah-wah* of an ambulance coming from the opposite direction. At the curve dead ahead he saw clusters of police cars, cops, civilians, their faces bathed a sickly pink from the wheeling domes' reflected light. No matter what the hour, there would always be people stopping to witness an accident. It must be one hell of an accident.

And the source of light was fire. A trooper was signaling him to pull over. He'd barely stopped the Jag before he flung open the door and yelled at Casey to stay back.

"What is it? What is it?" Her voice was raspy, her eyes wide and terror-stricken. "What is it, Chad?" She was starting to cry.

"An accident." He put his arm around her and told her, please, to stay in the car, knowing she'd get out and follow him. Chad had walked on a few feet before a trooper stopped him: "No farther, bud." Chad remembered the other cars, the two that had passed him, the teenagers, obviously high on something.

Chad swallowed. "Did anyone get out alive?"

The policeman ignored the question.

"Listen, man! Some of the people who were up ahead of me I knew. Christ, you could at least answer a simple question!"

Chewing gum, the cop adjusted his glasses. "No one would've got out of that hulk." He nodded towards what remained of an automobile. Chad had never seen a car so completely gutted. Parts of it were flung onto the highway—a tire, a smashed door; the chassis was burnt black.

"Look, officer, can you get any information for me? See, my—mother was driving in a car a few miles ahead of me." His tone was pleading.

"Just wait a minute." The trooper's voice was very sympathetic. "What kinda car was she in, son?"

"BMW." He choked from the heat and smoke.

The cop walked away, talked to a few of the others, then came back. "It wasn't a BMW." The trooper even sounded relieved. He was probably sick of relaying nothing but bad news. "Sports car. They think a Porsche." He stuck his hands under his armpits, went back to surveying the black hulk, adding, "Used to be red."

FIVE

Chad lunged toward the fire, but the arm shot out to hold him back was like a steel girder. "Jesus, kid, there is *nothing* anybody can do, unless you can maybe walk through fire." Then the trooper jerked his head around and said, "Take care of your little sister."

Casey was a few steps behind him, tears streaming down her cheeks. "It's Mommy, isn't it?" Her voice was clotted; she gulped in air.

Chad put his arms around her again. Through the thickness of the bathrobe she felt small and bony.

"It's not your mom."

In another few minutes the flames had nearly subsided. All of them—police, ambulance crew, onlookers—stood transfixed, watching the outline of the gutted car turn to cinders, smoke and ashes drifting up as the flames went down. Cars were still stopping, their drivers and passengers getting out. One of them walked slowly toward the wreck through the shimmering heat.

It was a woman. It was Eva.

She stopped a good ten paces from them, looking over the top of Casey's head directly into Chad's eyes, her own eyes horrified and then, in the play of the last vestige of fire, dark, hollow, gutted. Chad first put his cheek against Casey's soft hair and then dragged her arms from his waist and turned her around. Casey yelled and ran to her.

It was as if the positions had simply reversed, he thought, finding it almost impossible to keep from dropping his eyes.

His thoughts scattered, his eye traveling across the crowd, across the debris, the wet trails left by the hoses, the throbbing lights of police cars, black cars as shiny as patent and headlights streaming across the road. He had misunderstood; he had misunderstood the whole thing.

He looked back at the woman in the old coat who had come here obviously alone, whose silvery hair was suddenly whipped in a wind, and whose white scarf loosened and fluttered away.

He did not know how long they stayed there, watching the fire die in the spill of oil that had run in a jagged circle around the burned-black automobile where the still-persevering firemen in their heavy oilskin kept turning their hoses and moving about.

Under hats that seemed too big for them, the last of the flames reflected across their faces, forming delicate webs of light and dark, and Chad thought of Shadowland.

Ramon Fernandez

ONE

A perfect stranger, thought Sam, looking down at the body of
Elizabeth Hooper lying on the blood-caked ground. Or what
was left of her. Not just her throat was slit; the whole of her had
been ravaged, the knife trailing from neck to pubis. She lay in what
was left of her slip, brassiere, and panties. Her white coat had been
tossed aside. There was no sign of her dress.

All of Sam's men and half the Elton County force were here,
even though it was Sam's territory. He had called Sedgewick and
asked him for reinforcements, and to bring along his forensics
people; the local police hadn't got either the equipment or the
expertise that the county police had. His real reason for buttering
up the sheriff was to get him over here to see firsthand what
Elizabeth Hooper looked like.

Sedgewick stood there, fat and frowning, warming his hands
under his armpits, shaking his head. "This here's going to get all
the women in a panic. There ain't no way to keep it quiet, her
being an out-of-towner. We got reporters from here to kingdom
come on our backs."

"Is that high priority? Don't you think the women around here
should be locking their doors and not taking midnight walks?"

Sedgewick was hitching up his pants preparatory to an argument, but couldn't get the belt over the beer belly.

"Elizabeth Hooper was from the city, like you said," Sam continued. "Very quiet, very nice. Had nothing to do with anyone.
Just came through once a month on the way to visit her son.
Nothing like Perry or Butts—but she was carved up like them,
wasn't she? Like them and Nancy Alonzo."

Sedgewick knew where this was heading now. "Wait one little *minute*, DeGheyn. You trying to tie this up with those others again? You still trying to clear Boy Chalmers? Shit, I'd as soon believe he ex-caped again than go along with your cock-and-bull theories."

Angry though he was, Sam pulled out his cigarettes, offered one to Sedgewick, who took two and put one behind his ear. They lit up. "But he didn't, did he? This time Chalmers is locked up tight as a tic's ass." He kept all traces of sarcasm out of his tone and tried to talk in Sedgewick metaphors. Anything to get the sheriff, the mayor, the state's attorney to simply admit the obvious: it'd been somebody else all along, not Boy Chalmers.

It was not going to be easy.

"*Jee*sus, DeGheyn!" Sedgewick tried to shrug it off with an artificial little laugh. "You'll not be satisfied until you can turn up a serial killer, will you?"

"I'd be satisfied, Sheriff." Sam's smile was thin. "But would he?"

Sedgewick looped his thumbs in his wide belt and ignored that. "Four homicides in . . . what? Three years? Hardly New York City, is it?"

"Five, Sedgewick."

"Huh?" He chewed his tobacco a little more slowly, studied Sam warily, as if Sam might try and put something over on him.

"Eunice Hayden."

"Wha . . . *hell* you talking about?"

"Five murders in four years. Kind of a distressing regularity to it, wouldn't you say?"

Sedgewick's jaw stopped working, and he spat. "Shee-it. That girl was totally different. She was just a kid. And she wasn't raped, neither," he added lamely. To get off the Hayden murder and to show Sam the wheels were turning, he said, "What I wonder is, where in hell's Hooper's clothes? Her dress, I mean? Now *that* ain't never happened before, so this one maybe makes me think the killer's got—what d'ya call it? Got a fetish. Yeah. A fetish." He licked his lips and chewed his gum faster, as if savoring the word. "Know what I think? I think this might've been one of them city psychos followed the woman here. Maybe she had problems with some weirdo back in the city. After all, what do you know about her?" He seemed rather proud of that insight and even favored Sam with a tight smile because he thought he'd put another dent in Sam's argument. Then he moved away when one of his men called him.

Sam didn't reply. He supposed he should be thankful that this homicide had happened in the woods, away from the La Porte citizens, who all still slept snugly in their beds. And the police ambulance had come from the other direction, the direction of Hebrides. Why Dr. Hooper had been walking along this narrow dirt path, he couldn't imagine. Walking this path in the woods, at this late hour . . . Maybe she couldn't sleep.

And Sedgewick did have a point. What did he know about Elizabeth Hooper? Only that she'd been stopping in La Porte for over a year, it must be, stopping on her way to her son's school. Maud had told him that. Sam had seen Dr. Hooper ten, maybe a dozen times, usually in the Rainbow, where she appeared to have carved out a little niche for herself, sitting there at the counter beside Ulub and Ubub, or Dodge, or Wade, or Sims. Being polite when Dodge addressed a question to her. Polite as could be, but not really answering.

She talked to Maud, though; whatever Sam had learned about her, he'd learned from Maud. How she'd given up custody of her son, behavior that to Maud might as well have been extraterrestrial. Otherworldly stuff, something as foreign, Maud had said, as that spacecraft in *Close Encounters*. Sam had told her he thought that was a peculiar analogy.

Well, she'd said, people just floated off, came back, floated off again, so that you'd almost think that there were these other worlds they went to, places we had no knowledge of. (It always came to "we"; Sam had to be as ignorant of these things as Maud herself, he'd noticed.) There was this place Chad's friend lived—Belle Harbor. Maud in her fantasies would have Belle Harbor on another planet. Sam had reminded her that it was a place pretty much the size of La Porte, only a little over a hundred and fifty miles up the coast. It was inland, too, like La Porte. But it was much, much richer.

Looking down at the body of Elizabeth Hooper, he thought about Fate. Rarely did Sam think fatalistically, and never about Fate with a capital F, as he did this night. Why had she stopped here in La Porte? Elizabeth Hooper could easily have chosen the rich, chic Belle Harbor as her getting-off point. Its huge lots, spangled with lakes, were full of large, dazzling white houses, marinas, slips for yachts on the bayside—a rich person's paradise. Dr. Hooper looked rich; Dr. Hooper had class.

Dr. Hooper was dead.

Right now there were twenty or so men fanned out through the wood. No one had come up with anything. Sam stood there looking down at the body, at the face that bore no sign of a hellish attack. He always thought she'd been a truly beautiful woman, and likable too, even though she didn't start up conversations, just came into the café once a month, like clockwork. He heard the soft plop of a pine cone, thought about her son. Jesus, how was the kid going to handle this?

Was there anything much worse than the death of your mother? Mothers weren't supposed to die. He thought of the way his own mother had one night slipped away in her sleep. It was he who'd found her, and he went on and on, talking to the woman in the bed, raising the window blind, telling her it was a perfect October day, denying, denying, denying. When his sister had come into the room, Sam was still talking, asking questions. *"Right, Mom?"* Stuff like that. His sister was ten years older, and strong, but it took all of her power to get her screaming seven-year-old brother out of the room.

The stretcher bearers had moved the body onto the canvas and were taking Elizabeth Hooper away. It just didn't make any sense; there was no order in it. Maybe, he thought, as he watched the stretcher disappear into the woods, he could get Sedgewick to postpone the inevitable telephone call, either to the ex-husband or (God help us) to her son. He could drive up there. Maybe he could get Maud to go with him; if anyone could feel her way into a kid's head, it was Maud.

Sam wondered if he should call Chad. Maud was going to be horribly upset about the murder of Elizabeth Hooper. Elizabeth Hooper was perhaps Maud's favorite person, next to Sam, next to Chad. Sam was unreasonably irritated that Chad wasn't here right now, as if in some way Chad's presence could cancel out the terrible sorrow of Elizabeth Hooper's son. For Sam bet that in the last analysis the boy probably loved his mother, who'd left him, more than his father, who'd stayed.

And he wondered, as he had often done, what it would be like to be a father, a parent. That kind of love was very strange. It was almost like the better you were at it, the less you were needed. It was like a judgment.

"Well, well, I do declare. Never seen a grown man cry."

The sheriff was back. Sam's collar felt damp, and when he put his hand to his face it came away wet.

"Even you, Sedgewick—even you must have had a mother. Fuck off."

Sam turned and walked to his patrol car.

TWO

He had washed the blue dress carefully and was nearly finished ironing it, and just as carefully. He wasn't used to ironing, and it would be sacrilege to leave a scorch mark on it.

Finally, he held it up. Clean as clean could be. Not a wrinkle. He took pillows from the couch and from one of the other bedrooms and, together with the blue dress, went to his own bedroom.

Very carefully, he stuffed the dress. The smaller pillows he shoved up to near the neck to fill out the bustline. The bigger ones he put up the skirt. He wished he'd taken the bra and panties, too, but he hadn't, so you make do with what you have.

Once it was stuffed, he laid it down on his bed. Then he undressed and got into the double bed himself. He wound his arms around the blue dress and started crying, crying for all he was worth.

She would understand. *She* would say the right thing. *She* could explain how life wasn't crazy, even if it looked that way, that God had a pattern and, crazy as life seemed down here, it would all come out. It would come out almost like sins did in the confessional. How he wanted to crawl inside her. He could cut a hole in the first pillow underneath the skirt; he could get the scissors and cut a hole, he could

THREE

Some of the guests were leaving the party in twos and fours, and Maud was getting anxious. It was only two in the morning, and she knew how long those parties could go on; still, the ones who were going down to the dock signaled that at some point the lights would go out. It was Labor Day right now, she thought. And Labor Day marked the end of things. The house over there would be winterized; Raoul and Evita would go back to Manhattan; and Chad would be back at the university. His last year. Sam wasn't allowed to say it, but she must have said it a dozen times a day to herself.

She could feel an anxiety attack coming on. "Panic" was a better word. She wished to God Dr. Hooper were here. Yes, this would be one of those things only Dr. Hooper could handle. Usually the panic hit her when she was just about to either go to sleep or wake up. And that was probably because her defenses were down. She could feel the onset, a slight whirring noise and a rush of wind. Soon it engulfed her completely; her hearing went, her eyes started to cloud over. Unable to move, unable to latch onto anything, not the arm of the chair, not the lamp; there was nothing to hold her down, to hold her onto the pier. Maud could hear nothing outside this alien space, where the distant whirring grew until all she could hear was the beating of huge wings.

It was horrible. It was horrible. It was like being in the eye of the storm—worse probably, because at least a tornado was a natural disaster.

The only person she had told about this was Sam. He said he'd like to think about it for a while, that it reminded him of something he'd read. A few days later he'd come into the Rainbow and given her a book that had to do with life after death.

"I don't believe in life after death," she had said with some rancor in her voice. "I don't believe in death."

"Interesting," Sam said.

"Not for me, at least, or Chad."

"Then how do you account for the money Sonny Stuck makes at that big funeral home? The best-looking building in La Porte?"

She wiped the counter hard with a dish rag, frowning. "I don't know. It's a trick or something. But I guess that's not the point. What does the book say?"

"Read it," Sam had said, and then left.

It was surprising. There were countless other people who had felt a rushing wind of wings. It made her feel better to know she wasn't alone. It made her feel worse when she read that this was one, usually the first, of several steps towards an out-of-body experience. Maud sometimes felt that something was trying to drag her off the pier. Like some people during an operation could float above the table and watch the doctors and nurses hacking the hell out of what was left. No, thanks. Then a brilliant light was reported by all of them. That was usually the last step. Or at least the last step before the first step you took into the land of the dead.

If she just stuck it out, she knew the panic would end; and it did. The pier was firm beneath her feet, and everything was as it should be. Except she was sure she was dying. Oh, not in that stupid soul-leaving-the-body sense. There would be no bright light, no sight of the dead whom she had loved.

She was now thinking about Dr. Hooper's son. She had seen a snapshot of him and thought him very handsome; he looked just like his mother. Maud wished suddenly that she'd invited Dr. Hooper down to the pier tonight. Well, that was a stupid thought; imagine asking someone like Dr. Hooper, "Hey, would you like to come down to the pier for a drink?" Really.

Dr. Hooper stayed overnight sometimes at Stucks' place, or "the

Brandywine," as they liked to call it. Perhaps she'd gone out to dinner at one of the places the lake people frequented, such as the Silver Pear, a restaurant that specialized in quaint. It was quaint and expensive, and she and Chad disliked it intensely. Dr. Hooper probably would dislike it too, although she could easily afford to eat there instead of the Rainbow Café. You could tell she did very well in her profession just from her clothes. Or maybe she'd just stayed at the Brandywine and gone to bed; she probably didn't feel like being among people any more than Maud herself did. Yet Dr. Hooper could at least look forward to four or five more years of seeing her son on weekends and vacations, since he was only in the second year of prep school.

Maud lit a cigarette and envied Dr. Hooper. No, she didn't, for on the minus side was that the boy lived with his father. Lived with his father and might even *like* his father better, for hadn't his own mother given up on him?

She felt for Dr. Hooper's son. And she wondered if he'd forgiven his mother. To Maud she seemed such a wonderful woman—calm, quiet, intelligent. Sweet—yes, sweet. Sam had said that. Maud thought about that movie with Meryl Streep and Dustin Hoffman in it, where Meryl Streep had left the husband and the little boy. She remembered how eloquently Meryl had pled her case at the end, and she was sure Dr. Hooper could too, if she'd wanted.

She herself could never in a million years have left Chad like that, but she did not at all think this a point in her favor. She did not think that Meryl Streep and Dr. Hooper had loved their children any less. They had simply been able at some point to imagine themselves as existing separately from them. Maud couldn't.

Well, the father might well be the favored one with the Hoopers' son. But what right did *Ned* have after he'd run off with the Toyota saleswoman to come trooping back into their lives and pick up almost as if he'd never left? Achieving, she thought sometimes, for Chad, almost a certain glamour. The Prodigal Dad. He who should be favored over old stay-at-home Mom, the lady who was always boringly there . . .

Oh, Christ, don't be ridiculous. Still, she stayed on the alert for signs of Chad's switching his affections.

She squinted across the lake. There came another couple away from the party down to the dock.

After all, Chad didn't know why his father had gone off, and occasionally he hinted around that maybe it was her fault. It was an idea Maud knew he liked to toy with, seeing how he could divvy up the blame. She had never told him his father had run away with another woman. It wasn't because she was noble. She was just saving that particular little morsel in case Chad showed signs of bolting, of going over to the enemy camp.

Maud chewed the skin around her thumbnail. Well, maybe that wasn't precisely the reason she hadn't told Chad. Actually, it embarrassed her that she hadn't really cared that much when Ned had taken off with that saleswoman at the Toyota dealership, the one who'd sold them their last car. Maud remembered her as wearing draped and silky dresses of the sort that Velda favored, with big belts and shoulder pads. Maud couldn't recall whether she'd looked like Velda—probably not, since Velda was a fashion model. Maud never did know where Ned had met Velda, or what had happened to the Toyota saleswoman.

Maud much preferred the way Dr. Hooper wore her clothes. That blue dress she'd been wearing today was perfectly plain linen, cut on the bias, and probably cost a fortune. Maud could tell; she used to sew. Maud wondered again if Dr. Hooper had gone out to one of the lake restaurants for dinner. Maybe the Silver Pear.

At the Silver Pear you didn't simply eat, you had a "dining experience." It was one of those restaurants that offered large promises and small portions. Chad had needed another basket of bread just to fill up. It was in an old Victorian house about a mile farther up the lake. The owners were Gaby and Julian (restaurateurs, Maud had noticed, always had names like that, never "Mary" and "Bob"), and they'd carefully kept to the original structure, turning the several downstairs parlors into separate small dining rooms. Between the fireplaces and the candles in hurricane lamps, the rooms were masses of flickering shadows, an effect that pricy restaurants often strove for. Besides the glass-enclosed candle, each table seemed littered with the detritus of some New York designer's notion of rustic splendor. Chad had taken her there two years ago on her birthday. All through dinner she had moved things around—vase, little silver basket of potpourri, silver-painted pear (one on every table)—trying to get to the silver salt and pepper shakers, also pear-shaped. It was like maneuvering through a tiny silver-plated orchard.

The argument had been over Chad's Christmas vacation and where he was going to spend it. Ned and Velda wanted him to go to Vail in Colorado. Even though Maud knew it wasn't them Chad wanted to cozy up to, that it was the blazing fireplace in some swanky lodge in Vail where they would be Christmasing (Velda's word; in constant motion, all her nouns were verbs). Chad had never skied in his life, but what difference did that make when there were all of those blond girls in ski boots and heavy sweaters with reindeer designs sitting by the fire with drinks, après-ski-ing?

Maud knew she'd lose, she knew she'd have to agree; still, there must be room for negotiation. "Well, all right—but not the *last* half of the vacation."

Oh, what a trial, his sigh had said. "Mom, that's when they'll *be* there."

"And I'm supposed to Christmas without you?" She was shoving the poached salmon around her plate, appetite gone. Then she worried the silver pear, moving it here and there, imagining the silver orchard, trying to remember that fairy tale that silver pear trees figured in . . .

"Of course not Christmas Day," Chad was saying. "I'll be here

Christmas *Day*." He was being eminently reasonable—couldn't she see that?

"But you'll be New Year's–ing there, is that what you mean?"

"Well, yeah . . . 'New Year's–ing'?-What kind of word's that?"

Maud looked at him narrowly. She was growing increasingly suspicious. "So how long do you mean to hang around the slopes?"

Very casually, he said, "Oh. Well, we thought I could just fly back to school from Vail."

The other diners, lake people who all appeared to wear white, probably flew back from Vail, or at least talked about flying back from Vail, all the time. "Vail" was falling just a little too trippingly off Chad's tongue, as if he'd been careening all over the slopes in his mind and it was hardly to be borne that he might have to return to La Porte. "Vail" grated on her ear. More important, her stomach felt hollow: Chad would be spending the last part of his vacation with Ned and Velda.

"Why can't you Christmas with them the *first* week of your vacation and New Year's with me?"

"For Christ's sake, Mom, stop talking like that. And I just said: how can I if they're going to be in Vail the second week, not the first?"

Of course it shouldn't make any difference; but it did, and he knew it. It was always harder to endure his absence at the end, for then she had nothing to look forward to. Nothing but absence.

Maud remembered gazing at the room, at the diners there, the couples and the foursomes, the women in pastels from which the firelight had drained the color, so that everyone seemed dressed in white, white attendants at yet another of her deathbeds. Every departure a death, so of course she had to negotiate: a few more days, please.

The couple at the next table, the man lighting cigarettes, then slipping the slim silver lighter into his white duck pocket: these summer people did things in smooth, single motions, like swimmers cutting seamlessly through water, or skiers slanting down mountains, or players sliding across the court to make their perfect returns. Maud heard, in her mind's ear, tennis balls plop like pine cones in the snow.

And she thought: their lives must be soft like that, for they reeked of privilege. Their voices, their modulated laughter seemed to float toward Maud like mist rolling over the lake.

Did the four at that table by the window, the panes starry with reflected points of light—did they have children?

Yes, of course they did; but they were smooth, ornamental children, maintained for giving pleasure much like the little boats that slipped by on the water, or docked for the night, berthed along the water's edge. Maud could envision the children asleep now, floating in dreams, bobbing up and down to the rhythm of dream imagery.

And if they got divorced, there would be no predicament. Maud could see that woman in the filmy pastel dress back in New York, now separated from him, living her own life in her vast, muse-umlike Manhattan apartment, where she had a Life of Her Own as a painter or perhaps an editor with some literary sort of publisher. Maud could see the son shamble in, tan, cashmere-sweatered, plopping down in a soft armchair, breezily greeting his mother and saying he might be Christmasing with a few friends in Portofino; and then, here comes the daughter: *"Daddy wants me to Christmas in the Hamptons. It sounds super . . ."*

And the mother, the woman with the pale hair, so absorbed in her paints and canvas or else her brilliant first novel, or an author she's discovered, barely hears this, for it barely matters, and thinks, "Ah, now I can Christmas with Kyle." Or Robert. Whichever lover she feels is deserving of her Christmas company.

No, this beautiful painter-editor-with-lovers mother—she didn't need to strike bargains. But for Maud, it was always like that: the little trade-offs, negotiating and renegotiating.

Then she had started wondering about the birthday dinner itself: was it simply a sop, a way of getting her in a good mood so she wouldn't give him a hard time about Vail? That was painful, not being sure.

"I've got to spend *some* time with them, for god's sake."

"I didn't say not to. I'm just talking about *which* time, which part."

She hated herself, felt ashamed for sounding like some haggling purveyor of beads and silks in a Baghdad bazaar, trying to raise the selling price a rupee at a time, just a little more, a little more. The argument had escalated, not in raised voices but in rancor and bitterness. He couldn't understand, or said he couldn't, why she had to make such an issue of it.

It was odd, though, he never gave as a reason that, after all, his dad was paying for the university. Sometimes she thought it was because he knew it would be taking unfair advantage, and other times she thought it was because they both knew it was not really an issue. If Maud had had all of that money, these arguments would still have gone on. Ned probably thought he had staying power because he had buying power. In a way Maud almost wished it were true; it would make her and Chad's relationship much easier to understand.

She watched several more of the party-goers try to get into their boats, with a lot of whoops and hollers and laughing when one nearly went over the side. But the music went on. They'd probably be up until dawn, especially since this was the last party.

The ice in the bucket had melted except for a few pieces, which she chased through the water and put in her glass. Sam said he'd be back, so he would, even at this hour. It was after two a.m.

It was wonderful: no more had she thought it, she heard the car, the door slamming, and he was coming down the walk. She hoped he wouldn't start some depressing talk about the end of the season.

"Hello, Maud."

She turned. "Wade Hayden, for the Lord's sake! What are you doing wandering around at this hour? I expect you couldn't sleep, either." She did not want to make it appear that she sat down here for any other reason.

"Mind if I set down, Maud?" She nodded. He sat in Sam's chair and put a brown paper bag beside it. He looked at the forgotten can of Coors. "I don't drink as a rule, but I wonder, would you mind. . . ?"

Actually, she would: if the last beer were drunk, it might mean Sam wouldn't come. Oh, for pete's sake. "Go right ahead, Wade." Then she thought Sam would get a real thrill out of this—Wade Hayden taking the Coors out of the cold water and popping the top.

"Someone having a party over there, Maud?" His smile was just a twitching up of the lip. "And never invited us?"

There was something slightly chilling about the way he coupled them. "Us." She drank the weak martini.

"Something I got here to show you." He reached into the brown paper bag and brought out the blue dress. "Pretty, ain't it?"

Maud sat dead still. She felt very fragile; were she to move, she might splinter apart. She was cold with fear. The dress was Dr. Hooper's. Maud always looked carefully at her clothes, wishing she herself could wear such simple things and look as good as Dr. Hooper. She had to respond. Her mouth was dry, but she said, "Wade, that is *very* pretty. Is it a present for someone, maybe?" She didn't know how she got her mouth to move; it felt that tight.

Wade Hayden smiled that unfelt smile again. "It sure is. It's for you."

She had never seen Wade Hayden anywhere but in the post office or the Rainbow, and he never said anything except hello and goodbye. Something was horribly wrong; she had to be careful of what she said . . . but not so careful he would hear the fear in it. "Well, that *is* a nice dress, Wade. But why should you be giving me a present? It's not my birthday." She managed to bring to her frozen mouth a little smile.

"Oh, you'd never guess what it's for. I know your boy's left for school, and I know you miss him. This is just a little something I brought you for being a good mother. There's not a better mother for miles around; there's not even one *as* good. You could say that being postmaster, you know an awful lot about people. Can't help but." His look at her was oddly kind. "You want to try it on to see if it fits?"

Without looking at him, she took the dress and held it on her lap. And without speaking to him, she looked up and over the water and saw that it was quiet, all quiet, no one except for a man—she could make out the glimmer of his white jacket—standing on the dock over there, smoking a cigarette. The tip made a tiny glow, a pinpoint of light winking on, then off. But he was too far to call to, might as well have been in a plane up there in the black night whose winking red light meant people were going somewhere, places she couldn't follow—back to school, to the city, to that room whose balcony hung over the sea.

Maud smoothed and smoothed the dress. Two tears made their way down her face, fell on the dress. Dr. Hooper.

"No, Wade. I don't think I can try on your dress, thank you all the same."

Elizabeth Hooper would never come through La Porte again, never sit at the counter eating pie again, never see her son again.

FOUR

Sam hadn't moved the car, hadn't done anything. Stupid to get on the bad side of Sedgewick. But everybody has their limits, he thought, and he was sick of kowtowing to blind bastards like the sheriff.

He switched on the engine as if he knew where to go and let it idle.

If it had been his kid . . . He thought of Wade. Stony, silent except to try and go over the murder of his own daughter again and again. No wonder. What else would go through a man's mind after something like that happened?

Sam suddenly thought of Rosie. He thought of Rosie strolling down Fifth on her lunch hour, looking in shop windows, eyeing a Spanish shawl, brilliant splashes of reds and orange for her red-gold hair, something to toss over her shoulder in a grand gesture, go sweeping down Fifth Avenue in the soft air of one of those perfect spring days to which even New York City gets treated—

A spasm caught at his hand and he dropped the cigarette when he realized he'd been thinking of an imaginary girl. Watching her, following that bright Spanish shawl worn by a girl who didn't even exist until he'd said her name to Maud. There had never been a Rosie.

Grinding out the cigarette with his heel, Sam wondered, was he going Maud-mad? Maud-Mediterranea-mad? He smiled. The thought and the smile revived him a little, enough to go back over the whole damned business.

He leaned his head against the head rest, closed his eyes, and thought about the women. To him, they were different. Tony Perry might have been an out-and-out whore (though he loathed the word), a woman with children she didn't pay much or any attention to. Loreen Butts, according to the mother, was shy and quiet; according to the husband, could be hard to handle; according to Boy Chalmers, ditto. Carl Butts was away most of the time, leaving her the care of the son. *Not that the son ever got much care* . . . Sam frowned. But how could Elizabeth Hooper even be compared? Or Nancy Alonzo? Nancy had been a local, yes; but that was about all she had in common with Perry and Butts. He lit a cigarette; his frown deepened. But wait a minute. Yes—yes, she could, if she'd walked out on her son and husband. Eunice Hayden. Eunice hadn't been raped, no . . . Still, he *knew* all of these killings had been done by the same man; knew it as well as he knew that his headlights were running twin paths of smoky light through the woods, sectioning off trees, undergrowth, rocks. What else did the victims have in common except they all had kids? Not Eunice, though.

They all had kids. They all had kids who a lot of people saw as neglected at best and abused at worst.

The thought simply stuck. Well, it was ridiculous. Most women did; and there was Eunice—she didn't fit. As much as he tried to rid himself of the answer, it still came rushing toward him, insane and senseless. Neglected children. Tony. Loreen. Nancy. Elizabeth. In the mind of the murderer, neglected. But Eunice? Her mother, Molly, watched over her like . . . her mother, Molly, hated Eunice. Eunice starts rolling in the hay like a common whore, some would say, maybe to spit in her mother's face . . .

Dear God, the one person who might be able to see in this insanity some sort of design was one of the victims . . .

He was still trying to piece it together when his radio started squawking, bristling with what sounded like overlapping voices. But it was only Donny, his deputy. He lifted the mike and pushed the button. "DeGheyn."

"Sheriff? Sheriff?" Donny always seemed to be questioning just who that was.

Sam sighed. "Yes. It's the sheriff."

"Listen, Sheriff. Maud Chadwick's kid—you know him?—her kid's trying to get in touch."

Sam held the handset away from him. Donny was shouting. Donny always shouted, because he didn't appear to believe contact was ever being made over airwaves, radar, whatever. "Stop shouting. What about Chad?"

"What? What?" Donny bellowed. "Okay. Listen, the Chadwick kid needs to talk to you."

Sam frowned. "Did he say why?"

There was a silence.

"Did he say why? Donny?"

Nothing. Had the damned fool signed him off? He did it all the time.

"Sheriff? You there? No. He didn't say."

"Where was he calling from?"

Fade-out again. Then the voice crackled back. "From Meridian. I think that's where."

Meridian was about fifty miles out of Belle Harbor, about a hundred miles from here. What the hell was Chad doing there? "Donny?"

Nothing but static and distant, tinny sound. Donny could have been beating a plate with a spoon for all Sam knew. He hadn't been Sam's first choice for deputy, certainly. "Donny?" Now Sam was shouting.

"Jail."

"What're you talking about? Chad's in jail?"

Dead silence. Donny was probably messing with the board and he'd cut Sam off again.

He replaced the mike and switched on the engine. The car lurched along the dirt road and took the turn onto Main with two wheels an inch off the ground.

He banged the door of the office shut and told Donny to get his feet off the desk and go and help out Sedgewick's men.

Recognizing this was indeed the sheriff, Donny yanked his belt and holster from a shelf and scrambled for the door.

Sam didn't bother sitting down; he placed the call to Meridian.

"No, he ain't exactly arrested."

Involuntarily, Sam put his hand on his holster. His nerves were on edge, and the Meridian police force—if you could call it that—was a cluster of Donnys. "Well, if he ain't exactly, then how about letting the kid go?"

"It's this car. The kid was driving this Jag that was reported missing."

"You're saying Murray Chadwick stole the car?"

"Not exactly."

"Then what, exactly?"

"This real bad accident out on twenty-nine. About ten miles from here, you know?"

"No, I don't know. What's that have to do with the Jag?"

"It's all the same people. I mean, the Jag owner—well, some family member—was in the accident. We're just trying to put it together. It was reported, see. This Jag that the kid was driving. Some car, lemme tell you. No wonder it got stole."

Jesus. "I thought you said he didn't steal it."

"Yeah. Well, not exactly."

"Let me talk to him."

Chad told Sam what had happened. "I wasn't stealing the fucking car, Sam. And I don't think Mr. Bond ever reported it that way. I don't think he'd do that, and anyway, he wouldn't care about a fucking car at this point." He was close to weeping; he sounded like he already had, and a lot.

"They don't think you did. They're just trying to get the whole thing figured out. That might take them some time, and I don't see why you should have to hang around for it."

"I was on my way home. I tried to call Mom, but no one answered. Is she down there on the fucking pier?"

He sounded little-boy enraged. It would all be, in some part, Maud's fault. Sam smiled. "Yeah, she's down on the fucking pier. If there's any problem about leaving there, just tell them to call me. They know me. It's probably as much excitement as Meridian's seen in a year."

Chad laughed. A weak sound, but better than before. "Right. It shouldn't take me more than a couple of hours."

"For Christ's sake, you might have a Jag, but don't get picked up for speeding. I'm going to see your mother."

There was a brief silence. Then he said, "Listen, thanks, Sam."

"Don't mention it. Just get here."

"You going to tell her?"

"Tell her what?"

Now there was a longer silence, an in-depth silence, as if the boy were turning over the years.

"I don't know." He sounded puzzled.

FIVE

"No, of course you can't," said Wade. "Don't know what got into me. Course you can't put on the dress. Sorry—I guess I wasn't thinking, Maud. A lot's happened."

Maud felt relief for a second, loosened her grip on the arms of the rocking chair, but tightened up again almost immediately. It was still Dr. Hooper's dress, wasn't it? And Wade was looking at her, a look she did not return; she just kept her profile to him, her eyes on the dock opposite.

He was still there, the man or boy, the tiny red eye of the cigarette winking on and off. *Chad.* She concentrated as hard as she could on the name and the figure over there. *Chad.* She closed her eyes tightly, trying to project the name across the water.

"Things that's been happening, Maud, I thought maybe you'd understand." He paused. "What's wrong? You got your eyes shut tight as a baby."

"Baby." The word sounded, in his mouth, obscene. But she opened her eyes. Her throat worked. Maud raised her fisted hand to cough delicately, to see if any words would come out, for she'd seen, and given no sign whatever she'd seen, the knife. "Why, nothing, Wade. Nothing at all. I guess I'm just surprised you'd be out this late." It amazed her that she sounded perfectly natural. Amazed her she had the control—even the control to smile a little. "You strike me as someone usually in bed at sundown. With the ch—" She coughed. And then she knew why she'd not said the word "chickens." Because of Eunice out there in the barn. He'd killed Eunice, too. All of them.

Now she even forced herself to rock the chair; it creaked on the rotting planks, and she felt her neck creak, too, as she ever-so-slowly turned her face to look at him with that same stiff smile. Wade Hayden was grinning crazily back at her, but she didn't look away. She dared to look straight at the knife. "Wade, what've you got that old kitchen knife for? You can't hunt with that." She said it slowly and almost dreamily, her mouth curled up in that memory of a smile. The way, she thought, Joey smiled.

Shirl would go on seeing Joey in the Rainbow Café forever. But she was never going to see Chad again, never.

Somehow she managed to go on rocking, holding Dr. Hooper's blue dress, and saying, while he was looking down at the knife with a puzzled expression, "What things, Wade? Why don't you tell me what things have been happening?"

"That's what I was meaning to do, Maud. Bad things." Now the knife was between his thumb and forefinger, dangling, swaying slightly. "Things I did. I thought you might hear me out."

She tried to bring her son's face to mind and she couldn't. It was blotted out by the fear.

She felt a momentary reprieve. Yes, she assured him, she would hear him out. If she didn't look at him, if she concentrated on the dock over there, she might be able to convince herself that this wasn't really happening. Beyond that row of little boats she had no future. She wondered if she even had a past. It was all unreal. "What things were those, Wade?" she asked again, conversationally, her fingers pleating the blue dress.

Wade was crossing his legs, clearing his throat, as if to get comfortable and in voice.

"You didn't know me and Eunice very well."

No, she hadn't. Her tongue felt thick. He'd murdered his own child.

"We was like *that*." He held up two fingers close together. "Much more'n her and her mother. Yeah, Eunice and me, we understood one another. Trouble was, Eunice took herself off whorin' around."

It jolted her, the way he said this, his voice so measured and calm. Maud's hair was a cap of perspiration; her scalp prickled. She would have to hide her terror.

". . . whorin', and got herself pregnant." He turned it into three syllables—"preg-a-nant." Now his voice, almost guttural before, became high and thin and whined like a saw as he brought his fist down on the arm of the aluminum chair. "You can't have that goin' on, not in your own house—not your own flesh."

She could feel the heat coming off him; it was like the shimmering heat that can rise, miragelike, from baked surfaces—a road, the desert. She had to answer him: "No. No, you can't, Wade." Keep saying his name. Did he even hear her? Did he even know where he was?

"Eunice, she'd've turned out like that Loreen Butts or that Tony what's-her-name."

He had forgotten. Maud shut her eyes. He'd actually forgotten the name, as if Tony were only some lost acquaintance, someone he'd known casually.

"Did you ever know Loreen Butts?" His tone was conversational, casual, as if they'd just stopped on the pavement to exchange a bit of gossip.

No. The word did not come out; she choked on it, swallowed. Maud cleared her throat. "No," she said firmly.

He turned to her. "You coming down with something, Maud? You're all over sweat. Nothin' worse'n a summer cold."

Nothing worse. She clutched her book. Behind her, twigs snapped. Sam.

It's not Sam. You didn't hear a car. Forget Sam. She tried to shut out Wade's voice. He was talking about Loreen Butts.

"Thing was, she took up with that Boy Chalmers. He's queerer than a three-dollar bill, everyone knows that. In a way it's just as well that sheriff in Elton County arrested him. Boy Chalmers." Wade leaned over, spat onto the boards. "His kind shouldn't be walking around. Don't surprise me trash like that Loreen Butts would take up with Boy Chalmers." Now he was back to talking about Eunice again. "Thing is, Eunice's ma never really knew how to raise her, though I expect she tried. Not like my own momma. You should've known her . . ."

His angel of a mother. Maud gripped her book, the blue dress now lying folded over the chair arm, and listened to this peculiar, disjointed tale, about how wonderful his angel mother was. It was all a lie. Wade's mother had gone off when he was just a little boy. Sam had got it from Molly Hayden; even Molly, so tight-lipped around nearly everyone, even she would talk to Sam.

Where was he? Was he coming back?

"Dr. Hooper." Maud didn't know she'd said it aloud until Wade turned to her, turned as if he were still with cold, his whole torso, not just his head.

"She had you all fooled, didn't she, that woman? Probably just because she was a doctor, you thought she was better than other people? You know them letters she used to write? Well, you ought to have read them letters and I bet you wouldn't think she was so wonderful."

His voice, Maud thought, had taken on the rancor and bitterness of an invalid, a sick old woman like Aunt Simkin.

"You didn't know she walked out on her boy, did you?" His tone had deepened. "Letters is bad news, most of the time. Being postmaster, well, I should know. Postmasters got a sacred trust."

She felt him looking at her, wanting her to ask. "I expect they do, Wade. I'm not sure just what it is, myself." She coughed.

"It's a sacred trust to know. To *know* what goes on in your town. That Billy Katz—you know him? He's postal clerk over in Hebrides. Billy Katz is a disgrace to the profession." Wade leaned forward, spat into the dark water, then continued, conversationally. "Yeah, that Billy. If it wasn't for me going over there to pinch-hit him, well, that town'd hardly get any service at *all*. Don't think I didn't know all about Loreen Butts and that Antoinette woman. Ain't much goes on a postmaster don't know about." He took a pull at the can of beer, laughed as he swallowed, and wiped the spittle from his mouth. "Sam DeGheyn thinks I was over to Hebrides all that afternoon. You remember? Afternoon Eunice was murdered?"

As if this were just another to-be-forgotten date on the calendar. Maud's fingers were tight around the blue dress. She couldn't answer.

"Sam DeGheyn thinks he is the cat's pee-jays around here." His tone became sly. "He was carrying on with that Alonzo woman, did you know that?"

Maud shook her head. She knew it wasn't so, and yet a flicker of jealousy spurted up within her. It was astonishing that in the midst of all this fear, she could feel something as clear as jealousy.

"Oh, hell, yeah." He kept his eyes on her. "Fooled around over there in the courthouse after hours. I bet he had her in just about every—"

"How'd you fool him, Wade?" She blurted it out in a voice that sounded tight as violin strings. "How'd you put one over on Sam?"

His laugh was more of a giggle. It was awful. "Easy as pie. All I had to do was jump in my pickup and come back to the farm and then go back again. Only took an hour, not much more. Anyone'd come into the post office, all I had to do was say I was in the john or was sick. No one come in, I guess. Who wants to talk to Billy Katz, anyway? He don't know his ass from—excuse my French."

The giggle was frightening, almost worse than his thumb running the blade of the knife.

"Dr. Elizabeth Hooper . . . Dr. Elizabeth Hooper . . ."

He repeated the name again and again as if he were stroking it, tasting it. He told Maud how he had watched, that very night, from inside the dark post office. "She wasn't nothin' but a whore, Maud." His voice had taken on again that whining petulance. "Had to do her, didn't I? Just like I did the others. What the hell did she care about her boy? She just walked out on him, didn't she?

Like Loreen Butts left that baby of hers time and again so she could go with that Boy Chalmers." The voice had changed to that high, rasping whine again, as he talked about standing at the window of the post office. It was down the street a little from the Brandywine Guest House, but he could look up that way and watch.

"Don't . . ." Maud held up her hands to stop him telling her about what had happened.

It was crazy to challenge him, to suggest he'd done something wrong, but she couldn't help herself. Not when it came to Dr. Hooper. "She was here because of her son. Because of him she came through here like clockwork, once a month, just to see her son."

Maud was weeping now, looking out over the water. All of those people across the lake and not one of them could help her. Sam.

"It's too late."

The change in his voice jolted through her like an electrical shock. Out of the corner of her eye she saw the knife move, no longer forgotten. She had said just the wrong thing: it was not her place to argue Dr. Hooper's case; it was her place to tell Wade he was right. Wade Hayden needed absolution; he might be going to kill them both, but he needed something from her. That was the reason his voice was so cold with rage.

Suddenly the fear left her. She couldn't understand why or how it had fled to go and watch her from some other place. She squinted, looking across the water, and saw either the same figure returned or another much like it. The figure was no more than a black stick, but she could still see the tiny light of cigarette or cigar. It was as if the fear had fled across the water to stand way over there and observe her.

Maud just sat there waiting, smoothing her hand over her book of poetry as if it were some kind of talisman. She did not fully understand this new feeling; here she was sitting on the end of the pier with a madman, a psychopath, a murderer, and she felt lightweight. Looking across the water, she felt the scene before her dissolve into particles of light and then reform itself into something the same yet subtly different, something that couldn't be seen with the naked eye but could only be *felt*. "Ramon Fernandez, tell me . . ."

Wade was saying something.

"What?" she asked.

" 'Ramon,' you said."

She must have said the name aloud.

" 'Ramon Ferdinand,' you said. Who's he?"

"Not 'Ferdinand.' Fer-*nan*-dez."

"What kinda name's that? Is that a Spanish name?"

She smiled slightly, smoothed her hand over the book. "Maybe it's Cuban."

"Sounds like a spic." Angrily, he spit into the water. He seemed to have forgotten why he was here.

She smiled again. "Well, he's not."

"It's one of them spic names," he said sulkily.

Maud thought for a moment, and then she started to rock. It was as if this were a night like any other night, just the two of them sitting on the end of the pier, chatting. The *three* of them, she thought, thinking of Ramon.

"He's a friend."

"Well." His voice held a note of apology, but he was still sulking.

"A good friend. Yes, I've known him for—oh, years and years." She turned to look at him now, at the thin and craggy profile, the nail-bitten hand that was now loose on the knife.

"He ain't from around here, is he. I guess I'd remember a name like that."

"No, he's not." She paused. "He lives in Key West."

"Key West, *Florida*? That place where all the queers go? I hope you're not goin' to tell me he's a queer."

"He owns a marina. You know, where people berth their boats."

Wade was working up to spit again. "Kinda work queers do."

"It's beautiful, the marina. All the boats."

"*You* never been to Florida, have you?"

Maud kept on rocking slowly and studying the line of boats across the water. "Just the once. It's so beautiful. The sun goes down right behind the marina. You've never seen such a sunset in your life, not up here in the North."

"Hell, sun goes down here just like everywhere. What's so special about Key West? All it is is full of queers."

He'd forgotten everything, it seemed. Forgotten the blood, the knife, the reason he'd come here; and she kept on rocking and talking about the Key West she'd never seen except in her mind. And then she felt that what happened didn't make all that much difference. The most Wade could do would be to take the knife and stick it into her. And in the long scheme of things, of wars and famines, floods, fires—that wasn't very much. What people thought was important was important only in the way a rattle is to a baby: something bright that makes a pleasant noise, something the baby simply wants. That knife wasn't much more than a rattle. If he suddenly plunged it into her, it would merely move through particles of light. For the first time in her life, Maud felt free.

Something would have to be done, nevertheless. She turned and looked at him. "Wade, I guess it's time for me to go in."

He was still little-boy sulky. "I was hoping we could just set here and talk more."

"Maybe some other night."

She rose. He didn't move.

"I've got to take the things in." Maud moved the bottle from the Colonel Sanders bucket and dumped the melted ice out. All Wade did was to look up at her, blinking, as if his eyes were trying to adjust to a new darkness. "You could help. You could just fold up that chair and bring it along."

He got up slowly, sighing with impatience. Still holding on to the knife, he folded up the aluminum chair as Maud pulled the bead chain on the lamp. They were in darkness. She flicked it on again, and there was a tiny dazzle of moonlight on the knife, the chair, the silver bucket-stand. She picked up the stand and reached for the lamp. "Do you think you could carry this?"

"I guess," he said, his tone still truculent. His big-knuckled hand closed around the lamp.

Maud looked at him, at the pathetic and rather silly picture he made. He was standing with the chair under one arm, the knife still clutched in that hand, the lamp in the other, holding it by its wrought-iron stem. He was squinting at the light, his thumb and forefinger about to pull the bead chain.

She shook her head. It was so sad and so simple. No way in the world he could keep his balance, she thought, as she suddenly swung the bucket stand and caught him a glancing blow across the shoulder.

Wade weaved, looking at her, surprised and puzzled. Then he pitched over backwards into the lake. There was an awful, terrible sound, and she shut her eyes and clamped her hands over her ears.

Maud stood there, eyes squinched shut, when she felt a softness against her ankle. She looked down to see the black cat had been rubbing against her foot and now had trailed over to the very end of the pier to poke its head over the edge.

She guessed if the cat could stand it, so could she, though it would help if your eyes were cloudy. Testily, she leaned over. What she had expected to see, she didn't know: devastation far worse than this. The body of Wade Hayden floated face-down on the water, his work shirt ballooning upward as if someone had pumped in air to inflate it. The lamp, of course, had disappeared, but left behind it the memento of its flowered shade, which floated near Wade's head . . . as if it were a party hat come off when the silly, drunken fool fell into the lake.

Out on the black water, another speedboat ripped by. And Maud, sinking into this strange dream of death and water, watched to see what its wake would do to the body, almost as if the pull of water could drag it out to sea. The body barely moved; the rose-colored shade bobbed.

She picked up the cat for comfort and wondered: Why didn't you simply turn to ash? Ashes should be scattered there. Tears ran down her face and dropped onto the cat's fur; it whined and struggled out of her arms. She stood there, arms straight down, looking at the figure of Wade gently tugged by the little waves.

Someone seemed to be calling her name from a great distance. She barely recognized the sound of it; and she registered the other sounds behind her—the spitting-up of gravel, the car engine cutting off, the thunk of a shutting door—as alien rustles from another universe.

"Maud? *Maud?* Are you there? What the hell happened to the lights?"

Sam came, hurrying, onto the pier. She stood there clasping and unclasping her hands, not speaking.

"Maud? What's going—?"

The overturned chair, the fallen bucket-stand, the bottle lolling . . . He walked over to the edge. "Jesus God!" he breathed, down on one knee. The body rose slightly, fell like a resting swimmer on the ruffled waves. "What in hell *happened*? Maud, are you all right?"

Holding her book and the dress tightly against her, she said, "Where are the cops when you need them? It was him all along. It was Wade who murdered them."

"Jesus," Sam breathed. Then he put his hands on her shoulders. "Got to get to my radio. Maud?"

She merely nodded and stood there looking off at the boats, at the party-goers drifting towards the dock. Drowsy laughter floated across the lake.

Sam was back and taking off his leather jacket. "What the hell happened?"

"You're the loot; figure it out. What are you *doing*?" She was shaking the jacket away from her shoulders. "Why in hell are men always tossing their coats at women? You see too many movies."

"Are you going to tell me? What happened?"

"I had to push him, didn't I? There wasn't anybody else around to push him. Here—here's her dress." Before Sam could react, Maud said sternly, "Don't tell me about it; I don't want to hear." Then she looked at the old boards at her feet. "What about him—what about her son? It's not right he should hear it from his father." Maud's shoulders started to heave, and she felt her face burning, get puffy, as if a squall of tears were coming. "It's not *fair* he should hear it from his father. I don't *care* if she felt she had to walk out; she was a good mother." In a moment, she would start wailing, crying.

"I thought maybe," Sam said calmly, "I'd just drive up there, maybe tell him myself."

There was a silence. Testily, she said, "You won't do it *right*. You'll probably read him the autopsy report." She looked off towards the little line of boats, their number diminished now.

"I thought maybe you could come with me."

Maud took in a deep breath of night air, puffed out her cheeks, let it go. "Well . . ." For a long moment, Maud looked across the lake. The lights of the Japanese lanterns still glowed softly. "Are their names really Raoul and Evita? I bet you lied."

Sam winced. "For Christ's sake, Maud. Wade Hayden just got— you were down here with a *killer*, Maud. Who cares about Raoul and Evita? Come on. Let's go up to the house."

"Gee, thanks." She shook his arm away as she had done the jacket.

"Christ, you're grumpy. You're grumpy because I didn't come back."

Maud ignored that. "I guess you'll get a vacation. You finally solved it. Even though it was really me." She sighed and started walking toward the house. "Will my picture be in the papers?" she asked, over her shoulder.

Sam came abreast of her. "I expect."

"After we see Dr. Hooper's son, I want to go to the university and see Chad. To let him know I'm still alive." She sounded rather proud.

Chad. Sam had forgotten about Chad. He stopped and looked up at the night sky, purpling now along the horizon. Was it that late? Was it almost dawn?

"Listen, Maud. I talked to Chad. He telephoned to say he was driving back here this morning."

"What? What do you mean, driving? He doesn't have a car. And why would he be, anyway? He's in Belle—"

"Belle Harbor, I know. Well, he called from Meridian. He borrowed his friend's car."

Impatiently, she said, "Meridian? What's he doing in Meridian?"

"I thought I just told you. He called from there."

"That still doesn't explain why he's coming home."

Sam thought for a moment as he tried to settle his jacket around her shoulders, with her fidgeting like that blind black cat that was stealthily slinking around the end of the pier. "He forgot his books."

Maud shouldered off the jacket. "Oh, for god's sake. He wouldn't come all the way back for that; he'd make me FedEx them. Anyway, he can't read. It's not a nice thing to lie to me about." Leaving the jacket on the ground, she walked away.

"Maud, god damn it! I'm not lying. He'll probably be here in a couple of hours." Sam picked up the jacket. He felt like slinging it at her.

She turned. "You're sure you're not making it up?"

"No. Go ahead—ask Donny if you don't believe me. Or stand out on the road until he comes." He was getting pretty impatient with her.

"You don't have to get tetchy."

"I don't?" He brought his face down close to hers. "Listen to me: I don't like seeing women get murdered. Dr. Hooper—I *liked* Elizabeth Hooper. I don't want her lying there spattered with blood. I feel pretty goddamned *tetchy*. Out there, if you've forgotten, a dead man's floating belly-down in the lake!"

"I should know. I just had a martini with him." She started up the path again.

"Oh, for Christ's sake . . ." Sam caught up with her, put his arm around her shoulders. She didn't shake it off.

Then, as if none of this exchange had occurred, she went on, "So after we see Dr. Hooper's son and after Chad goes back to school, I want to go to New York."

She kept on walking, but Sam stopped dead. "New *York*? What for?"

In the distance a siren sounded. It was far away, a ghost siren. "To see Rosie."

Then she turned and stopped, and Sam thought her smile glimmered like the lights in the little boats across the water.

"Unless you lied."

He caught up with her on the path, and as they walked away from the end of the pier, he thought she must have said (but he couldn't be sure because of the music drifting over the water), said or sighed, "Dear boy."